to know you!
With love and
best wishes always,
Sue
LeDoux

THE
DIVINE
MEDDLER

Sue LeDoux

Printed in the United States of America
Hardcover ISBN: 978-1-959096-50-4
Paperback ISBN: 978-1-959096-51-1
Ebook ISBN: 978-1-959096-52-8

**Canoe Tree
Press**

4697 Main Street
Manchester Center, VT 05255
Canoe Tree Press is a division of DartFrog Books

This is a work of fiction. While I placed the action in Texas counties and the Huntsville prison system, the towns, Craigmore College, and St. Dismas Monastery are fictional. The Houston Forensic Science Center exists, but the expert testimony is fictional and not derived from there, nor are its characters. All other characters in *The Divine Meddler* are products of my imagination, with one exception. I named the town of Raider's homicide detective after my grandfather, Charles Yockel, who was a detective in the Rochester, New York police force. I wanted to honor his memory.

I dedicate this novel to my husband, Gene LeDoux. He supported me in every way possible and shared my enthusiasm for all the people that inhabit St. Dismas Monastery and beyond.

CONTENTS

ACKNOWLEDGMENTS

I am grateful for all the kind, knowledgeable people who generously offered their expertise and time to help make this book worthy of your investment.

First, I would like to thank my husband, Gene LeDoux, whose unfailing support kept me going, even when I occasionally forgot to start dinner because I was in the monastery.

The members of my Greece, NY, Writers Group have walked alongside me from Chapters 1 to 43 several times. Excellent writers themselves, each brought something special to my effort. Prolific author John Caligiuri not only encouraged me, but set an example of hard work and commitment to the craft. Tippi Young encouraged me always to dig deeper. Pat Embury, fellow writer and nurse, brought spot-on criticisms along with her expert knowledge of orthopedics. Liz Voll, chemistry professor by day, and romance writer by night, cheered me on and found all those hidden glitches. Sherry Van Slooten, a poet, had a way of getting to the heart of matters. Finally, Steve Yates, master of alternative fiction, removed most of my exclamation points, and when he was not doing that, his careful critiques proved invaluable.

I am grateful for my insightful beta readers — Reverend Kirk Dueker, Pastor of Hope Church, for his theological review, and Michael Raha, whose ministry in jails and prisons in New York State, helped me populate St. Dismas Monastery with believable characters. Finally, Robert Zinnecker, a talented author whose work I enjoy and respect, contributed his expertise as well.

I am indebted to other professionals who graciously shared their knowledge in so many areas. Retired Greece Police Lieutenant Lou Buduson explained police procedures at crime scenes.

Beth Guterman, former Assistant Attorney General of New York State, assisted with courtroom procedures and that the dialogue in the courtroom between the attorneys, witnesses and judges was consistent with real- life courtroom experiences. Andy Embury contributed his expertise relative to courtroom procedures as well.

Captain Todd Smith, Municipal Training Officer for the North Greece Fire department, gave me detailed information about fighting a barn fire.

Dr. Karen Usselman-Booth VMD (my dear god daughter) who asked me, "Why on earth do you want to know about tularemia?" From bunnies to bulls, her veterinary expertise proved invaluable in pivotal scenes.

Most of all, you would not be holding this book without the insights and commitment of my friend and editor, David J. Rhodes. He devoted hours and hours to help me polish *The Divine Meddler.* Thank you, David

PART I

VIGILANTE JUSTICE

CHAPTER 1

DEADLY DISCOVERY

Strong, chilly winds blowing off the lake did not cause Richard Brock's trembling. Still in his pajamas on this Texas dawn, he leaned against Franklin Abbington's boathouse door, as if to contain the horror within. But flashing red and blue lights told him he had summoned the whirlwind with his call to 911.

Houston County Sheriff, Cyrus McCoy, strode toward Richard. Middle-aged, gray at the temples, he looked like he had seen it all. He would soon discover he had not.

"Mr. Brock, you told the 911 operator there was a dead body in your neighbor's boathouse," McCoy said after introducing himself — as if he needed an introduction. Everyone in the small town of Raider, Texas, knew the Sheriff of Houston County, having re-elected him for years.

Richard nodded.

"Frank and Cam are out of town, and…"

"Frank and Cam?"

"Sorry, I'm… I'm upset. Franklin and Camilla Abbington. Anyway, I couldn't sleep because of the wind. When the lake's riled, it gets like that. Constant banging woke me. My bedroom is right there." He pointed a shaking finger toward his house. "Their boathouse door was slamming open and shut. I thought their son Beau would have heard it, but apparently not. I got up and went to shut the darn thing myself so I could get some sleep. Then I saw, I saw–her."

He shuddered and wiped his face with his hand. "It's awful. I'll never forget it. Poor girl."

McCoy led him away from the boathouse, while the police cordoned off the area with yellow crime scene tape. Officers began searching the grounds in the dim light for evidence. In the most reassuring voice he could muster, McCoy asked Richard if he noticed anything else.

"No. I just ran home and called it in."

"Does anyone else besides Mr. and Mrs. Abbington live in the house?"

"Like I said, their son, Beauregard. He comes and goes at all hours when he's not on campus. Ask me, he's a spoiled only child."

"Campus?"

"Craigmore College. I think he's in his second year."

"Do you have a key to their home? We'd rather not break down the door."

"Sure. I'll get it. Then can I go home?"

Cyrus nodded. "Yes, but stay in town in case we have more questions."

After the police secured the boathouse, Cyrus McCoy entered and immediately recognized the dead teen. He moaned. She was Becky Skalney, Lou and Sally Skalney's only daughter. He knelt next to the girl's body and wished he could cradle her back to life. She was so young, too young to die such a death. She'd been such a happy child. Over the years, he had watched her grow from a toddler into a beautiful young lady, and an ache lodged deep in his chest.

He and Lou had been friends since high school and had spent many pleasant weekends hunting and fishing together. When Lou went into construction after graduation, McCoy worked for the Abbington Piano Company, making wooden hammers for their grand piano line. After a mind-numbing year of doing the same thing every day, Cyrus joined the sheriff's department, where no day was the same.

Now Lou Skalney's daughter lay on her back on the boathouse floor, her head resting at an unnatural angle. Blue eyes with dilated pupils stared unseeing at the ceiling. Her corduroy jacket was open, and her blouse looked like someone had pulled it out of her jeans. The bottom buttons, ripped off, had landed in front of a chair in the corner. Seems there was a struggle, but with whom? And why here?

It looked like the Abbingtons had converted the boathouse into an outdoor entertainment center. A bar dominated the room, with club chairs and end tables situated here and there. A fishing net, decorated with shells, a bamboo fishing pole, and assorted fishing lures, hung from the wall behind the bar.

He noticed strands of blood-stained hair caught on a splinter jutting from the edge of the bar.

Were the tall stools that lay scattered on the floor collateral damage from a struggle? If she had fallen or been pushed against the bar, striking her head before falling, would that account for the blood? Hitting the side of her head when she fell could result in her awkward head angle. Why was she in Abbington's boathouse at this hour? Where was Beauregard Abbington?

An officer poked his head in the doorway. "House is empty, Sheriff."

"Thank you."

McCoy called the station and told the desk Sergeant to check the DMV records for Beauregard Abbington's license and put out an APB to haul him in for questioning.

Cyrus reckoned Becky must be about 17. The thought of telling Lou and Sally their daughter was dead, made those dull, hammer-making days look good, but he would do it himself. He did not want a strange police officer telling them their worst nightmare had come true.

Grateful for police procedures that checked his rising emotions, McCoy called the medical examiner and the county's homicide liaison officer for Raider, Detective Charles Yockel.

After the experts arrived, were briefed, and the crime scene preserved, Cyrus left to do what he most dreaded.

At 7:48 a.m., Cyrus pulled his cruiser far into Skalney's driveway. A raised voice and Sally's cries greeted him as he approached the side door. It sounded like Sally and Lou had already discovered Becky had left the house sometime in the night. Lou was vowing to bring Becky home after he "beat Beau senseless."

McCoy banged on the door and called, "Lou, open up! It's Cyrus."

Sudden silence, then footsteps. The door opened, and Lou stood in the doorway, wearing jeans and his pajama top. His hair stood on end, and he had yet to shave. His face crumpled upon seeing his friend standing in his uniform at the bottom of the steps.

"What happened to Becky?" Lou's voice croaked.

"May I come in?"

Lou turned and walked silently into the kitchen while Cyrus followed. Sally, still in her bathrobe, stood next to the kitchen table, eyes wide, hands clutched against her chest. Both Skalneys stared at McCoy as he gently as possible told them what had happened.

Sally screamed and sank into the nearest chair. Lou stared, open-mouthed, at Cyrus and pulled a chair, with a shaking hand, from the table and dropped into it. Cyrus took the opposite seat and waited while horror made its first inroad into his friends' hearts.

After a while, Lou spoke, his voice a barely audible growl. "Beauregard Abbington."

"What about Beauregard, Lou?"

Cyrus slipped a notebook and pen from his jacket pocket and placed them on the table. Lou's hands formed fists, and he leaned toward his friend.

"You don't have to take notes. I'll tell you what happened. Beauregard Abbington killed my daughter. Get out there and get to him before I do!"

Sally placed her hand on Lou's arm. "Let Cyrus.... Don't do something we'll all regret."

She took a ragged breath. "When we found out she'd been dating Beauregard, we grounded her."

Cyrus folded his hands, ignoring his notebook. Neither had absorbed Becky's death nor the last violent moments of her life. Reality was yet to shred their hearts.

"How did you discover they'd been dating?"

"The scumbag gave her marijuana. Sally found it in Becky's room. It all came out then."

"Way too old for her." Sally shook her head. "Becky said it made her gag, but everybody was using it. We told her to break it off, but she didn't." Sally brought a fist to her mouth and sobbed.

"If only she'd listened to us!" Lou buried his face in his hands, his shoulders shaking. After he regained control, Cyrus asked, "How did you find out she was still seeing him?"

"I was on a scaffold at H.E.B.'s grocery on a siding job. Saw them kissing in the lot behind the Raider High football bleachers. I ran there, sent Becky home, and told Beau to stay away from my daughter. When he laughed and said Becky wasn't daddy's little girl anymore, I decked him. The weasel looked at me from the ground and said I'd be sorry I'd punched him. Lucky I didn't kill him then." He made a fist. "Wish I had."

With tears streaming down her cheeks, Sally said, "We grounded her, except for school. She said she hated us, and we were terrible parents. Becky told me she wanted a more exciting life than I had and called me a doormat. We stuck to our guns, but what good did it do? Were we supposed to stand guard all night?"

She stared at Cyrus as if seeking absolution.

"Of course not, Sal. You and Lou did what all parents would do. Listen to me, this is not your fault." Cyrus let that sink in and then asked, "When do you think she left the house last night?"

Sally looked at Lou. "I looked in on her just before we went to bed, around 11, didn't I, Lou? She must have snuck out after midnight Saturday morning while we were sound asleep."

Lou nodded and leaned toward his friend. "Cyrus, Beauregard Abbington is dirt and his sidekick, Floyd Armbruster, isn't any better. He did this, and you'd better throw him in jail before I get my hands on him."

At 4:36 p.m. that same Saturday afternoon, Patrolman Matt Parker observed a car weaving side to side in its lane as it was entering Raider. The license plate number told him he had found Beauregard Abbington, the target of the APB, and a "person of interest."

Matt called it in, flicked on his lights and siren, and pulled the driver over. He cautiously approached Abbington, wondering what the story on him was.

"S'matter officer?" Beau said, blinking up at the cop as he rolled his window down.

"You were driving erratically, weaving in your lane."

"Nah," Beau denied in a long, alcohol laden breath.

After checking license and registration, Parker ordered him out of the car.

"Wassa, wha, wha for?"

"Sobriety test."

"Ooooh. I don't think so."

"I'm telling, not asking."

"Aright, aright. Do what you want. Chill, man."

Beauregard opened the door, lurched out and took two wobbly steps. Parker caught him before he fell, glanced over Beauregard's shoulder, and noticed the edges of two plastic bags jutting from the space between the driver's seat and the side console.

"Man, how much booze you got on board? Let's get you settled where you won't hurt yourself." Matt continued a one-sided conversation to keep Beau compliant until he could get him into the squad car.

"Where were you coming from?" Matt asked in a conversational tone. His left arm supported Beauregard while he guided him to the patrol car.

"Fishin' lodge in Possum Creek."

Parker opened the cruiser's door and poured the affable drunk into the back seat.

"Here, breathe into this, will you?" He handed Beauregard the breathalyzer.

"Why?"

"Want to find out how much booze you're holding, man." Matt said, as if challenging Beau's manhood.

"You'd be sprized," Beau boasted.

Parker watched him take a deep breath and blow into the mouthpiece. A look at the result confirmed driving while intoxicated.

"I'm going to get your car keys from the ignition and then check out your car. Someone can pick it up later."

Beau murmured "kay" and closed his eyes. Matt shut the door.

When Parker reached the Land Rover, he grabbed the two plastic bags he had seen. One looked to be full of weed, and the other held several blue tablets. After checking the rest of the interior, he opened the trunk but found nothing suspicious. When he returned to his squad car, he woke Beauregard, who was too groggy to resist, as Matt fastened handcuffs on his wrists.

"Whachdoinsofer?"

"Sorry man. You blew point one-two on the breathalyzer, and I found two bags of drugs in your car. I'm arresting you for driving while intoxicated and drug possession. Anything you say may be held against you in a court of law. You have a right to an attorney. If you cannot afford one, one will be provided for you. Do you understand what I told you?"

"Understand! Course I do. Hear it on TV."

"This is not TV."

"Course not. I'll call Russ…. Russ…. what's his name… my folk's pet lawyer."

"Good idea."

By the time Matt parked his cruiser at the station, Beauregard Abbington was snoring. Parker smiled.

Just gotta know how to reel 'em in, nice and gentle, and you get yourself a fine catch.

CHAPTER 2

LAMENT

Beauregard Abbington sat at the defense table with two lawyers at his side, and armed for battle. Not one brown hair was out of place, and his gray suit, with crisp white shirt and blue striped tie, created the image of a serious university student. He smirked and nodded in response to a whispered comment from his lead attorney and family friend, Russell Blake.

Lou glared at his daughter's killer. Fortunately, a rail separated Lou and Sally Skalney from lawyers, jury, judge, and especially Beauregard Abbington.

It was the second day of Beau's trial, and so far Lou was not impressed with Eric Reed, the Houston County, Texas, District Attorney. The man's opening statement had sounded as worn as Lou's oldest pair of jeans.

How much work was there to just listing the facts he would present to prove Abbington's guilt?

Russell Blake's opening statement promised to blast every one of those facts. He sounded confident, dressed in his silk suit and flashy gold signet ring. Lou watched the jury hang on every word. Flash and dash.

When the D.A. turned to offer him a perfunctory greeting, Lou engulfed his outstretched hand in an iron grip. *See that my daughter gets justice.*

Reed pulled Lou closer and whispered, "Sally will be my first witness this morning. I'll question her like I did when we prepped for this. Don't worry, it will be fine."

Lou had his doubts.

For a small town like Raider, parked on the southern edge of Houston County, this trial would make local history. People packed the courtroom to watch the only son of the town's wealthiest family defend himself against the charge of murdering a construction worker's daughter. It was standing room only.

As owner of the Abbington Piano Works, Franklin Abbington was the biggest employer in Raider. He could well afford Houston County's most prestigious criminal law firm, Blake, Wilson, and Perry. The Blakes and Abbingtons ran in the same circles that publicly supported socially acceptable charities. Only the best lawyer for his son would do, the best lawyer and an old friend.

Harvard educated Russell Blake took first chair and his associate, James King, with the University of Texas law school honors, took second chair. The choice of lawyers was not lost on Lou. Blake would blend his 20-year Ivy-League expertise with King's familiarity with his hometown, Raider.

Legal beagle and family pet. Good Lawyer, bad lawyer. They're both bad.

Lou groaned and ran a finger under the collar and constricting tie that chafed his neck. A muscular man, with a growing paunch, Lou preferred jeans and loose work shirts. When he felt tears forming, he tightened his hands into fists. Rebecca Skalney's father would not shed one tear until he won justice for his little girl, until he took care of business.

Hadn't my old man, drunk or sober, drilled that into me? A man takes care of business. Always. Beauregard Abbington will pay. The whole damn family will pay.

"It's almost time to start," Sally whispered to Lou. She rested her hand on his thigh. When he did not respond to her touch, she pulled off her glasses and opened her purse. Strands of straight brown hair fell over one eye as she rooted around to find a reasonably clean tissue, which she vigorously applied to her glasses. She shifted in her seat, straining at the seams of her skirt. Comfort food numbs pain.

Lou looked over his shoulder. Just behind them, Sally's friends from St. Stanislaus parish were filling empty seats. Ceiling fan blades cranked to life at exactly 9:00 a.m.. Sunlight poured through open Venetian blinds that covered three long windows on each side of the courtroom. Lou felt beads of sweat forming on his forehead while more people filed in, adding to the room's warmth.

The bailiff walked to the front of the courtroom. "All rise! The court is now in session. The Honorable Ramos Navarro presiding."

Following the bailiff's announcement, Judge Navarro stood behind the judicial bench. The contrast between his curly white hair and black judicial robe made him look younger than his 69 years. Silence reigned while his gaze crept across the courtroom. He frowned.

"This trial is not a three-ring circus. While I appreciate the civic concern shown by Houston County citizens, spectators will not exceed seating capacity. The bailiff will escort those with no seats or business in this trial out of the courtroom."

After the murmuring from exiting spectators ended, Judge Navarro allowed those remaining to be seated.

Turning to Eric Reed, Navarro asked, "Is the prosecution ready to proceed?"

Reed stood. "Yes, Your Honor. I call the victim's bereaved mother, Sally Skalney, to the stand."

Russell Blake shot to his feet. "Your Honor, I object to the defense's misuse of the term 'bereaved.' He's shamefully playing on the jury's sympathies."

Judge Navarro sighed, frowned, and pointed his glasses at the D.A..

"I will not tolerate drama in my courtroom. Objection sustained."

"I apologize, Your Honor."

After taking the oath, Sally perched on the edge of the witness chair. She clutched her hands together and rested them on her lap. Eric approached her warily, as if to avoid spooking a wild animal. He gave her his warmest smile before he spoke.

"Mrs. Skalney, please tell the court how you discovered Rebecca was dating Beauregard Abbington."

Sally took a deep breath and looked at the ceiling as if searching for an answer. Lowering her gaze, she said, "I was putting laundry away in Becky's dresser when I found a plastic bag of marijuana tucked under her clothes. When I asked Becky about it, she said a friend gave it to her. I asked her what friend, and she admitted she had been seeing Beau Abbington."

"And how did you respond?"

Reed faced the jury as Sally answered.

"I was upset. I told her Beauregard Abbington is too old for a seventeen-year-old girl. A college sophomore has no business fooling around with a high schooler."

Sally squinted at Beauregard and raised her voice. "Everyone knows he runs with a fast crowd. It didn't surprise me he gave her marijuana."

"Objection!" James King leaped to his feet. "Conclusion on the part of the witness."

"Sustained."

Eric Reed barely managed to hide his satisfaction. Point made.

"And What did Becky say to that?"

"That he was more mature than the boys in her class, and the gossip about him wasn't true. She said she didn't want to settle down and get married like I did. She wanted excitement and fun." Sally shook her head. "We talked some more, but I got nowhere. Finally, I told her I would tell her father. She begged me not to because she knew he would forbid her from seeing Beau."

"Thank you, Mrs. Skalney. No more questions. Your Honor, I reserve the right to recall Mrs. Skalney."

Navarro looked toward the defense. James King rose and approached Sally.

"Mrs. Skalney, please accept my condolences for your loss. I realize this is difficult for you, so I have only a few questions."

"Do you know, chemically or botanically, anything about cannabis sativa?"

"What is cannabis sativa?"

"Marijuana or weed, as they call it."

"I'm not a chemist, but I've seen pictures of it."

"Have you ever smoked marijuana?"

"No."

"Have you ever seen a marijuana plant?"

"Not until I saw it in Becky's drawer."

"So you don't know, but presumed it was marijuana. Thank you, Mrs. Skalney. No more questions."

Reed stepped forward.

"May I redirect, Your Honor?"

The judge nodded.

"When you were talking with Becky, did she deny it was marijuana?"

"No."

"Thank you. No more questions."

After Sally returned to her seat, Reed turned to Lou. "I'm calling you to the stand next. I know you despise Beau and believe he killed Becky, but just answer the questions asked of you without editorializing."

"Yea, yea." Lou frowned, but nodded his head.

A few minutes later, he was on the stand.

"What did you do when Sally told you what had happened?" Reed asked a stone-faced Lou Skalney.

"I forbade her to see Beau Abbington or his friends anymore, for the reasons her mother gave her."

"How did Becky respond?"

"She cried, said she was old enough to pick her own friends. I told her in my house what I say goes. If she continued to see him, I would ground her. When she is over 18 and independent, she can do what she wants. Until then, she will follow my rules."

"What did she do?"

"She cried, ran into her room and slammed the door. She appeared to obey me."

"Appeared? Did she, in fact, obey you?"

"No."

"How did you determine that?"

"I was on a scaffold working a construction job for the H-E-B supermarket a few doors down from Raider High. I could see the empty lot behind the school's bleachers, and I saw Becky and Beauregard holding hands and kissing."

Lou scowled at Beauregard until Reed's next question brought him back to the moment.

"What did you do?"

"What did I do? What any good father would have done. I went to the lot, sent my daughter home and told her to stay there. After Becky left, in tears, I told Beauregard Abbington that he would have me to deal with if he so much as looked at my daughter again."

Stepping closer to the jury, Reed asked what Beauregard's response had been. Lou fixed his gaze on Abbington and announced, "He informed me that Becky was not daddy's little girl anymore, and then smirked, just like he's doing now."

Russell Blake quickly jumped in. "Objection. Move to strike."

"Overruled."

Lou pointed a shaking index finger toward the defense table.

"I wanted to beat him senseless right then. Instead, I grabbed him by the neck and threw him to the ground. He threatened I would be sorry I did that. I wasn't afraid of that punk, but worried he might try to get to me through Becky."

"No more questions," Reed said, not wanting to push his luck and poke an angry bear.

Lou concluded he had done a magnificent job of testifying. But then Lou Skalney was not an attorney.

CHAPTER 3

ARM OF THE LAW

Eric Reed approached Sally as they were preparing to exit the courtroom at noon recess.

"I want to compliment you on your testimony, Sally. You did an excellent job, and I liked how you slipped in Beauregard's reputation. If I know Blake, he won't be able to leave a potential slur on Beau's character alone. If he tries to fix it, I'll have him where I want him."

After lunch, the D.A. called Officer Matthew Parker to testify. Lou leaned forward and grasped the railing in front of him.

"Why did you pull Mr. Abbington over while you were on road patrol?"

"His vehicle was weaving dangerously in its lane. I suspected he was driving under the influence. Also, the license plate matched the number on the APB."

"Did you ascertain he had been driving under the influence?"

"Yes."

"Please tell the jury how you did so."

"I asked him to step out of the car and he almost fell over. His breathalyzer showed point one two."

"Did you arrest him for DUI?"

"Yes, and also for possession of possible controlled substances I found in his car."

"Was the defendant confrontational?"

"Not at all."

"Did he agree to allow you to search his vehicle?"

"He did. Just before he fell asleep in my cruiser."

"What did you do after permission?"

"I checked his vehicle and found two bags of possible drugs, locked the vehicle and took possession of the keys. I went back to Mr. Abbington, handcuffed, and mirandized him. Then I drove him, his car keys, and substances straight to the station."

"Thank you, Officer Parker. No further questions."

Judge Navarro turned to Blake. "Any redirect?"

Blake half rose from his seat. "Not at this time, Your Honor."

Lou snorted. *That's smart. Wouldn't touch that testimony either if I were you.*

Next, Reed called Detective Charles Yockel, of the Houston County Sheriff's Department, to the stand. He testified he was the liaison investigation officer between Raider and the Houston County Sheriff's Department, which has authority in homicide cases. In answer to Eric Reed's first question, Detective Yockel described the scene where Richard Brock discovered Becky's body.

"When did you interview Beauregard Abbington?" Reed said.

"At 3:46 pm Saturday afternoon, October 16th, eight hours after Officer Parker brought him into the police station."

"Why did you wait eight hours to question him?"

The detective cleared his throat. "According to Officer Parker's report, he was too sleepy to respond to questions at the time of his arrest. His breathalyzer at the scene registered point one two. Also, substances in his possession included tablets and what appeared to be marijuana. Without a toxicology report, I didn't know if he was under the influence of other drugs when he was processed. I waited until he could respond appropriately to questioning."

Reed handed the previously submitted breathalyzer result, Evidence P-1, to the jury.

Lou balled his hands into fists. A low growl escaped him as his face turned beet red.

That lowlife was about to turn my Becky into an addict. I should have killed him behind the bleachers when I had the chance.

He rose, as if to leap over the rail, when Judge Navarro banged his gavel.

"Sit down now, Mr. Skalney, or I will have the bailiff remove you. There will be no emotional display, or worse, in my court. Is that clear?"

Lou looked at the judge and blinked. "Yes, Your Honor. I apologize. I didn't realize how…"

Reed quickly jumped in with his next question for Detective Yockel.

"Did Mr. Abbington have an alibi for Friday night and early Saturday?"

"He said he was alone at his friend Floyd Armbruster's fishing lodge from Friday afternoon to Saturday morning."

"Did you corroborate that with Mr. Armbruster?"

"Yes, I did. He said Mr. Abbington had called Friday afternoon and asked if he could spend the night at Floyd's family's fishing lodge in Possum Creek. Said he wanted to get some early morning fishing in. Mr. Armbruster agreed and reminded Mr. Abbington where the family kept the key to the lodge. Mr. Armbruster added he would have joined him, but he had a game on Saturday. He is a linebacker for the Craigmore Lions."

"Did you ask Mr. Abbington if anyone saw him at the lodge?"

"Yes. He said he was alone and did not see anyone."

Lou crossed his arms. *What else would he say?*

"Did you question anyone at Possum Creek?"

"Yes. I questioned Craig Farley, the manager of Tubbs General Store, if he saw Mr. Abbington at any time from Friday afternoon to Saturday morning. Mr. Farley said he did not see him at all during that time."

"And why did you ask the store manager if he had seen Mr. Abbington?"

Yockel leaned forward. "Since the store sells bait and fast food, it would seem likely Mr. Abbington may have stopped there for provisions."

"What further investigation did you do?"

"The security camera at the only gas pump in town did not show Mr. Abbington or his Land Rover on the premises at any time. I also questioned the neighbors on either side of the lodge if they saw the defendant, or any sign of life in or around the lodge."

"And what did they tell you?"

"They said they did not see Mr. Abbington but would not have seen him or lights in the lodge, anyway, because of the woods separating all three properties."

"So Mr. Abbington has no alibi because his statement that he was alone cannot be corroborated. No further questions."

Russell Blake approached Detective Yockel.

"Detective Yockel, How long have you been working homicide cases?"

"Twenty-five years."

"Impressive. Have you ever worked a case where the accused could not prove he or she had the alibi they said they had? Yet it was later proven they were innocent after all?"

"Yes."

"About how many times?"

The detective waited a moment before answering. "That's hard to say after 25 years on the job. I'd estimate about ten percent. Thirty cases in three hundred, maybe."

"So, about ten percent of the time, the accused had an alibi, but could not prove it. Would you say that is correct?"

Yockel nodded. "I need to hear your answer, Detective," Navarro said.

"Yes, Your Honor. I would say that was correct."

Reed bolted from his seat. "Objection, conclusion on the part of the witness. He has no hard data to support his answer."

"Sustained."

"No further questions," Blake responded.

As Detective Yockel unfolded his six-foot plus body from the witness chair, Lou almost chuckled at the expression on the officer's face. *Lawyers!*

CHAPTER 4

SCIENCE AND SLEUTHING

Before court ended for the day, Reed called what he referred to Lou as the "lab geeks."

First up was Eugene Cosentino, fingerprint expert from the Houston Forensic Science Center. After he stated his education and credentials, Reed asked about the fingerprints found at the scene.

"I identified fingerprints consistent with the samples I took of Beauregard, Franklin, and Camilla Abbington. In addition, I found prints that were smudged or not in the database. I found one clear print on a button attached to the corduroy jacket the victim was wearing."

"Did you find a match?"

"No."

"Thank you, Mr. Cosentino. No further questions."

Russell Blake rose and swaggered toward the witness stand.

Lou held his breath. *Even I see where the defense is going. Maybe Reed had to include the fingerprint testimony. That's probably why he left off questioning Cosentino as fast as he did.*

"Mr. Cosentino, did you obtain samples of Beauregard, Franklin, and Camilla Abbington's fingerprints?"

"I did."

"It's the Abbington's boathouse. Isn't it reasonable the family members' prints would be all over it?"

"Yes."

"Could the unknown and smudged fingerprints simply belong to Abbington's guests?"

"They could."

"Did you find any other fingerprints on Rebecca Skalney's body?"

"I found some smudged prints on her body."

"Why would they be smudged?"

"A struggle likely would cause smudged prints on skin, and prints are difficult to pick up on heavy material, like the victim's jacket."

"And you testified that the one clear fingerprint found on Rebecca's jacket button was not in the database and did not match Beauregard Abbington's fingerprints."

"Correct."

"Thank you, Mr. Cosentino."

Later in the afternoon, Reed called the Houston County Medical Examiner, Carolyn Brown MD, to the stand. The redheaded expert appeared young for her position, but her courtroom demeanor said otherwise.

Eric asked if she had determined the cause of Rebecca Skalney's death.

"Yes."

"And did you determine the time of death?"

"Somewhere between midnight and three a.m. Saturday morning, October 16th."

"And what was the cause of death, Doctor Brown?"

"The victim suffered a subdural hematoma in the occipital portion of her head, most likely caused by blunt force trauma.

"A subdural hematoma in the occipital region is right near the brain stem, and there isn't much room in that area for the blood to accumulate. It would cause intense pressure and compression of, and possibly movement, of the brainstem, affecting the respiratory and cardiac centers of the brain. It can kill within minutes."

"So, in English, what caused her death?"

"Asphyxia secondary to head injury."

"How hard would a person have to hit her head to cause a brain bleed that severe?"

"For a bleed that size, there would have had to have been a great deal of force. She also had bruises on her neck and arms, indicative of a struggle. Bar stools were knocked over, further signs of a struggle."

Reed approached the evidence table.

"Your Honor, I would like to present as state's evidence P-5 of photos taken at the crime scene."

He passed the photos to the judge. Navarro frowned as he studied the pictures. Silently, he handed them to the bailiff to give to the jury foreperson.

Tears streamed down Sally's cheeks. Lou closed his eyes and recalled those horrendous photos he had insisted on seeing. Only Navarro's last warning kept him in his seat. Everything in him longed to leap over the railing and strangle Beauregard Abbington. He jiggled his legs, jammed his fist into his hand, and took deep breaths, forcing himself to remain in his seat.

He looked toward the defense table. Beau's head was bowed, and his shoulders were shaking. Even from a distance, Lou heard muted sobs as King placed his arm around his client.

Crocodile tears. Going for the sympathy ploy.

When Sally placed a restraining hand on his thigh, he brushed it away.

Lou focused on the jury as they looked at the photos. Some closed their eyes after the first glance. One woman bowed her head as if in prayer, another gasped. One juror passed it along with barely a glance.

What in blazes is wrong with him?

The last witness for the day was Dr. Edna Lewis, toxicologist, who testified that Beauregard's toxicology screen confirmed the point one two blood alcohol level. In addition, his blood was positive for marijuana. The other drug found in his possession, but not in his blood, was methylenedioxymethamphetamine, or Ecstasy. Rebecca Skalney's blood was negative for any drugs. Lou smiled.

My Becky was nobody's fool. She knew better than to take that poison.

The next day, Rudy Kowalski perched on the edge of the seat behind Lou, leaned forward, and spread his forearms along the back of Lou's bench. Short, with a body like a fireplug and a head topped with a buzz cut, he whispered, "When the judge calls a recess, meet me in the coffee shop on the main floor—alone."

Rudy raised a hand against questions his friend may have and settled back in his seat. He looked past Lou and stared at Judge Navarro.

Word in Raider's halls of justice was that Ramos Navarro was a stickler for protocol and did not tolerate courtroom theatrics. It was said he runs a courtroom like his father had in Mexico until the cartel assassinated Ramos Senior. After his mother took her two sons and emigrated to Texas, she settled in a Hispanic enclave. Most lawyers quickly learned that, while he could be empathetic to the struggles of minorities, Navarro possessed no sympathy for murderers, and contributed yearly to the population of Huntsville's death row.

Waiting to hear what Rudy had to say added to Lou's anxiety. He knew his oldest friend was on to something, but what?

Bullied for stuttering as a child when they both attended St. Stanislaus School, Rudy had grown into a formidable reporter who could ferret out hidden details of any story. Lou feared whatever Rudy had discovered would not be good.

Yet he was ready to believe what Rudy had to say. They had become friends the day he finally pummeled the kid who had been making Rudy's life miserable. Of course, he paid dearly for his actions with an order to mow the school's lawn for a month as penance. He wondered why he had to end the bullying, and not the principal. Lou Skalney gained a friend for life at the same time he learned the world was not fair.

Not then and not now.

Relieved Sally was with her friends during recess, Lou nabbed the last open table in the coffee shop. He took a sip of coffee, grimaced, and loaded the brew with sugar.

"Shouldn't be allowed to call this sludge coffee," he muttered and looked around. The line for donuts slowly snaked past steaming carafes and vending machines that offered bottled water and sodas. Rudy had little competition for his hot water, tea, and fruit before settling across from Lou.

After fiddling with his tea bag, Rudy leaned across the small table and asked, "Have you noticed the third juror in the front row on the right?"

"Yeah. He barely looked at the photos Reed passed around. He seems kind of fidgety and keeps looking at Abbington. Maybe it's the first time he's been on a jury or seen an actual murderer up close."

"Alleged murderer."

Lou reared back and glared at Rudy. "Not you, too."

"I'm just pointing out that, as a juror, he is required to see Abbington as an alleged murderer until they prove his guilt beyond a reasonable doubt," Rudy said, dismissing his friend's accusation with a wave of his hand.

"So?"

"So, what if Juror Number Three never reaches that conclusion, no matter what evidence is presented? And I gotta say, Lou, this case won't be a slam dunk. Not with Russell Blake as the defense attorney. When I overheard Franklin Abbington whisper something to Blake about insurance, I did some digging, because a hung jury would be better for them than a guilty verdict."

Lou's gaze hardened, and he leaned over the table. "You think that juror's been bought? I'm a construction worker, not a lawyer. But even I know you have to have more to go on than just a fidgety juror who stares at the defendant." He frowned. "I wouldn't put anything past Abbington."

"So when I investigated the matter," Rudy said, ignoring his friend's comment. "Low and behold, Juror Number Three is dirt poor but rich in kids—ten, to be exact. Most are pretty much no-account, but the youngest one, well, he's got potential. Graduating with top honors this year and was accepted at Texas A&M. No way Juror Number Three can afford that tuition."

Lou shrugged. "Probably a scholarship or two."

"My contacts at A&M said he's in the running for a full four-year football scholarship."

"So? This is Texas, Rudy. God and football. What's so odd about the kid applying for a full ride?"

"It would be odd if he got it, since he played only four games this year and his stats are not impressive."

Lou sniffed and considered Rudy's argument. After a moment, he nodded.

"Makes sense. They're one of the richest families in the state and probably have contacts all the way to the Governor's office."

"Beyond, actually."

"You should tell Reed," Lou said, hope in his voice for the first time in months.

"I did. Apparently, that's not enough. Kid hasn't gotten the scholarship yet, so officially there's no money trail to connect to this case. He wants more proof."

"Can you get it?"

"You know I'll blow a vessel trying, buddy."

CHAPTER 5

SAINT OR SINNER?

It was Monday morning and Eric Reed had just rested the prosecution. Lou and Rudy were sitting side by side in the gallery.

"Did you find any proof about the scholarship pay-off deal?"

"Sorry, buddy. Nada."

Judge Navarro turned to the defense table. "Do you wish to testify on your own behalf at this time, Mr. Abbington?"

"I do not, your Honor," Beau said, without rising.

"Did your attorneys explain your options?"

"They did, and I choose not to testify."

"Then is the defense ready?" Navarro asked Blake and King.

"We are, your Honor," they replied in unison.

Lou raised an eyebrow at Russell Blake's first witness for the defense.

What could Harvey Walker, the best car mechanic this side of Houston, have anything to add?

After establishing that Harvey was the Abbington's mechanic for all their vehicles, Blake, holding a notepad and pen, approached the witness and asked when he last serviced Beauregard's Land Rover.

"First thing Friday morning. The air conditioning system needed repair. Beau, Mr. Abbington, picked it up just before noon on Friday."

"That would be Friday, October 15th, the day before Rebecca Skalney's body was found in the Abbington's boathouse?"

Harvey cleared his throat and leaned forward, as if ready to throw a punchline.

"Yes."

"Did you note the mileage on Beauregard's Land Rover the morning of the 15th?"

"11,483 miles."

"Did you have a reason to check the mileage after Mr. Abbington's arrest?"

"Yes. Your office called me and said you were Beau's lawyers and wanted me to check the mileage again. I did. It was 11,607 miles."

Blake made a show of scribbling the math on the notepad. He looked up, as if astounded.

"Your Honor, I would like the Court to stipulate the distance between Raider and Possum Creek, the location of Armbruster's lodge, is about 62 miles."

"So stipulated. I have a cottage at Possum Creek myself, Counselor." He looked as if he wished he were there now.

Blake raised his notepad and asked Harvey, "If the distance between Raider and Possum Creek is 62 miles, the round trip would equal 124 miles. Would you state for the jury once again the difference between the mileage on Mr. Abbington's Land Rover Friday morning and when you checked the mileage at our request?"

Harvey smiled a crooked smile, leaned back, and announced, "It was 124 miles."

Punchline delivered.

Lou whispered to Sally, "Doesn't mean a thing. Why isn't Reed challenging this? I'll bet the Abbingtons bought him off too. Even I could do a better job."

"Who knows? Maybe he has a good reason we don't know about."

Lou grunted and crossed his arms.

King stepped forward. "I call Dr. Ian Peterson."

A statesman like gentleman, wearing a three-piece suit and rimless glasses that perched precariously on the tip of his nose, strutted to the witness chair. Once settled, he cleared his throat and looked at King as if giving him permission to speak.

"Dr. Peterson, would you describe to the jury your current position?

"I am currently Dean of Men at Craigmore College."

"And are you acquainted with the defendant, Beauregard Abbington?"

"I am."

"What can you tell the court about Mr. Abbington?"

"Mr. Abbington is a business major with a 3.2 grade point average. I have received no reports of behavior that would require disciplinary action. To my knowledge, he has consistently comported himself like a gentleman of Craigmore College."

"Thank you, Dr. Peterson. No more questions."

Eric Reed approached the witness for redirect.

"Dr. Peterson, can you describe the first time you met Beauregard Abbington?"

"Yes. Every semester, the faculty hosts an all-day reception for incoming students. I met Beauregard in the Fall of his freshman year."

"And when was the last time you interacted with the defendant personally?"

"I believe it was at the beginning of this year."

"Have you spoken with the defendant at any other time in the last year?"

He frowned and, after a long pause, said, "Not that I recall. I had no reason to"

"So, you interacted with the defendant only twice, and both times at public functions."

"Correct."

"Based on those two interactions, can you tell the court if he is involved in any campus activity? The debate team, or college newspaper, for example?"

Peterson folded his arms across his chest, as if to protect himself from the obvious conclusion. "No."

"In other words, you have nothing to add about Beauregard Abbington today other than the testimony you just gave. Correct?"

Eric did not wait for a reply. "No further questions. Thank you Dr. Peterson."

Blake and King huddled at their table while the dean made a quick exit.

"Do you have a plan to address Beau's DWI and drug possession charge?" King whispered.

"That's another trial. I don't want to remind the jury about it if I can avoid it. We know Beau's no angel, so the less said, the better. Frankly, Reed has nothing, and he knows it. Grasping at straws. I'd rather rest now while we're still ahead."

"Makes sense," King agreed.

When Blake announced the defense rested, Lou shot a look at Reed, as if to say, is that all? Do something!

Reed rose and said, "I would like to call Margaret Ames to the stand as a rebuttal witness."

Blake sprang to his feet. "Your Honor, the defense knows nothing about Ms. Ames, or what she has to do with this case. She is not on the witness list."

Lou watched King and Beauregard, head-to-head, in what seemed a heated conversation. Neither looked happy. Lou smiled.

This is going to be good—finally.

He leaned forward. Judge Navarro beckoned Reed and Blake to the bench.

"Your Honor, Ms. Ames came forward early this morning. We had no time to add her to the list."

Blake harrumphed. "That ploy is as old as my grandfather's whiskers, your Honor."

"We will discuss this in my chambers before we proceed any further."

Navarro banged his gavel and called a fifteen minute recess.

Lou grabbed a quick cup of coffee from the vending machine while waiting for court to resume. Eric had told him earlier this morning about Margaret Ames and the slim possibility of getting her testimony admitted. *Please, God, make the judge allow her testimony.* In the next second, he wondered why he had just prayed to a God who either did not exist or was useless. *Habit, I guess.*

Upon returning to the courtroom, Judge Navarro announced, "The defense opened the door to character with Dr. Peterson's testimony. I will allow the testimony of Ms. Ames." He gave the D.A. a warning look. "Proceed with caution, Mr. Reed."

Trim, to the point of anorexia, Margaret's hand shook as she raised it to take the oath. Once settled in the witness chair, she waited for Reed's first question.

"Ms. Ames, are you a recent graduate of Raider High School?"

"Yes."

"When did you graduate?"

"Last year."

"And did you know Rebecca Skalney?"

"I'd heard her name in school, but never met her."

"Do you know Beauregard Abbington? Can you point him out?"

"Objection. Compound question," Blake said.

"Sustained."

"Ms. Ames, do you know Beauregard Abbington?"

"Yes."

"Where did you meet him?"

"Jill's Diner. Most of the kids from Raider High hang out there after school. A few guys from Craigmore too. That's where I met him."

"Could you point him out?"

"Yes." She flicked her forefinger in the direction of the defense table.

"Let the record show the witness pointed to the defendant, Beauregard Abbington," Reed said.

Navarro responded, "So noted."

"What was the nature of your relationship?"

"Last year, I dated Beauregard Abbington for a while. At first, he seemed nice, like a gentleman, you know? He was like, opening doors for me and taking me to nice places. Not like the cheap places other guys take you to, you know?"

"Objection. Narrative, your honor."

Lou smirked. *You don't like where this is going, do you, Blake? Too bad.*

"Sustained." Judge Navarro responded. "Ms. Ames, please try to answer questions concisely."

"I'm sorry, your Honor."

Eric Reed's voice was gentle as his questions led the jury through her experience.

"I realize this may be difficult. Please tell the court if you and Beauregard had a sexual relationship."

"Yes. I mean, no. We, like, made out a lot, but that was all." She turned pleading eyes to the jury. "I'm a good girl. I never… you know."

"The jury does not know, Ms. Ames. Did you have consensual intercourse with the defendant?"

Margaret's "No!" was as loud as Blake's objection.

"Irrelevant, your honor. This has nothing to do with the case before us today."

"Where are you going with this, Mr. Reed?" the judge asked.

"It goes to character and probability."

Navarro sighed. "I'll allow it for now, but you'd better make your point soon."

"Thank you, your Honor. Now, Ms. Ames, you testified you did not have consensual intercourse with Mr. Abbington, correct?"

"Right. We were alone in his boathouse. He said they called it the 'Boar's Nest.'" She sniffed. "Now I know why. He came on to me, but

I said no. He grabbed me and ripped my blouse open. We fought, and I screamed. He punched me in the stomach and called me a name. Then he ran out of the boathouse and slammed the door."

"What did you do then?" Reed asked.

"I couldn't do anything. It hurt so much, I couldn't move. After a while, I left. Never spoke to him again. Don't want nothing to do with him!"

"Did you tell anyone about this incident? Your parents, for instance?"

She laughed. "Not on your life. They would kill me, or him."

"Yet you are testifying today. Why is that?"

"Because he may look like a nice guy, but I couldn't keep quiet when I heard what happened to Becky Skalney. Like it's the 'me too' time, isn't it?"

She nodded her head, agreeing with herself.

"No further questions," Reed said. He returned to his chair wearing a hint of a smile.

Blake rose slowly and spoke calmly.

"Ms. Ames, do you have any firsthand knowledge of the relationship between Beauregard Abbington and Rebecca Skalney?"

She paused before sheepishly answering, "No."

"No further questions, your Honor."

Reed rose quickly to redirect.

"Ms. Ames, what was your reaction when you heard about the death of Rebecca Skalney?"

"Objection, your Honor. Ms. Ames' reaction is completely irrelevant." Blake waved his hand in the air as if to brush Reed's question away.

"Overruled. The witness will answer the question."

"I thought Beau did the same thing to Becky that he tried to do to me, except this time he killed her."

Blake slammed the defense table with the palm of his hand. "Your Honor, move to strike!"

Navarro turned to the jury box. "The jury will disregard Ms. Ames' last statement."

But the damage had been done. Lou kept a poker face while inwardly he cheered.

Maybe Reed graduated from law school after all.

CHAPTER 6

VERDICT

Russell Blake's smile looked genuine as he approached the jury for his closing remarks.

"Ladies and gentlemen of the jury, I thank you for your careful attention and patience as you listened to testimony in this trial. While we lawyers labor to present our cases, it is you, the jury, who have the greatest task. And that is to determine innocence or guilt, the very future, of a young man whose life has just begun."

He spun toward the prosecution's table and jutted out his arm. "My esteemed colleague has presented evidence you must not ignore." Turning back to the jury, he continued. "Yet, the prosecution's evidence is only circumstantial when examined closely. Mr. Abbington has no motive for murder. In fact, backed by Mr. Armbruster's deposition, he was nowhere near the scene of the crime at the time of Rebecca's death. When the police arrived at the Abbington home on the morning of October 16, Mr. and Mrs. Abbington were out of town, and so was their son. Although no one in Possum Creek saw the defendant during the time in question, that does not mean he was not there, as Detective Yockel admitted on cross-examination.

"Mr. Harvey Walker, the family's mechanic, testified as to the mileage on the defendant's Land Rover. It is consistent with the round-trip distance between the town of Raider and Possum Creek.

"Officer Parker's testimony about his conversation with Mr. Abbington during the traffic stop confirmed the defendant's statement about his recent stay at Abbington's Possum Creek lodge.

"Mr. Cosentino testified that Beauregard Abbington's fingerprints were not found on Rebecca Skalney's body.

"Simply put, you do not have enough solid evidence to find Beauregard Abbington, an upstanding student at Craigmore College, guilty of this heinous crime. Dr. Peterson, a respected educator, has testified to Mr. Abbington's character. I place little value on the testimony of an inexperienced eighteen-year-old girl, who may have testified because of any number of possible perceived insults before her relationship with the defendant ended.

"I am sure when you look at the weak, so-called facts the District Attorney presented, you will conclude that while Rebecca Skalney died at the hands of a predator, and we grieve with the family, that predator was not Beauregard Abbington."

After Blake took his seat, Eric Reed approached the jury. In a "it's-just-us-folks" tone, he picked up on Blake's last words. Reed leaned forward, resting his hands on the jury box.

"The defense is correct. Rebecca Skalney died at the hands of a predator. And that predator sits before you in this courtroom. Oh, he appears to be a Texas gentleman, but what goes on behind that cultivated facade? Predators do not wear signs. Upstanding citizens do not drive drunk while transporting drugs.

"Mr. Blake said the defendant lacked motive. But he had a motive. It was the same motive that left Margaret Ames immobilized with pain after she rejected Beauregard's sexual advances.

"As for the round-trip mileage on his car that Mr. Blake believes proves Mr. Abbington's alibi, it proves only that he had driven 124 miles somewhere at sometime between Friday and Saturday afternoon. He could have driven those 124 miles anywhere after killing Rebecca Skalney and leaving her body in the boathouse.

"He had motive and opportunity. His parents were out of town. Rebecca was angry at her father's order that she could no longer see her boyfriend. It would make sense she would sneak out of the house to see him again. Smart college student that he is, Beauregard could easily have arranged for a meeting in his boathouse through several means, including the old pebble thrown at the window schtick.

"Indeed, it is their case that is circumstantial, not ours. The defendant had motive. It was sex. He had opportunity. He was alone with her after midnight, in his boathouse, while his parents were out of town. And he had means—brute strength of an aroused male against a young girl. He had tried this before and failed. This time, it was fatal.

"Ladies and gentlemen, you must find Beauregard Abbington guilty. For the sake of other young women, for the sake of justice, this dangerous man must be removed from society.

"I thank you for your service and believe you will reach the only correct conclusion."

After Judge Navarro charged the jury, Lou's life stood still while the twelve took two days to deliberate. His home grew as quiet as Becky's tomb. Lou paced through the house, stopping often to stare into space, or sit motionless, alone, in the garage. He ate little and spoke less, trying to make sense of his loss.

Questions swirled in his mind as he lay on their bed.

What good is a God who can't watch over a 17-year-old? Why did he let this happen? Let Sally mumble her prayers. I'm through with God.

Lou rose and yanked the crucifix that hung over their bed off the wall and looked at it briefly before flinging it into the wastebasket.

Lou was relieved Sally no longer reached out to him for comfort, since he had nothing to offer her. He had entered a dark cave, leaving only his body behind.

When the telephone's ring ripped through their home's black curtain of grief, both jumped from their seats at the kitchen table.

Lou grabbed the receiver. His legs turned to rubber when he heard Reed's voice. He leaned against the doorjamb.

"Jury's in."

Silently, eight men and four women filed into the jury box, all absorbed in taking their seats. Lou focused on Juror Number Three. He seemed intrigued by his fingernails and never looked up, even when the judge asked for their verdict.

"On the first charge of felony murder, we find the defendant, Beauregard Abbington, not guilty."

The jury foreperson's voice sounded flat and formal, and it did not change as he responded to the lesser charges with the same decision.

Sally gasped and silence cloaked the courtroom until the judge thanked the jury. The bang of Navarro's gavel drove an auditory spike into Lou Skalney's heart. His vision darkened, as if he were looking at the world through black smoke. He struggled to control his breathing as he glared at the handshakes and shoulder pats among the defense team.

That's right. Celebrate now while you can.

CHAPTER 7

TWO FACES OF GRIEF

Fall surrendered to winter, and now winter was giving way to spring.

Sally suffered sleepless nights while mechanically cooking and cleaning her way through endless, silent days. Becky's door remained closed, like a band-aid covering a raw wound.

Every morning, she watched Lou turn his head away from the door as he walked from their bedroom to the bathroom, his lips compressed into a thin line.

He's afraid memories will tear him apart.

After Lou left for work one day, Sally faced Becky's door. She held the crucifix she had salvaged from the wastebasket months ago, close to her heart. She forced herself to take several deep breaths before she slowly turned the handle. Sally stood at the threshold and braced for memories to attack like a colony of rabid bats. Instead, the open book lying on her daughter's flowered comforter next to Esmeralda, Becky's first and favorite doll, filled the hole in Sally's heart with a dollop of sweet memory. After placing the crucifix on the nightstand, she fell onto Becky's bed and clutched Esmeralda.

Tears turned into wracking sobs. Sally wailed into the abandoned room, shrieking her pain, as she had never done before. She thought she would never be able to stop and did not care. Becky's life rolled past in a kaleidoscope of memories, each more precious than the one before. Could there be any pain greater than that of a parent bereft of her child? While she rolled side to side, still clutching Esmeralda in a death grip, Sally sobbed until there were no more tears. Her throat was raw. Drained from her emotional torrent, she dropped to the floor on her knees and leaned on the bed.

"Dear God, you took Becky, and I don't know why. Lou blames you, but they say you give and take away. I want to see her. Holy God, I want to be with her. Help me get through this, because right now, I don't want to live without Becky."

Sally crawled onto the bed, curled into the fetal position, and slid into an exhausted sleep.

A few days later, Sally looked out the kitchen window at their detached garage. In the gathering dusk, she saw a strip of light lining the bottom of its closed door. She assumed Lou was tinkering with a project that lately occupied his evenings. She grabbed her sweater to tell him dinner would be ready in twenty minutes.

Patches of green grass and tiny daffodil tips dotted her path through melting snow to the garage's side entrance. She sniffed the air, searching for hints of Spring.

Without knocking, Sally opened the door and poked her head into the clutter. With no room to park a bike, let alone a car, the garage offended her sense of order, so she rarely entered it. Boxes containing God- knows-what lined three walls, and the workbench where Lou stood claimed the fourth. Lawn equipment, car parts, machines she could not name, and metal objects, as mysterious as they were plentiful, lay strewn about.

She noticed the corkboard Lou had nailed to the studs behind his workbench and gasped. Photos of the Abbingtons covered every inch. Some were cut from newspaper articles, but others were informal pictures, like paparazzi would take—or a stalker.

Lou turned to her, his hand covering a legal pad. He forced a smile.

"So you braved the mess, did you?"

"Dinner will be ready in a few minutes. Lou, what is all this?" She waved her hand at the corkboard.

"Nothing."

"It doesn't look like nothing. The trial's over and we've got to go on. Lou, you can't stay fixated on the Abbingtons. It's not healthy."

He stared at Sally for a long moment.

What's going on in his mind? He does nothing without a reason.

"Lou, talk to me. Are you going to do something you will regret?"

"Of course not. I just haven't had a chance to take down these old photos, that's all. You're worried about nothing. What's for dinner?"

Why does he think distracting me with a dumb question would work?

"High test or decaff?" Sally asked Kathy as she reached for the coffee canister.

Kathy Kowalski rested her arms on her friend's kitchen table and sighed. She glanced up at the kitschy black and white cat clock on Becky's wall. A flick of the tail, a flick of time. Kathy smiled.

"I think high test today. Didn't sleep a wink last night. It's Saturday and I have a ton of outdoor spring clean-up ahead of me."

Sally filled the percolator's strainer with freshly ground coffee. Nothing like hot coffee shared with a friend. The rich aroma teased her nose, and she breathed it in. She was up to eight cups a day now, just to push through the hours. Her kitchen sparkled with its blue and yellow French Provincial décor. It had become her safe harbor.

"What kept you awake?"

"I guess lots of little things." Kathy sighed. "Usual teen stuff with Gabe and Lisa. Rudy just got back from out of town, chasing some sort of lead. I worry about him all the time, especially when he goes undercover for a story. Sink's dripping. I need to call a plumber. Just stuff. What goes through *your* mind while you stare at the ceiling?"

"I'm worried about Lou," Sally answered as she placed steaming mugs on the table and settled into her chair. "He's acting weird, more withdrawn and quieter than usual, and spends hours fiddling around in that mess of a garage. When I went in there to call him to dinner the other night, I saw a wall full of pictures of the Abbingtons. I think he's been stalking them with his camera. He'll never admit it, but I think he's fixated on Beauregard and that entire family. When he saw I noticed the pictures, and asked him if he was planning something, he denied it and changed the subject. Tried to sound reassuring."

"Maybe counseling would help."

Sally snorted. "We're talking about the same person, right?"

"Well, for most people, that would help."

Sally leaned against the back of her chair. "Yesterday I found him in our spare room, cleaning his father's Colt.45. When I asked him why, he said it reminded him of when his father taught him how to shoot at the target range." She sniffed. "I think that's the only time those two did anything together. Target shooting. Sometimes I wonder…"

"Where is he now?"

"Said he had a few errands in town. Kathy, we're like roommates sharing the same space, but not the same life. He never talked much, but it's worse now. I feel so abandoned, just when I need him the most."

Sally burst into tears and groped in her pockets for a tissue. Kathy grabbed a paper towel and pulled Sally close.

"Let it out, Sally. You have Rudy and me, and close friends that love you from St. Stan's, and your neighbors, too. God did not abandon you. Didn't we learn that in religion class when we were kids?" Kathy grinned as Sally offered a weak smile.

"I guess so. But it's not just about me. Something is wrong with Lou. I'm sure he's depressed and that fixation he has about his father's gun scares me."

"Where does he keep the gun?"

"In a locked tackle box in the spare bedroom."

They looked at each other and conversed wordlessly, as close friends do. As one, they walked to the spare room. Sally stood on tiptoe to reach the top shelf in the closet and brought down the tackle box. It was unlocked. She lifted the lid and turned wide eyes to Kathy. "It's gone."

CHAPTER 8

TAKING CARE OF BUSINESS

Kathy gave Sally a departing hug. "Maybe he took it target shooting. Don't think the worst."

As she watched Kathy walk to her car, Sally knew her friend tried to be reassuring. But to her, it sounded like whistling in the dark to keep fear at bay. It was getting harder to silence the warning echoing in her head. *What if he's planning revenge?*

At first, she attributed Lou's withdrawal as grief. But rather than fading over time, it became a part of him like his drive to take care of business.

He's a good man, even though I wish we were closer. Surely, he wouldn't be so stupid to throw away our life, his life, just for vengeance. Maybe I'm overreacting. But then, there's that wall of photos in the garage and the missing gun.

She wished she could believe Kathy's parting words. Sally dreaded the long hours ahead until Lou returned home this evening, when she would demand the truth. No more guessing. She needed certainty, and by heaven, she was going to get it.

By the time the evening's newscast ended, her dinner had cooled in abandoned pots. She punched Lou's cell number on her iPhone.

The least he could do was call me if he's running late. I've had enough.

"Hi Sally. I was just about to call you. Ran into Harry at the hardware store and one thing led to another. Don't hold dinner for me. I'm playing poker at Harry's tonight. Don't wait up, either."

"Thanks for letting me know before I cooked dinner," Sally growled.

"Sorry. I guess I lost track of time."

"Lou, where is your gun?" She held her phone in a death grip. *No more waiting until the right time to talk to him because there hasn't been a right time for months now.*

"Why were you looking for it?"

Is he stalling for time?

"I was cleaning the closet in the spare room and noticed the tackle box was empty."

"Yea, well. Town's not safe anymore with that killer loose. I'm packing."

"Lou, please tell me you won't hurt him. You're scaring me. You can't…"

"Haven't I always taken care of you and Becky? You think I'd do anything that would cause harm to you? I'm just protecting me and mine."

"And that's how you do it? With a gun? "

"If that's what it takes."

Sally snorted. "The new you."

And I don't like him.

Sally had never sounded so cold. Lou realized he'd crossed a line.

She'll never understand.

But right now, his black Ford F150 sat parked behind Beau's Land Rover. In the darkness, a canopy of tree limbs hid the truck along the side of Abbington's driveway.

Lou had stalked Beau for the last month. Now only one light remained on in the house, and Lou knew Beau would soon step outside to wait for Floyd Armbruster. Abbingtons had paid the fine for his DUI, and Beau spent all of three days in jail. Only the drug possession charge remained. Meanwhile, he and Floyd spent Friday nights wherever they could find action at 11p.m and the start of the weekend.

He smiled when he saw his prey step onto the front portico. Just like clockwork, but he had to move fast. Lou figured Floyd would show in about 15 minutes.

He again fingered the handcuffs. By now, he could apply them one handed with his eyes closed. It had surprised Lou they were so easy to purchase online. He felt the Colt.45 in his waist holster for the 90th time.

Quickly, he exited his truck and squatted below the Land Rover's passenger window and watched Beauregard stroll to his car. Beau was about to turn to lean against its door to wait for Floyd as usual. Lou stood and pointed the Colt.45 at Beauregard's head.

"Do–not–even–think–of–moving. And don't make a sound, or I'll blow your brains out. Understand?"

Beau froze and stared at Lou, wide-eyed. When he nodded, Lou walked around the Land Rover and poked the Colt's barrel against his neck.

"Put your hands behind your back."

With practiced ease, Lou hooked the cuffs on Beau's wrists with one hand and clicked them shut. "We're going for a ride. Get in the truck and don't make a sound or it will be your last."

He shoved him towards the Ford, opened the passenger door, and ordered Beau inside. With the gun pressed against his prisoner, Lou fastened the passenger seatbelt — another restraint. Once behind the wheel, with the windows rolled up, Lou started the engine.

"Do you know why I'm doing this?"

"Yea, you still think I killed Becky, but I swear I didn't. She was the most amazing girl I ever dated. She had a great sense of humor and sweet, quiet ways. Mr. Skalney, I loved her! You've got to believe me." His voice cracked. "I miss her so much."

Lou looked at Beau for a long moment.

I could almost believe him. He looks like he's about to cry. Crocodile tears, that's all.

"She's not daddy's little girl anymore," echoed in his mind.

Lou looked away from Beau, and over his shoulder, as he pulled onto the road. "Yeah, right. You'd say anything to save your skin."

"Where are you taking me?" Lou heard fear in Beau's voice. It fed something deep inside, and he craved more.

"Where you deserve to be."

"What does that mean?" Beau's voice cracked.

Let him stew.

Houses and buildings gave way to fields and woods. Lou flicked on his bright lights.

"Hey man, I wasn't even in town when someone killed Becky."

Beauregard twisted his body side to side, pushed frantically against the floorboard and back of the seat. But with his hands behind his back, he soon tired.

More fear. More pleasure.

"Please, Mr. Skalney, I respected Becky. I wouldn't have hurt a hair on her head."

"Wouldn't hurt a hair on her head? You gave her drugs. On top of being a murderer, you're a drug pusher."

Lou reduced speed to a crawl and eased onto a dirt road, hidden, unless someone knew it was there. The truck slowly navigated ruts and high grass until it arrived at an abandoned barn.

It was still an imposing structure, although sagging on two sides and with double doors barely clinging to their hinges. Even in the dark, Lou made out the stone foundation of what was once Miller's farmhouse. He recalled trespassing on old man Miller's land to hunt with his friend Cyrus, and in all those years, they never saw the recluse. No one in town knew much about him, and he died alone. People guessed he was in his nineties. Now all that remained of a solitary life was a falling down barn and a pile of stones.

Lou's lips imitated a smile as he parked the Ford 150 and eased himself out. He walked to the truck's bed and pulled a flashlight and roll of duct tape from a bulky satchel and placed them on the truck's cab roof. With his gun in one hand, he yanked the passenger door open and unfastened the seatbelt.

"Get out."

Beau shot him a terrified look, stood down from the cab and frantically looked around.

Lou sneered. "Looking for a place to run? Go ahead, take off," he said with a malicious grin. Beau looked from Lou's face to the gun he held. Not an athlete like Floyd, he cast a fearful glance into black woods. Lou, flashlight and tape in hand, easily marched him to the barn.

Once inside, Lou flicked on the industrial sized flashlight. Its powerful beam showed abandoned stalls, an old milking stool leaning against one wall, and an overhead hayloft. He pointed the gun barrel toward one of the two poles propping up the hayloft.

"Sit against that pole."

Beau eased himself to the barn floor, his back against the pole.

"Come on, Mr. Skalney, please believe me. I did not kill Becky. If you let me loose, we can find the killer together. I'll help you." He began to cry.

Lou broke off a long length of tape. "Here's how you're going to help me. You will hold still while I tape your ankles together. And then you will hold still while I attach your wrists, handcuffs and all, to the pole. If you do not hold still, I will blow your brains out. Got it?"

With tears streaming down his cheeks, Beau nodded. Minutes later, Lou smiled at his handiwork. He retrieved his satchel from the truck bed. Back in the barn, he grabbed the milking stool and eased his weight onto it. It held.

With an audible sigh, he pulled a thermos of coffee and a deli sandwich from his satchel. He checked his watch. Midnight. Just on time. Lou rested the gun on his thigh while he sipped with one hand and ate with the other. He savored each bite, feasting on the moment he had planned for months, and relishing the fear written on Beauregard's face.

After a while, Beau begged again. "What do you want from me? What are you going to do to me? Why won't you believe me? The jury did. Why can't you admit you are wrong and find the actual killer?"

"I found the actual killer. Now we are enjoying some time together in this barn like you and Becky spent time in your boathouse, until you, you—"

Lou left the sentence unfinished and gulped the last of his coffee. He balled up the sandwich wrapping and threw it over his shoulder. When Beau opened his mouth to respond, Lou aimed the gun at him. In desperation and terror, Beau shook his head frantically.

"No, no! You got it all wrong. We can work together. I swear. I know who she hung with besides me. Please!" He pulled his knees up and writhed furiously from side to side, rubbing his ankles together. But with all his struggling, he could not undo the duct tape and finally gave up.

After an hour, Beau said, "I need to pee."

"So pee. I'm not stopping you."

"Come on, man. You know I can't run away. You have the gun."

"Forget it."

It was a long night.

When Sally awoke after a fitful night's sleep, she looked to Lou's side of the bed. Empty. Her lips formed a determined line.

This is it. I won't hide from the truth any longer.

She threw off the blanket, jammed her feet into slippers and grabbed jeans and a top from the closet. Once dressed, she marched into the kitchen, made a pot of coffee, and waited for it to perk.

Lou's not a womanizer, and he's not a drinker. He didn't spend the night at a poker game. Poker game my foot! And who is Harry, anyway?

Sally grabbed her cell phone and pressed Lou's number. When it went to voice mail, she knew what she had to do. She poured the brew into a mug and called Cyrus McCoy on his private cell.

The Sherriff answered on the second ring. "What is it, Sally?"

She skipped the preliminaries.

"Lou's been stalking the Abbingtons, and he didn't come home last night. He has his gun, and I'm terrified he's out to kill Beauregard."

"What? Why didn't you tell me this before?" Cyrus' concern terrified her because it confirmed her nagging inner voice.

"I didn't want to believe he would really do something like that. And every time I questioned him, he'd say something reassuring. I so wanted to believe him, I ignored my suspicions. Cyrus. I'm scared to death."

"Did you try to reach him?"

"Went to voice mail."

"I'll get back to you."

By the time Sally finished her second cup, the phone rang. It was Cyrus.

"Beau's car is still in his driveway. He and Armbruster had planned to get together, but Floyd said Beau wasn't there when he got to his house."

Sally's heart skipped a beat, and she felt blood rushing to her head. "Oh dear God! What are you going to do? You have to find them!"

"Sally, calm down. I'll put out an APB. Meanwhile. I have a hunch where he may have taken him."

Lou stood, stretched, and limped on stiff legs to look out the barn door. The sun was rising, turning black night to early dawn. He heard a car motor growing in the distance. The world was awakening. It was time.

Lou walked to Beauregard, whose mouth hung open in sleep. When he kicked him in the thigh, Beau's eyes flew open. Relishing the terror reflected in them, Lou jammed his Colt.45 against Beauregard Abbington's forehead.

"It's time to take care of business."

He pulled the trigger. He held his breath shot again. Blood and brains floated from Beauregard's shattered head to paint the pole and wall behind it.

Lou exhaled as he looked down at Beau's mutilated body. Instead of satisfaction, a deep sorrow crept into his heart. He blinked away sudden tears. A car door slammed shut as death's artwork oozed toward the floor.

Lou heard footsteps growing closer and turned to see Cyrus standing in the doorway. Wordlessly, he dropped his gun and raised his hands.

Cyrus shook his head. "Oh Lou, no."

CHAPTER 9

TWO PATHS

Cyrus mirandized Lou, who offered no resistance to his arrest. His hands shook, and he gritted his teeth as he fastened handcuffs around his friend's wrists.

Did Lou plan this part as well? In a million years, I wouldn't have thought he could do such a terrible thing.

He stood beside Lou as his deputies, forensics, and the medical examiner swarmed onto the scene. Cyrus waved over a deputy, and as the officer headed their way, Lou whispered, "I had to do it, Cyrus. I had to take care of business for Becky and his other victims."

"Shut up, Lou. Save it for your attorney."

Lou raised his voice. "No. I did it, and I don't care who knows it."

Stop talking, you idiot, Cyrus thought, and quickly handed Lou over to his deputy. Before returning to supervise the crime scene, he blinked away tears as he wrote every word of Lou's confession in his notebook.

Sally watched half a dozen police officers cordon off her property with yellow crime scene tape, while a man in a rumpled suit approached her front door.

Oh dear God, this can't be happening.

She held her breath against a sudden wave of nausea and froze when the doorbell rang. She forced herself to walk to the door, and with a shaking hand, turn the handle. Her heart pounded as a tall, sad faced, middle-aged man showed his badge.

"Are you Mrs. Louis Skalney?"

"Yes."

"I'm Detective Yockel, homicide liaison for Raider and Houston County. I have a warrant to search your home and property."

Homicide! Warrant!

Sally barely opened the door further to let him in.

"Thank you," Yockel said as he entered her living room. "Perhaps you may want to sit, Mrs. Skalney. May I call you Sally?"

"Y-yes," she whispered and sank into the club chair near the door. She trembled while every neuron in her brain flew into panic mode.

"Sally, we have taken your husband, Louis, into custody for the murder of Beauregard Abbington this morning."

Her hands flew to her mouth. "Oh, dear God!"

"Do you know where your husband was last night?"

She shook her head. "I talked to him on my cell around seven last evening. He was late for dinner and said I shouldn't wait up for him. He was going to a poker game with Harry."

"Harry who? What's his last name?" Yockel pulled a notebook from his pocket and put pen to paper.

"I have no idea who Harry is. He could have met this Harry person in a bar for all I know."

"Have you noticed any changes in your husband's behavior lately?"

Cameos of the photos Lou had taken and pinned on the corkboard in the garage, memories of his remarks about justice withheld, and of his rejection of all her efforts to bring normalcy back into their lives, flashed through her mind.

I was so blind. I thought it was a good sign when he said he was going to take the photos down last week, but they're still there.

Looking back, Sally realized all the terrifying hints, covered by his assurances that all was well, reflected the battle that had raged in her husband for the last year. She wanted to believe in Lou so badly, she had told herself his innate goodness would win in the end. Despite the warning signs, the image of Lou taking a life was too unreal to believe. But today, truth wore a suit and carried a badge.

You waged a long battle, Lou, and lost.

While her love had hardened into resignation and then anger, she had remained silent. She would be silent no longer.

After a deep breath, she said, "He has photos of the Abbingtons on a corkboard in the garage. When I noticed his gun was missing, I asked him where it was. He said with Beauregard out free, the town wasn't safe anymore. Said he was carrying his Colt."

Detective Yockel listened without interrupting as Sally described the last two years of their lives. He nodded sympathetically and occasionally asked a question. His empathy, and her fury, overrode the voice in her mind that shouted, "betrayal!"

I can't believe this is really happening. It's like a nightmare.

When Sally finished, he asked, "Was last evening the last time you spoke with him?"

"Yes. He never came home last night. That scared me, and why I called Cyrus McCoy this morning. I worried because no matter what he was doing, he would always come home."

Sally frowned and struggled to find the words for her question. "Can you tell me, um, where he killed him? Could there be a mistake? Is it possible someone else killed him and Lou found the body?"

"We're putting together the pieces now. It appears he shot Beauregard in an abandoned barn."

"On old man Miller's property. Right"? Sally studied Yockel's face for confirmation.

"Yes. How did you know?"

How did I know? I know because the man I married left when Becky died, and an angry stranger took his place.

"Lou used to hunt there with Cyrus when they were young. He would have remembered it's been abandoned for years. Cyrus said he had a hunch where Lou had taken Beau. I'm afraid to ask, but how was Beauregard killed?"

"He was shot."

"By a Colt.45?" Sally shuddered, fearing the answer.

"We are still investigating. I can't tell you more right now, Sally."

She sagged in her chair and threw her head back. *Probably best not to know right now. This is all too much.*

After answering every question Detective Yockel asked, three police officers joined them in the living room. He stood and said, "Please show us where your husband kept his gun."

Sally led them to the spare room and handed the detective the empty tackle box with three lonely bullets rolling around in it.

She surrendered every personal record they asked for and did not object when they photographed practically everything but the bathtub. Walking outside with the officers and Detective Yockel, she saw curious neighbors standing in clusters on the sidewalk. Sally's anger trumped her shame. She raised the garage door so the police could search it, and then her Saturn parked in the driveway.

Take a good look, friends.

Three hours later, Detective Yockel said they were done for now and asked if she had family or friends she could call.

"Friends. My relatives live in Dallas. My parents are dead."

"Why don't you call a friend to stay with you for now? Meanwhile, take my card. Call me if you think of anything else that may be relevant."

Sally called Kathy when the detective and police drove away. After updating her friend, she concluded, "I suppose I should go to the jail to see Lou and call a lawyer, but right now I don't even want to look at him."

"No, you don't have to go to the jail. I'm picking you up right now and bringing you here."

"But…"

"But nothing. In fact, pack for a couple of days. You need distance from your home right now, and lots of it."

"I won't argue." She sighed as she looked around her home and shivered. The police had violated it and it would never be the same.

Half an hour later, Sally turned her face away from the yellow crime scene tape as she made her way to Kathy's car. She tossed her suitcase onto the back seat and climbed in.

"Holy tamales!" Kathy said, looking at the Skalney home as she put her car in gear.

"And that's only what you see." Sally made a face as she described the interrogation, and hunt for evidence. "They violated my home. Every day I walk past Becky's empty bedroom and now, everywhere I look, I will see those strangers plowing through every inch, looking at every record, ripping apart the last of my life. And for what? So Lou Skalney could take care of business?"

"Oh Sally, I can't imagine."

Kathy handed Sally a glass of wine after getting her settled in the family room. They sipped in silence until she said, "I should have spoken up sooner. I told you how weird Lou's been acting. Maybe if I'd said something, Beauregard would still be alive." She brushed a tear aside.

"And what would you have said? You had nothing concrete to go on. A man cleaning his gun? This is Texas, Sally. Lots of guys carry. And what if you had been wrong and landed Lou in a ton of trouble? Stop second guessing yourself. This is on Lou, not you."

"Maybe." She offered Kathy a weak smile.

"Let Rudy help Lou get a lawyer. One good thing about being a reporter, he knows everyone."

Sally rested her head against the back of the sofa and stared at the ceiling. "What would I do without you and Rudy?"

After a moment, she leaned forward, put her wine aside, and pulled a tissue from her jeans' pocket. After a spate of crying, she wiped her eyes and sniffed.

"It's not only Lou's defense, if you can defend what he did. It's the rest of my life. My child is dead. With Lou in jail, or worse, I have no money coming in without his paycheck. I see a looming pile of legal fees. How will I pay the mortgage, the groceries? I'll need to find a job. Who's going to hire me in this town? I'll have to move. Where will I go? What will I do?"

She searched Kathy's face for answers while shredding her tissue. Kathy took Sally's hand. "One step at a time, my friend. Rudy and I will always be here for you. Right now, you need to trust in God more than ever. Rely on us too. Eat, sleep, and tomorrow we will find answers."

Rudy's raised voice bounced off the jail's visiting room walls. "Lou, don't use a public defender when you don't need to."

Lou shrugged and gave his friend a blank look from across the table. "Why not? It doesn't matter."

"You say that now, but just one visit with Mark Edwards will change your mind. He's the best criminal lawyer in Houston County and I got him to agree to take your case. For half his usual fee, I might add."

"Really? Where were you when I bought my truck for a small fortune?"

"Hiding. You were taking care of business and wouldn't have listened to me anymore than you are now."

"Probably not," Lou said, and went on. "You're my closest friend, and I'm grateful you and Kathy are helping Sally. I killed Beauregard, but I'm not insane. I knew it was wrong, and I did it anyway. And I would do it again. The so-called justice system failed, and I don't trust it to do right by me either. In fact, they should find me guilty. I won't leave Sally to deal with a pile of legal fees."

"We'll help…"

"No!"

Frustrated, Rudy blew out a long breath. "If you're so worried about legal bills, why did you kill Beau in the first place? How did you expect Sally would manage without you?"

Lou's head jerked back as the truth hit home. He covered his face with both hands and shook his head. Neither spoke until Rudy leaned toward Lou and asked, "Is this your way of committing suicide by trial?"

"When did you become Dr. Phill?"

"When you became Crackpot of the Year."

Lou stood. "Just watch over Sally."

CHAPTER 10

JUDGMENT

Lou's attorney barged into the visitors' room at the jail. He was out of breath and holding an open briefcase bulging with papers. He nodded at Lou and landed on the chair across from him while pulling out a legal pad. After a quick smile, he said, "Mr. Skalney, I'm Cal Holder, your public defender. I only recently learned I would represent you, so I apologize for this." He waved his hand over his briefcase, from which several papers threatened to erupt. "You are charged with kidnapping and first degree murder. Your arraignment for the murder charge is scheduled two months from now. Tell me what happened and leave nothing out."

Cal lifted his pen and focused on his new client. After Lou gathered his thoughts, he described everything he had done and why he had done it.

"I'm sorry for your loss, Mr. Skalney. I can't imagine your pain. But you shouldn't have said anything, let alone confess to murder. It's bad enough Sheriff McCoy found you in the barn, standing over Beauregard's dead body, with a gun in your hand. Hopefully, we can keep you from the death penalty by pleading temporary insanity. Otherwise…" He shrugged his shoulders.

Lou snapped at Cal. "Are you nuts?"

"Well, one of us better be, and it's not me."

"Look, Cal. Cyrus caught me holding a gun over a dead body in an abandoned barn. I knew what I was doing and why. I wasn't insane and am not now. Period."

Cal drummed his fingers on the jail's visiting room table, then ran them through his thinning hair.

"Look, you have one chance to save your life. Between the scene you just described, and your brilliant announcement to everyone within earshot that you are guilty and don't care, the only way I can keep you breathing is if you plead insanity, like I said."

Lou folded his arms and leaned on the table. Looking Holder in the eye, he said, "Plead what you want. Knock yourself out. I'm not changing my story. It's exactly what happened."

Holder grunted. "I'm not Clarence Darrow, you know. It's this or nothing. I could get a mafia don the Good Citizen award easier than I can save your butt without an insanity plea."

Lou snorted a laugh. "Probably been done."

Cal stood and packed his briefcase with the papers he had hoped to fill with defense motions.

"You're tying my hands, Lou. I will enter a not guilty plea for you at the arraignment, anyway. From there, we and the prosecution will request psychiatric evaluations. Here's my card. If you change your mind, call me. Otherwise, I will see you in two months."

Lou Skalney stood beside Cal Holder in Judge Ramos Navarro's courtroom as Eric Reed read the state's charge of first degree murder. Lou studied Reed for any sign of their previous connection from Beauregard's trial.

I wonder if down deep he understands.

But the District Attorney's face was as much of a mask as was Lou's when Holder entered a not guilty plea for his client.

I'm as guilty as they come. What a farce.

Holder requested to approach the bench and Reed rose to join him.

"Your Honor, the defense does not deny Mr. Skalney killed Beauregard Abbington. The question arises whether he was sane then and if he is sane now, so I will request a psychiatric evaluation. I entered a not guilty plea in his best interests, but he has indicated he does not wish to offer a vigorous defense. Without his cooperation with an insanity plea, it will be impossible for me, or any other public defender, to represent him adequately."

Reed nodded. "The prosecution would request its own evaluation as well."

"Requests granted, gentlemen."

As they returned to their respective tables, Navarro checked the court docket and announced the date for opening arguments to begin in 97 days after they completed both psychiatric evaluations.

Three months later, Sally listened to Eric Reed's opening remarks. She cringed as he described Lou's simmering fury after Beauregard Abbington's acquittal, and his actions leading to the night of the murder. Guilt flooded her again.

Thank God I can't testify against him.

She wanted to plug her ears when Reed described the murder and charges against this stranger who once shared her bed.

In his opening statement before Judge Navarro, Cal Holder did not deny Lou had killed Beauregard. Instead, he focused on Lou, a tortured father who struggled to deal with his daughter's murder. A father, watching the man he believed had murdered his child walk free, sought justice in the only way he knew. He aimed his remarks at the jurors' hearts, not minds, hoping his words would hide the fact he had little else to say.

After a brief recess, Eric Reed called his first witness. Dr. Angela Markham stated her credentials and experience as a forensic psychiatrist.

"Did you examine Mr. Skalney?"

"Yes I did. At the time of the murder, Mr. Skalney knew what he was doing. It was a premeditated act based on false assumptions. Dreadful as his actions were, they were logical, and he carried out his plans in an orderly fashion. He stated he knew what he was doing was wrong and against the law. He said he did it anyway because the justice system failed his daughter. He has symptoms of depression and dysfunctional grief, and based his actions on a false belief. However, that does not make him clinically insane. Troubled and in error, yes, but not insane. His choice to refuse to defend himself, although indicating depression, does not rise to the legal definition of insanity. He is aware of what he is doing and the probable outcome."

"Thank you Dr. Markham."

As she walked to her seat in the audience, she cast Lou a sympathetic look. He did not raise his eyes to her.

Reed next called Cyrus McCoy to the stand. Settling in the witness chair, McCoy turned a blank face toward the D.A. After he testified to his professional background, Reed asked him, "Sheriff McCoy, please tell the jury what you saw when you entered Mr. Miller's barn."

"Mr. Skalney was standing next to Beauregard Abbington, who appeared deceased. Lou, Mr. Skalney, was holding a gun in his hand."

"And?"

"And what? That's what I saw."

"Was Mr. Abbington's body intact?"

"No."

Reed walked to the table that held evidence, lifted the gruesome crime scene photos and said, "If it pleases the court, I submit these photos as evidence labeled A-1 through 3 for the jury."

Lou stared out the window while twelve good and true citizens examined them. Unlike his close observation of the jury's reaction to Becky's photos, he did not bother to watch this jury's response.

After all had seen the evidence, Reed continued to question McCoy.

"What did you do upon finding Mr. Skalney holding the gun over Mr. Abbington's body?"

"I handcuffed and mirandized him. I needed to remain at the scene, so I assigned a deputy to take Mr. Skalney into custody and transport him to the jail."

"Did Mr. Skalney say anything?"

McCoy pulled a notebook from his uniform pocket, took several seconds to find his place, and read, "I had to do it, Cyrus. I had to take care of business for Becky and his other victims."

Cyrus looked at Lou, who nodded his head as if to say it was all right.

"Would you repeat that louder so the jury can hear you?" Eric said.

Cyrus cleared his throat and repeated Lou's statement. Eric nodded.

"And did Mr. Skalney say anything else?"

"He said 'I did it and I don't care who knows it.'"

"Thank you, Sheriff McCoy. No further questions." Reed resumed his seat and glanced at Holder.

"Recross, Counselor?" Navarro said.

Holder stood. "No, your Honor. We reserve the right to recross later. I would like to confer with my client at this time."

Navarro nodded, banged his gavel, and declared a 20 minute recess.

Alone in the holding area, Holder wasted no time as he faced Lou.

"Our expert shrink will testify you had a grief filled psychotic break when you killed Beau. He also believes you are suffering from a psychotic depression, so we can plead insanity. If you do not submit an insanity plea, I guarantee the jury will convict you and the state will execute you. Now, do you want that? Consider your wife, your family and friends."

"My wife would be better off without me, and I have no family. For once, the justice system will work even if I must ram the truth down its throat to do it. I was not insane then and am not insane now, no matter what your shrink says."

Cal sighed. "Well, maybe I can gin up some sympathy for you if you testify how Becky's murder affected you and Sally."

"I will not spill my guts to a jury for a pity plea. I have nothing further to say and will not testify."

Holder stared at Lou for several seconds before shrugging his shoulders.

"It's literally your funeral, Lou. I will inform Judge Navarro of my recommendations for your defense and your decision to reject legal advice. You leave me no other choice."

There was little more to be said or done. Conflicting psychiatric testimony, coupled with Lou's stubborn refusal to engage in his defense, left Holder with no ammunition. He followed professional procedures, informing the court of the situation so he would not face censure. Reed presented a few other witnesses, and with nothing more to offer in Lou's defense, Holder did not recross. The prosecution rested its case, assured of the outcome. Navarro charged the jury and adjourned the court.

Having been found guilty of both kidnapping and first-degree murder, Lou listened to Judge Navarro instruct the jury on the punishment phase of the trial. They had two choices: life in prison or death by lethal injection.

Eric Reed approached the jury.

"Ladies and gentlemen, you are here today to determine the fate of a cold-blooded killer. You heard Sheriff Cyrus McCoy testify that Louis Skalney admitted, while he was being taken into custody, that he killed Beauregard Abbington. Those are the words of a man turned lethal killer because of his daughter's murder. We could feel sympathy, but he is not a man who is sorry for what he has done. According to expert psychiatric testimony, he was sane at the time of the murder and at his trial. He is no longer fit to remain in society, even the harshest prison society."

Reed pointed to Franklin and Camilla Abbington. "Mr. Skalney claims he was taking care of business. He does not know what taking care of business means. Mr. and Mrs. Abbington do. Their company has supported this town for years and so we in Raider have prospered because of them. And their only son, Beauregard, was about to step up and serve this community in the honorable manner of his parents — until Louis Skalney decided he alone knew how to take care of business."

Franklin Abbington folded his arms across his chest, as if to protect his heart. Camilla stared at Lou, tears streaming down her cheeks. Without turning to look at them, Lou felt their rage crawl up his back.

"Now it is your turn to take care of business. Justice demands the death penalty, and nothing less."

After Reed's closing, Holder approached the jury.

"Ladies and gentlemen, Louis Skalney is not a hired gun or a crazed murderer. He is a man whose heart was ripped from him and shattered into a thousand pieces. All his life, he worked to provide a living for his widowed mother and then his wife and daughter. His father taught him that an honorable man takes care of business. And so, for this terrible period in his life, taking care of business meant getting the justice he thought his daughter deserved and to protect other girls like his Becky."

He turned to the first juror on his left, and said, "Put yourself in Mr. Skalney's shoes. Think how you would respond if your child's body was found dead in a boathouse. Would you be rational? Wouldn't you scream and cry out in agony?"

He turned to the next juror. "Wouldn't you want to do to your child's killer what he had done to the light of your life? Lou Skalney did what his father had taught him to do, because he believed Beauregard had killed and would kill again. Mr. Skalney is not a cold-blooded killer who needs to be destroyed for the good of society. Instead, he is a devoted family man who acted in a state of excruciating pain and despair. Despite his psychotic depression, he had the integrity to admit what he had done and why. He is not a man so evil he should not live. Punishment? Yes. Even life in prison, but not execution. This is a time for understanding and mercy, not an eye for an eye. Thank you for your time and consideration."

It took only three hours to judge Louis Skalney's fate. After the bailiff presented the jury's written decision to Navarro, the judge asked them, "Do you find, beyond a reasonable doubt, that the defendant, Louis Skalney, would continue to commit acts that would constitute a threat to society?"

"Yes," the foreperson announced, looking at Lou.

"Do you find from the evidence, taking in all the evidence including the circumstances of the event, the character and background, personal moral culpability of the defendant, Louis Skalney, that there is a sufficient mitigating circumstance or circumstances, to warrant that a sentence of life without parole, rather than the death penalty, be imposed?"

"No."

After polling the jury, Navarro looked at Lou.

"The court sentences you, Louis Skalney, to death by lethal injection at a time to be determined. You will be remanded to Huntsville prison to await your execution."

Lou felt Navarro's words hit like a gut punch, and for a moment, he struggled to breathe.

It's what I wanted. Why do I feel like I was just struck by lightning?

The judge turned to Franklin and asked, "Mr. Abbington, do you wish to address Mr. Skalney now?"

Franklin slowly rose and looked at Camilla.

"My wife will speak for both of us."

Judge Navarro nodded. Camilla rose and walked, head held high, to take her seat in the witness chair. She looked into Lou's eyes. He wanted to look away, but forced himself to face her.

"Do you think you are the only parent who loved their child? Since the moment you…" She let out a sob, but quickly regained control. "Even now, you don't have it in you to feel any remorse for your heinous act. It is you who are a cold-blooded killer, not our son. Beauregard did not kill Becky. That is something you cannot grasp.

"Now, every day of our lives, we live with a hole in our hearts nothing can fill. Eliminating you will make Raider safer, but it will never compensate for what you did to us, to Beauregard. You ripped our lives apart with your vigilante justice. You are guilty.

"Unlike you, Franklin and I refuse to poison our lives with hate, to unleash pain and misery on those around us. We will not stoop to your level. May you someday realize the horror you inflicted on us, on the people of Raider, and confess your evil. May God have mercy on you because right now, there is none for you in this world. From now on, Franklin and I will never look at you again. We will erase you from our lives as surely as you erased Beau from ours. But he is not gone. He lives on in our hearts and some day we will be reunited."

Silence reigned in the courtroom after Camilla's last word. Lou bowed his head. Franklin gave Camilla a tiny smile and a nod. Without a glance at Lou, she returned to her seat.

Judge Navarro thanked Camilla and the jury, and the trial ended with the bang of a gavel. When the guard approached Lou, handcuffs in hand, Lou turned his back and heard them snap shut. As he walked out of the courtroom, he caught sight of Sally sitting between Rudy and Kathy. Lou watched Rudy put a supportive arm around Sally's shoulder and Kathy take her hand. Sally stared at him.

What is she thinking? Why doesn't she know I did this for our Becky?

PART II

TRADING PRISONS

CHAPTER 11

SHADOW OF DEATH

POLUNSKY UNIT OF HUNTSVILLE PRISON

Lou rested on his cot and stared at the cell wall. His thoughts again circled around Becky, the trial, and Beauregard Abbington's lifeless body. His stomach cramps were worse today. Where was the relief he believed getting justice for Becky would bring? Instead, waves of guilt washed over him. He turned on his side and drew his legs up to his chest.

Beauregard had to pay for what he did. He would have killed other girls. I had to stop him, and would do it again. I committed capital justice, not capital murder. And so, stone by stone, he built himself a fortress of rationalizations.

Some of his fellow inmates on death row insisted they were innocent, that their jury had it all wrong. Others admitted their guilt and claimed God forgave them.

Just like that, huh? God simply forgives? Get over it. If there is a God, you're going to hell.

He kept his thoughts to himself and conversed only superficially. *What difference did it make, anyway?*

The guard's gravelly voice roused Lou from a fitful nap. "You have a visitor."

"They tell you who?" he asked as he rolled off his cot and walked toward his cell door.

"Nope. Said to take you to the visitor's room. You expecting someone?"

Lou backed against the door and squatted, passing his hands through the opening. While the guard fastened the manacles to his wrists, he called to mind the two people on his approved visitor's list — Rudy and Sally. Rudy visited yesterday, so that left Sally. She had not spoken to him since the judge sentenced him to death. Lou would never forget the blank look on her face when the guards removed him from the courtroom.

There's no way I could have shared this with her. She would have tried to stop me, so I kept her in the dark. I can understand her anger, but why can't she understand the reasons I did this?

By now, Lou was familiar with the twists and turns to the visitation cubicle for death-row inmates. Since he arrived at the Polunsky Unit, he lived in his solitary cell alongside twenty other prisoners. They remained segregated from the other inmates, and allowed only short, daily, solitary periods outside. Having a visitor was a big deal.

The guard removed the manacles after he entered the secure visitor cubicle. Lou did not immediately recognize Sally. She had replaced her long straight hair with a brown curly bob, touched with blonde highlights, and traded her glasses for contact lenses. The woman looked thinner by at least two dress sizes. He recognized the skirt she was wearing. It was her favorite, before grief-driven plumpness consigned it to the back of her closet. Her pallor, as if her body's metabolism was barely functioning on standby, peeked out from the edges of her makeup. He saw pain in her eyes, and she looked uneasy, as if she wanted to be anywhere but here.

He smiled at her and lifted the phone off its cradle on the side of his cubicle. Without changing her expression, she did the same.

"Thank you for coming. I missed you." His voice held the hint of a question. *Why did it take you so long?*

As if reading his mind, Sally got right to the point.

"I need to tell you something, and it's taken me a while to get the courage to do it." She took a deep breath and continued.

"Our daughter was murdered two years ago. She wasn't only your daughter, she was mine too. When we met, you swept me off my feet and we got married when we found out I was pregnant. Maybe you never loved me the way I loved *you*. Sure, you liked me enough, but I felt no passion from you. I'll give you credit for supporting us, even if you did it out of duty. You were a super dad, but I don't think you were happy with our life together.

"When Becky died, you wallowed alone in your grief and anger, and shut me out. It was as if only you owned the right to mourn her, to want justice for her. You never saw or heard my pain, held me while I cried, or listened when I needed to talk about her. You walled yourself off, like always."

Lou looked away as her accusations hammered against his emotional fortress. He searched for words to defend himself.

"Aw Sally, I'm not a talker. I married you, for Pete's sake." He shook his head and frowned. "Didn't that tell you something? I could have given you money to—you know. Or I would have supported the baby. Instead I married you."

Sally swiped at her tears. "Lou, I never felt loved because you shared nothing with me. Didn't you trust me to understand? You decided Beauregard Abbington was guilty, and maybe he was. But then, you secretly plotted and carried out his murder. It was a self-centered, self-righteous, evil thing you did. Did you think about me for a second? I lost my daughter, I lost what little I had of you, and now I am losing everything else."

Sally fished in her pocket and pulled out an old-fashioned hankie. She covered her face and sobbed. The small cotton square, edged with a lilac design and lace, was too tiny to handle her torrent of tears. Lou wanted to reach out and comfort her. "Sally, Sally," he repeated. "I'm so sorry. I never thought." He covered his eyes.

Wadding the hankie in her hand, Sally lifted a tear-stained face. "What did you expect would happen when you killed Beauregard? Was that supposed to make a big statement and take away your pain? Will her father's execution give Becky justice? What if Beauregard was innocent? Did you ever consider that?"

Lou's jaw dropped. Sally's tirade was a riptide, dragging him into waters he feared would drown him. He desperately clung to Beauregard Abbington's guilt because otherwise he had committed the unspeakable.

The justice system failed, so I took care of business, he whispered in the depths of long, sleepless nights. *I probably saved the lives of other innocent girls like my Becky. Now Sally is questioning my motives? Beauregard killed Becky and hid behind his family's money and connections. Why doesn't she see that? I did this for Becky and for the both of us. And how can she say I didn't love her? The daily grind I've lived since we married was all for them. I would have chosen a different life, if not for family responsibilities — first taking care of Mother, then Sally and Becky. I wanted to work my way through college, be a history teacher, or even a professor. But no, I stayed and took care of business.*

Sally was relentless. "I carried my anger and grief alone, thanks to you. After a while, I realized they would steal my life if I didn't let them go. You think what you did took courage? I've got news for you. It took wallowing self-pity and no regard for anyone but yourself.

"I came to tell you I'm moving to Dallas, where I'll stay with my cousin until I find a job. Becky will live in my heart until I see her again in heaven. I will make a life without you, and in some ways, won't notice the difference. I've been without you from day one. You never needed me before, and don't need me now. Frankly, I can't stand watching you go through what you brought on yourself. If you want me here when they, you know, I'll come back for that. Otherwise, it's over. Thank God your mother is dead, so she doesn't have to live through this."

Lou did not stop his tears. "We could have shared so much between us," he whispered. "I guess I never listened. I assumed you knew I loved you because I stayed with you and Becky and put a roof over your heads and food on the table. I thought that counted." He raised a tear-stained face to the stranger behind the partition. "You wanted more of me."

Sally nodded.

"Let me do one loving thing for you from my heart. Don't put yourself through watching the execution. Even if I never said it enough, I love you, Sally. And I'm so sorry."

They placed their palms against the glass and cried. After a long moment, Sally stood and walked out of the room without looking back.

Sally, dear Sally.

The pain in Lou's stomach brought his head to his knees until it gradually subsided after several deep, shuddering breaths. Resigned, he stood and backed up to the opening in the door and extended his wrists.

Except for occasional letters and visits from Rudy, months passed without another visitor. Mourning the loss of Sally, the best thing in his life, thrust him into a black void. He turned to the prison library to find something, anything, that would divert his thoughts. Lou took refuge in all the history books he could lay his hands on. He learned to live under a leaden emotional weight that never left him except in sleep.

He was ready to die.

CHAPTER 12

ENDINGS

A YEAR LATER

Realizing he was no longer processing the words, Lou flung *Life During the Civil War* onto the floor. What did it matter if he finished the book? According to word on the cellblock, his would be the third shortest time on Huntsville's death row since they executed Steven Renfro after only 263 days. Lou lay on his mattress, folded his arms behind his head, and stared at the ceiling. His thoughts ran in a jumble.

By tomorrow night, I will be dead. I'm not a dangerous killer. I avenged my daughter, that's all. What father wouldn't? Beauregard Abbington was guilty as sin. But what if he wasn't? Of course he was! I shouldn't be the one to die. I saved other girls from that monster. Is there really a hell like they say? I'll find out soon enough. Or maybe there's just nothing. Yea, that would be best. An end to this agony. I'm scared.

"You have a visitor, Skalney."

Maybe Sally reconsidered staying away. Or maybe it's Rudy for the last time.

Lou knew better than to ask the guard.

Must be Sally or Rudy.

He smiled.

When he entered the visitors' cubicle, Lou saw a stranger wearing a clerical collar, looking at him from the other side of the glass partition. Lou turned toward the locked door behind him, thinking to call the guard, but stopped. Is this gray-haired priest someone from my past at St. Stan's? He remembered only two priests from the parish, and they probably retired or died by now. Although he no longer had any use for religion, his curiosity got the better of him. Lou warily settled in the chair and lifted the phone from its cradle. The visitor did likewise.

"I'm Father Mercer, Lou. I visit Catholic prisoners. Did the prison chaplain meet with you?"

"Yes. He told me what to expect tomorrow and offered to help me. I told him I didn't need anything, but he said he'd be with me, anyway."

Father Mercer nodded. "Good. Meanwhile, would you like to make your last confession?"

Lou watched the man draw a purple stole from his pocket, kiss the cross in the center, and drape it around his neck. His actions brought Lou a kaleidoscope of memories. Father Briscomb at St. Stan's calling down deadly retribution on them when the ball they were playing with broke a rectory window. Briscomb was far from the good-natured Father O'Malley in the old movie *The Bells of St. Mary's*. When the nuns herded them into church for weekly confession, they could choose to line up for Father Briscomb on one side of the nave, or the younger, cooler, associate priest, Father Hart on the other. If the church were a boat, it would have listed dangerously as the entire class moved to Hart's side.

So, is this guy a Briscomb or a Hart? What does it matter? I have nothing to say.

Lou said, "I really can't do this confession thing. It's been too long."

"It's never too long." The priest's voice sounded gentle. "Let's just talk. You can do that, can't you?"

Lou shrugged. "I guess so."

After collecting his thoughts, Lou spoke with gathering urgency, as if he had only a few minutes to make his case.

"Beauregard Abbington was a spoiled, sick, animal. That family squirms out of everything. They probably bribed a juror, and God knows who else. Innocent? Not on your life! I killed him because the justice system failed, and he needed to be taken out before he did the same thing to another man's daughter. Capital justice—that's what I did — not capital murder. They have it all wrong. I took care of business, the business they should have handled. And I'd do it again. So you can put your purple scarf away, Father."

Lou glared defiantly at the priest, surprised he had to catch his breath.

"Is it not possible that the jury was right, and this person was innocent?"

"My wife suggested that a year ago. No, I'm sure. And it's not the first time the Abbington family got away with murder."

"What do you mean?"

Lou frowned as he recalled the year he was 16.

"My father worked in the Abbington Piano Works factory. They made uprights for the mass market, but their specialty was grand pianos. He was working on the loading dock the night he died. Old man Abbington was too cheap to hire enough workers, so Dad and two other guys were trying to do the work of four men. Dad was backing up, dragging a piano, when he slipped off the loading dock. He hit his head and died instantly."

"I'm so sorry, Lou. Did your family get compensation? Was it just you and your mother left, or do you have siblings?"

"No. It was only Mom and me. Doctors said he could not have survived, given the way his head hit the concrete. Do you think he died in pain, Father?"

The priest shook his head. "I've seen many deaths in my life as a priest, and no one with that kind of head injury seemed to experience pain."

"Dad was what they call a functioning alcoholic. I don't think he ever drew a sober breath even while he was working. He was usually loaded enough to put anyone else out cold. And believe me, Abbington's lawyer made the most of the medical report he had a point two blood alcohol level when he fell. Mom and I never saw a dime. They got away with murder, just like now."

Lou's hands turned into fists.

"They didn't pay for my father's death, and I could see there would not be any justice for my Becky, either. No. I did what needed to be done." His lips formed a tight line as he looked directly into the priest's eyes.

Father Mercer nodded. "And that's why you were so sure he was guilty, even though he wasn't even born when your father died. Guilt by association."

"Not just that! There were facts. Facts their attorney twisted. I know they bought a juror, even though the D.A. dropped the ball and didn't tell the judge." Lou's voice rose to a shout. "I took care of business. Business no one else had the chops to do. You and God can deal with that as you like."

"Have you thought about what will happen when you die, Lou?"

"What? Judgment? I'm not sure I care about God's opinion of me when he let my Becky die and her murderer go free. Maybe God and I are better off not spending time together. I did what had to be done. I'm not sorry and I can't change that."

Father Mercer looked long into his eyes. Lou knew the priest wanted him to begin the sinner's formal ritual with "bless me Father, for I have sinned," so he could grant the absolution he believed Lou needed. After a moment, the priest spoke softly.

"Lou, as long as you have breath in your body, God is calling you. God did not murder your daughter. She is with him now. Don't take your anger and self-justification into eternity. Release them and ask for the grace of contrition and forgiveness. It's never too late."

Lou's eyes filled with tears. He shook his head. "It's too late for me, Father. I can't feel sorry. I can't say I was wrong, no matter what happens to me."

The priest bowed his head, lips moving in what Lou assumed was silent prayer.

Good luck with that.

With deliberation, Lou placed the phone in its cradle, stood, and turned away.

Lou felt as if he were moving in slow motion as he dressed the next morning. Every movement carried terminal significance.

This is the last time I will put on my shoes and socks; the last time I will comb my hair.

It felt like moving in a dream, while panic lurked at the edge of his rational mind. Lou kept terror from over-taking him by concentrating as much as he could on the details of everyday routines.

He recalled his last conversation with Rudy.

"I want you to take care of everything. If Sally turns up, be there for her. If not, don't call her. And I don't want any funeral. Just have me cremated. Don't come to my execution. I don't want you to have to watch. Promise me!" he insisted to his oldest friend.

With tears brimming in his eyes, Rudy nodded.

Rudy Kowalski slammed his fist against the steering wheel of his classic '67 red and white Ford Mustang. The car was old enough for him and his son, Gabe, to tinker with together, since it had no computer system to interfere with pleasant hours shared under the hood.

He eyed the waves of shimmering heat and the parking lot that was supposed to be the main expressway out of Austin. His last visit to Austin to tie up his investigation into substandard materials used on the city's infrastructure took him longer than expected. He was running late as it was, and now this.

Admitting defeat, he shifted the car into park, unfolded from the driver's seat, stood and stretched. He nodded to the fellow in the center lane, who was leaning against his Honda.

The stranger's smile turned down at the edges, and he said, "According to KKMJ, a truck overturned down the way, and we're being rerouted off 35."

The man folded his arms across his chest and peered down the road, as to confirm his pronouncement.

"Oh great. Just what I need."

He scowled, recalling how Kathy had reminded him months ago to arrange Lou's internment with the funeral home the prison used. She had been right, as usual, but somehow something always came up. If he were honest with himself, he simply had refused to believe Texas would actually execute his best friend. Rudy had hoped the Governor would step in like a superhero at the last minute and grant Lou a pardon.

Lou's not really a murderer in his heart. It's not like he would go around killing people from now on. Sure, what he had done was horrible, and I can understand Sally moving on. She put up with a lot in their marriage. Maybe not so much "a lot." More like too little.

Kathy had spared no comments one evening as they were getting ready for bed after going out to dinner for Lou's birthday.

"She could dress in red sequins and dance a jig, for all he'd notice," Kathy snapped.

"I'd notice if you dressed in red sequins," Rudy whispered in her ear as he wrapped his arms around her waist and pulled her close. She leaned her head back, and they kissed. "I'm so lucky," Kathy said.

He jerked his mind back to reality. He had put off dealing with Lou's funeral arrangements, and now he was out of time. It was easier to push the thought of his friend's execution to the back of his mind, where it didn't hurt so much. Instead, he had focused on his investigative expose' on graft and substandard materials for the paper. It had taken weeks to get people to talk to him, and even more time to get his editor to agree to their demands for anonymity. Time had slipped through Rudy's fingers, and today it would run out for Lou.

He hoped at least to get to the prison on time for the execution and meet with the funeral director immediately after. Now, with only a few hours to 6 p.m., Rudy was stuck on a highway going nowhere.

The State carried out executions in Huntsville Prison itself — "the Walls." Now guards led a manacled Lou to the prison van parked outside the Polunsky Unit. Constantly observed by armed guards sitting next to him, Lou watched Texas slip past his window, a montage of city streets and tall buildings, smaller towns, country roads and open fields. He'd grown up in a town like the one gliding past the car window. His mind sought solace in memory.

He recalled sliding down in his seat, hoping Sister Mary Teresa wouldn't call on him in math class, and later playing ball with the guys; coming home at dusk and smelling the magic his mother was creating in the kitchen. A 40-watt bulb cast a shadowy light in the simple room with an old farm table set for three. Elements of quiet comfort blended with unease as he waited for his father to come home. Would he be sullen or in an alcohol induced good mood?

Too soon, Huntsville's low, gray buildings loomed ahead. Lou noticed clusters of people standing along their way. Although the route to the Walls changed each time to keep bystanders at bay, protestors manned every street leading to the prison. They held signs that read "Capital Punishment is Murder," and "Mercy not State Murder." When the van stopped for a red light, Lou made eye contact with a young woman holding a sign that read, "Life not Death." He felt a lump in his throat at her compassion and he silently nodded his appreciation before he pulled his gaze away.

When the van slid to a stop, a guard stepped away from Huntsville's back entrance and opened the passenger door. Lou eased himself out and stood for a moment, gazing at the drab gray building. He felt another guard prod him and shuffled toward the door. Once inside, a guard searched him before leading him to a holding cell to await his execution.

Inside the cell, Lou paced, counting his steps, sometimes speeding up, then slowing when he felt short of breath. He did not know what to do with his body for the few hours he remained in it. He would sit, only to resume his restless pacing, trying to drown the voices of accusation in his head that never seemed to stop, and were growing louder by the second. The guard observing him offered a few remarks likely meant to be comforting. Lou barely heard him. He had entered a dark place where there was no exit. He had no appetite and refused food.

At exactly 6:00 p.m., the somber procession to the execution chamber began. Lou's eyes devoured everything and everyone. Painfully aware that death awaited him, he mentally recorded every fissure along the gray walls, every light bulb, and every person who shared his last walk. Shoulders curved forward and neck bent, he shuffled along. Lou resumed counting each step, as if he could leave his last seconds to posterity by mentally logging them.

The execution chamber was much smaller than he had imagined. A gurney sat in the center with a cart to its right, on which sat an EKG machine and equipment to start two intravenous lines. Two sets of IV tubing ran through an opening in the wall behind the head of the gurney and rested, capped, on the cart. Two small rooms, their windows covered by curtains, stood opposite the foot of the gurney.

The wall clock's clicking threw Lou's footstep count into oblivion. It seemed so loud. His knees buckled, and he sagged against the guard, who placed a supportive arm around his waist.

"We're going to the gurney now, step by step." The guard's voice was soft but firm. Lou allowed himself to be led and helped onto the thin mattress, where guards replaced his manacles with thick leather restraints. Lou was about to complain they were too tight, cutting off his circulation, but considering he was about to die, he merely grunted. The chaplain stood at his feet and placed his hands on his ankles. He gazed kindly at Lou, even though he had refused his help. One of two physicians secured EKG leads to his chest, arms, and legs. Sweat poured off Lou, and he felt his heart race. He heard whimpering and was disgusted when he realized it was coming from him.

I will not give the Abbingtons the satisfaction.

He took a deep breath and held it. When he turned his head, he noticed a man in a black suit standing beneath the clock. The man caught Lou's glance and said he was the Warden for this procedure.

Procedure. Is that what they call it?

With EKG leads secure, the doctor inserted an intravenous line. When Lou jumped and tensed at his touch, the man reassured him, "Just saline solution now." After the doctor inserted the other IV line, the Warden moved to the head of the gurney and asked, "Do you wish to make a last statement?"

The curtains opened. True to Camilla Abbington's statement at his trial, Beauregard's parents had erased Lou from their lives. Instead, Lou recognized old man Abbington sitting among others.

I thought the guy died years ago.

Lou turned his attention to the second room, filled with strangers. "Who are the people in the other room?"

"An AP reporter and a stringer from the *Huntsville Report*. Other media as well," the Warden replied, not unkindly. "Do you wish to say your last words?"

Lou had thought about what he would say. It would be the truth, and if it cut like a knife, so be it. The fury that burned in him like hot lava had solidified into a boulder.

"Beauregard Abbington murdered my daughter, Rebecca Skalney, in cold blood. The jury refused to convict him. When the justice system fails, people take the law into their own hands. I, her father, did what needed to be done, and, in doing so, saved other precious daughters." After a moment of silence, he added, "That's all."

Lou tried to numb his mind when the doctor retreated and joined others in the room behind him. The other physician, wearing a white lab coat and stethoscope draped around his neck, positioned himself beside the EKG machine.

At exactly 6:30 p.m., with no last-minute pardon from the Governor, the executioner in the room behind him released what was to be a lethal dose of sodium pentobarbital into the tubing. It snaked through the wall opening and into Lou's veins.

Everything turned black for Louis Skalney.

CHAPTER 13

QUESTIONS, QUESTIONS

Rudy screeched to a halt at the prison gate. He stuck his head out the window and watched the guard amble to his car.

"Have I missed the Skalney execution?"

"You're a little late, buddy," the gray-haired guard said. "The hearse is just about to pull out. You can park over there and wait for it." He pointed to a few empty parking slots between the road and gate.

"Okay. Thanks."

Rudy did not know what funeral home the prison used. That was another thing he was going to do.

Fine investigative reporter you are.

"Know which funeral home?"

The guard shrugged. "Park over there."

It was not a long wait until a black funeral limousine drove past. Rudy put the car in gear and pulled out to tail it.

The limousine sailed through a yellow traffic light at the edge of the prison road and left a cursing Rudy caught at the red. No! He inched forward and scanned the road for traffic and cops. Looking to the right and left, Rudy waited for a slight break in traffic. When it came, he floored it across the intersection, leaving a trail of honking accusations in his wake. By weaving in and out of lanes, fighting for every foot of pavement, he saw the limousine four cars ahead. He followed it, but became concerned when it passed a strip mall, a funeral home, and a family restaurant. It was headed out of town. What the…?

There's nothing out here except country. Where are they taking him?

Rudy turned the AC up full blast and vowed he would trail that vehicle to Mexico if need be.

After a while, it was just him and "Blackie," as Rudy had named the hearse. He spied the left turn signal flashing as Blackie stopped before a pair of solid wooden gates, surrounded on either side by stonewalls that looked about twenty feet high. A large bell with a pull-rope hung from the gate that held an unobtrusive sign identifying the property as the Monastery of St. Dismas. Rudy hung far back, pulled off the road, and killed his engine. From his vantage point, he watched the driver give the rope a hard yank. A monk in a black robe with a red cross emblazoned on his chest opened the gate and stepped aside to allow the hearse to enter. The monk closed the gate after glancing down the road.

Did he see me?

He pulled his cell phone from his crumpled suit jacket he had flung onto the passenger seat, and dialed home. "Come on. Come on," he whispered, imagining Kathy searching in their perennially cluttered kitchen to find where she had last left the phone. He eventually heard her voice.

"Rudy? Where are you?"

"You won't believe this, but I'm parked outside of a monastery in the boonies. The hearse carrying Lou just drove onto its grounds."

"What's it doing driving into a monastery, and why are you so late?"

Explaining his hold up on I 35, and admitting she was right about everything as usual, took up half an hour.

When the gate again opened, the limousine drove onto the country road and back toward town. Rudy said a quick good-by and tailed Blackie to Lindsy Brothers Funeral Home, only miles from the Walls.

Lou was only trying to spare me, but did he think I'd stay away? And now I've let him down. Never heard from Sally, but then I didn't expect to.

By the time he pulled into a parking space, he was hot, hungry, and angry. The day had been one big frustration, and now he wanted answers.

He got out of the Mustang and slammed the door. Still smarting from his personal failure, Rudy yanked open the front glass door of Lindsy Brothers Funeral Home and strode toward the receptionist sitting behind a small desk.

"I want to talk to the Funeral Director."

Probably used to wide ranges of emotions from their clients, the tidy blonde receptionist ignored his demanding voice, and smiled. "Of course. Mr. Lindsy is with a family now, but if you will take a seat." She pointed to a pale blue wing-back chair nestled against the opposite wall. "He will be with you shortly."

Rather than fume, Rudy settled into the chair, closed his eyes, and forced his mind to focus on his angle for the infrastructure exposé. Listing the major points, Rudy hunted for his opening lead. His mind circled the data like a hungry mouse looking for cheese, for any opening that would hook the reader. He had only three days to deadline.

"Shortly" turned into an hour and a half. Rudy startled when he heard a male voice addressing him. He blinked up at a middle-aged, slightly balding man of average height and weight. Dressed in a black suit and tie, he looked like a somber penguin.

"I'm Rich Lindsy." He extended his hand in greeting. "I apologize for making you wait, but I was with a family. Please, step into my office."

"Rudy Kowalski," he introduced himself as he trailed the Funeral Director.

Once in his office, Lindsy showed him to a plush leather chair in a conversation area across from his desk. "Can I offer you coffee or tea?"

"No… um, on second thought, yes tea, please," Rudy said as he sank into the chair. After his first sip a few minutes later, Rudy got to the point.

"I assume Lindsy Brothers will handle the internment of Lou Skalney, who was executed today." At Rich's nod, Rudy continued.

"I believe he left instructions I was to handle his funeral arrangements and, as it was, I didn't, couldn't–" Rudy coughed to fight unexpected tears. Lindsy nodded and murmured, "Understandable, understandable. It's an exceedingly difficult situation to deal with, especially when people were as close as I sense the two of you were."

"Friends since childhood," Rudy admitted. After a moment of silence, Rudy returned to business. "I believe he wanted to be cremated. The service will be small. Lou wanted nothing, maybe a few words at the graveside. I was caught in that mess on I 35 out of Austin today and missed his execution. Could I see him one last time before you cremate him?"

"We can certainly accommodate Mr. Skalney's wishes." After asking more questions, the funeral director said. "That should take care of all the details. Unfortunately, Mr. Kowalski, we do not have cremation facilities here at Lindsy Brothers. Mr. Skalney is already at the crematorium."

"I'm sorry, I must have misheard you. That can't be possible. I followed your hearse from the prison. And did you know the driver drove, with Lou inside, to a monastery before it returned here?"

Lindsy nodded. "Our hearse delivered his body to St. Dismas Monastery. They will cremate him there."

Rudy was speechless.

Monasteries do cremations? I don't think so. Never heard of such a thing. Something is wrong here.

CHAPTER 14

MONKS AND MURDERERS

Lou drifted in and out of consciousness. Voices sounded garbled, as if they were floating in overhead bubbles. If he could only reach up, catch a few and bring them to his ear. He willed his lips to form a question, but they would not obey. Then he heard, "One, two, three." Powerful arms yanked him from a hard surface and onto a mattress. He opened his eyes, but everything was blurry. He shook his head and blinked several times. Two men in black robes walked out of the room.

Is this what it's like to be dead? Where am I? Who are these men in black?

Lou tried to think of his last moments. They had strapped him to a gurney in the execution chamber and he said what he believed would be his last words on earth. And then—nothing.

There must be something else, man. Concentrate!

Instead, his eyelids drooped as sleep engulfed him.

When he awoke, he saw a curtain-covered window across from his bed. What lay beyond? Earth? Sky? Hell's landscape?

He turned to his left, where a sink and a long counter lined the wall. Open cabinet doors showed the usual clinic medical supplies. Lou tentatively moved his arm and felt tape pull at his arm hair. He looked up. A bag of intravenous fluid deposited measured drops into a small chamber above the tubing. Lou noticed he was still wearing his prison jumpsuit. He took a deep breath and closed his eyes as hope washed over him.

Maybe I'm not dead.

"You're awake."

Lou opened his eyes and saw a short man, engulfed in a black monk's robe. A large, red medieval cross rose from the cincture at the man's waist to his neckline.

"I'm sure you have questions, but first drink this." He handed him a glass of amber liquid. Lou raised an eyebrow.

"Iced tea. You need the caffeine and sugar right now," the monk answered his silent question.

Lou accepted the glass with a trembling hand and downed the sweet tea in seconds. "I'm not dead," he croaked, half statement, half question.

"Indeed, you are very much alive. And I think we can remove this." The monk teased the tape off the IV tubing and slipped the tip of the short catheter out of Lou's arm. "I'm Brother Luke, the monastery physician. The funeral home brought you here from the death chamber."

"Monastery? What am I doing in a monastery? Why aren't I dead? The funeral home brought me here? Is this the state's sick idea of a reprieve?"

"No. As far as the prison officials know, they executed you and removed your corpse for cremation."

"I don't understand."

Brother Luke smiled. The monk's brown eyes seemed to soften as he spoke. "Don't expect you to. In a little while, Brother Jerome will come to take you to Abbot Anselm, and he will explain everything."

Sometime later, a man in similar monk's garb helped Lou stand and pivot into a wheelchair. His legs felt like rubber, and but for the monk, he would have fallen.

Brother Jerome was a large black man, with a halo of white curly hair flowing from head to beard, highlighting his ebony complexion. Jerome spoke little as he guided the wheelchair through a labyrinth of stone corridors, dimly lit by wall sconces. Lou used the silence to marshal a list of questions for this Abbot—starting with why was he not dead, and what in blazes was he doing in this monastery?

When they arrived at a door leading to the outside, Jerome steered Lou onto a brick walkway surrounded on either side by open arches. A cool breeze washed over him, and he sucked fresh air deep into his lungs. He squinted at the bright sunlight and made a visor with his hand. He had not seen grass or trees in almost two years, and the only sky he had looked at was what loomed above the small prison yard enclosure.

It's so open, so green.

He watched a cloud float across an expanse of deep blue sky. Lou's eyes filled with tears.

"Stop. Please stop. I want to look."

Brother Jerome obeyed and turned the wheelchair so Lou could face the landscape. A rolling field, with a huge fenced in garden to the right, lay before him. Here and there, a few sheep nibbled on grass as they ambled from spot to spot. He heard birdsong punctuated by the piercing caw of an unseen crow. He soaked in every pastoral element of the real-life painting splayed before him. After several minutes, Lou nodded.

"Thank you."

The monk wheeled him through a doorway on the left, down a corridor and into a room. He parked him before a large tidy desk in the center of a sparse office, walled with stone. Jerome stepped back and leaned against the open doorway.

Light from a long, gothic arched window highlighted a bookcase on the opposite wall. Lou shivered. The room was chilly, despite glowing embers covering the floor of a massive fireplace. He studied the gray-haired monk sitting behind the desk. The man's robe hung on a lean torso, and his long face bore a sad expression. Pale eyes, as if most of the blue had drained away long ago, stared at him. Lou noticed a crooked scar running from just below the man's left eye, down to his chin.

"I am Abbot Anselm. How are you feeling?"

"Weak, relieved I'm not dead, and confused, for starters." Lou's voice felt raspy. He cleared his throat. "Why am I in a monastery? Who are you people?" His eyes flickered around the room before they returned to the Abbot.

The Abbot leaned back in his chair, as if settling in for a long conversation. "We belong to the Order of St. Dismas. Have you heard of the thief that was crucified next to Jesus?"

"Yes."

"Tradition has given him the name Dismas. He asked Jesus to remember him, and Jesus said he would be with him in paradise. Like Dismas, when death is near, no matter what you've done, faith in Jesus will save you."

Lou stared at the Abbot.

After a moment, he continued. "Our organization believes salvation is a far better option than death, and so we divert the process of capital punishment where we can. We have planted people within the penal system and beyond. The physician who declared you dead is one of ours. He had already replaced the drugs you were to receive with a lower dose of pentobarbital, so you only appeared to have stopped breathing. Your respirations were slow and shallow, barely observable. Our doctor declared you dead, turned off the EKG, removed the strip, and substituted it for another strip with a flat line from his pocket. Then our mortician brought you here."

Lou shook his head. He did not know if he should thank him or bolt from the room, not that he had the strength in his legs to bolt anywhere. Talk of shallow respirations made him take a deep breath, thankful for air, for life itself.

"Well, I guess I should thank you. But let me get this straight. As far as the prison and Texas are concerned, I died. And if I'm dead, according to them, what now? How do I make a living? How do I function legally if I'm technically dead? Does your organization have a plan for that too? Can they give me a new identity?" Hope fluttered in his heart for the first time in years. "When can I leave?" he asked, cutting to the chase.

"Lou, you will never leave here."

"But…"

Abbot Anselm cut him off. "How can we allow you to leave?" He waved his hand, indicating the room and everything beyond it. "Our order is non-denominational, but we are authentic monks. Because of our work, we live cloistered from the world, and every monk here has taken vows to accept the Rule of St. Dismas. Now, if you or any other prisoner were to leave, your return to the world would threaten the secrecy we require. We cannot allow that to happen."

Lou gripped the handles of his wheelchair. He opened his mouth to object, to swear he would not say a thing when the Abbot continued.

"More importantly, we could not do the work God called us to do."

"What work is that?"

The Abbot leaned forward. "This place is your last stop in life. No one on the outside believes you are alive. You have ceased to exist, except physically. The lawyers will probate your will and your wife can remarry if she wishes. You have no need for a lawyer, no need for a physician other than Brother Luke, because a dead man requires neither. You will work, eat, sleep, and die here. There are no phones, no internet, no computers, and no television. You cannot communicate with the outside world. We have a chapel and a library well stocked with Bibles and theology texts, and we encourage you to make use of both. Think of St. Dismas Monastery as the last leg of your life's journey, a journey to heaven or hell. It is your choice. We monks are here to guide you."

Astounded, Lou shook his head.

You are some crazy monks. This place can't be real. Maybe it's the purgatory the nuns talked about.

He looked about, thinking he might glimpse a demon lurking behind the furniture, or a pitchfork nestled in a corner. Flashes of his days at St. Stan's and Father Briscomb's ideas of discipline ran through his mind.

I've traded one prison for another. This is a thousand times worse. I will escape or die trying.

CHAPTER 15

GATE TO HEAVEN OR HELL?

Abbot Anselm rose, showing the interview was over. Brother Jerome stepped away from the wall to wheel Lou out of the office. Now that his fogged mind had cleared, he studied the monk more closely. He figured the man must tip the scales at almost 250 pounds, but he had difficulty guessing his age. The white hair and beard said elderly, yet the smooth black skin denied age. There was a quiet gentleness about this large man. He seemed to be a living contradiction; old and young, powerful, yet gentle at the same time. What was his story?

"How long have you been here?"

"Thirteen years this June." Brother Jerome's voice was deep and soft — another contradiction.

What was he doing that made him think coming here was a good idea?

"What did you do before?"

"I owned a bookstore."

Lou figured a restaurant owner would have made more sense. A bookstore? He didn't look bookish at all.

"You a reader?" Lou sounded hopeful.

"Yes. I read pretty much my entire non-fiction inventory. I'm the monastery's librarian now. Not that it's a full-time job." He chuckled.

"I like to read too," Lou offered. A kindred spirit. A small ray of light. The monastery has a library.

"How did you come here?"

The monk did not answer right away as he continued to push Lou in the wheelchair. When they reached the arched, outdoor walkway, he cleared his throat and replied, "God's will."

"That's all you got? God's will?"

"Yes."

A thousand thoughts flashed through Lou's mind.

How did this ex-bookstore owner find this place and then choose to live here? This is a glorified jail, a life sentence for prisoners. They have no right to shanghai people. Where do they get off directing the last leg of my life's journey? Of course they don't want to be discovered. It's not that they couldn't do their so-called "work," it's that they would be arrested. What's their real purpose?

As Brother Jerome pushed his wheelchair along the arched walkway, Lou scanned the pastoral scene once again. This time, he noticed that the high stone walls surrounding the monastery property lacked the crossed spikes that ran along the top of prison fences; nor was there a watchtower or armed guards.

Should be possible to climb those walls. I wonder if anyone tried.

Re-entering the monastery proper, Lou's eyes adjusted to the twilight of the inner corridors, and he tried to follow the labyrinth that led to a row of cells. Fury filled him at the thought of living in a cage again. Needing to stretch his legs before his world shrank again to twelve-by-twelve feet, Lou jammed his feet down on the stone floor to stop the wheelchair.

"I want to walk."

The monk placed both wheels in lock position. Before he could help him, Lou grasped the sides of the chair and rose. His legs still felt weak, and his knees ached, reminding him his arthritis remained, despite his recent resurrection. He took a few hesitant steps and soon fell into a slow but steady rhythm. Brother Jerome pushed the chair behind him.

He noticed that across from every cell occupied by a man in a long brown robe, a monk dressed like Jerome and the Abbot sat against the corridor's opposite wall. There were no doors on the cells. Apparently, the men in brown were prisoners like himself and the monks in the hall, their jailers. Lou shuddered. *What did those monks think the prisoners would do?*

Unlike in the penitentiary, where a new prisoner was subject to hoots, hollers, and profanity as guards marched him past occupied cells on the way to his own, these prisoners stared silently as he walked by. Lou kept his eyes focused on his steps to avoid eye contact. He was in no mood to talk.

Jerome interrupted his thoughts when he tapped him on the shoulder. "Here's yours."

Lou walked into the cell, turned in a circle, and felt the walls close in on him. It was like the Polunsky Unit where he lived like an animal in a cage, but at least there he had a little privacy. A monk would watch his every movement now.

How powerful are these monks? I don't see any weapons. How do they control the prisoners? How many prisoners are there?

He looked around his cell. It housed a metal cot with a thick mattress, a wooden chair, and a desk holding a battery-operated reading lamp. A large book with a gold cross etched on its cover rested next to the lamp. He shivered but felt reassured when he noted a wool blanket folded at the foot of the cot. A brown robe and pair of sandals lay on the blanket. Dim light from the hall flickered against the cell's windowless far wall. He turned to Jerome.

"Where's the toilet?"

"Toilets and showers are just off the common room down the hall." The monk nodded in the direction they had been walking.

"When are we allowed to go there?"

"Whenever you want. This is your home."

"My home!" Derision dripped from Lou's voice. "Aren't you afraid we'll gang up on you or escape?"

"No."

Lou noticed a smirk playing at the edges of Jerome's mouth, not that he could see it very well with the man's mass of facial hair. Was there a gleam in his eye as well?

"You don't need this anymore," Brother Jerome said as he folded the wheelchair. "You'll want a shower. Turn right when you leave your cell and go straight into our common great room. You'll see the door labeled 'Lavatory' on the far wall. After you shower, toss your prison clothes in the wastebasket and put on your robe and sandals. Dinner is in an hour."

With that, Jerome turned and pushed the wheelchair toward a monk who was bringing him a wooden chair. After a murmured conversation, the monk took the wheelchair and Jerome eased on to the chair.

For a while, Lou sat on his cot, head bowed. Hands, calloused from twenty years in construction work, hung limply between his knees. Lou shook his head. He wondered how he could live in this outlandish place. At least in prison, he learned to navigate the establishment and could reach out to his lawyer or Rudy. Now, locked away from civilization, surrounded by so-called monks who could be certifiable for all he knew, terrified him.

Maybe I died, and this is hell.

He remembered Father Briscomb calling Satan "the father of lies."

Maybe that Abbot was lying when he said they saved me from execution. Maybe pitchforks and horns are just props for the real thing. What if these so-called monks are demons?

Yet Lou could not deny he was very much alive. He felt grateful he was not dead and suffering the eternal fires that attending St. Stanislaus Church had engraved in his mind. Still, the thought of remaining a prisoner, even if not on death row, filled him with dread and fury at his keepers. They had managed the impossible — freeing him from a highly secure prison with the guards none the wiser, and the authorities believing they had executed him. Why wasn't he grateful?

If they wanted, they could release me and give me a new identity, but no. They have their own God agenda, and no matter how this so-called monastery differs from Huntsville, it's still a prison. They have no right to do this to me.

His mind turned to escape.

If it were possible, someone would have already done it and blown the whistle on this place.

He vowed he would find a way out.

There must be at least one phone somewhere and an entrance for supplies or garbage pickup. He could not imagine what the Abbot said was an organization of monasteries without a way of communicating with its members. Where there is structure, there is a weak link somewhere. Nothing is foolproof. He vowed to find the weak link at St. Dismas.

Lou rested his hand on the brown robe. It felt rough but thick enough to keep a person warm. He noticed there was no cincture.

So I don't hang myself with a rope belt.

The robe had no pockets, either. The sandals looked handmade and sturdy, with thick soles and broad straps to cover the instep and circle the heel. Jerome had told him to shower and change before dinner.

Food was the last thing on his mind right now. A hunger strike crossed his mind.

Maybe I'll starve myself to death. What could they do? Take someone who was supposed to be dead to the hospital for trying to die?

He snorted, and picking up the robe and sandals, walked toward the common area.

It looked like a grand hall in a castle, with a massive fireplace cut into the wall to the far right. Its maw was black from years of use, and even now, huge logs fed hungry orange and blue flames that sent waves of heat into the great common area. On the left, opposite the fireplace, a floor to ceiling stained glass window showing a hand reaching down from clouds toward a man standing below, threw prisms of light onto the tile floor. Small occasional tables and chairs dotted the room, while black-robed monks and brown clad prisoners walked in pairs or chatted in small groups. Some settled in chairs, reading, or resting with eyes closed.

Ignoring curious glances, Lou walked through the door labeled "Lavatory." For a monastery, it was quite modern. Toilet stalls and urinals lined the wall on the left, and separate shower stalls occupied the opposite wall. A bank of sinks and mirrors stood in the middle.

Either some of those monks had been plumbers in their previous lives, or skilled laborers modernized the bathroom.

"Here's your towel and soap."

Lou jumped and spun around to face a monk standing behind him.

"What the... You people are everywhere," Lou accused him, snatching the soap and towel.

"Yes, we are everywhere, Lou. I'm Brother Cornelius. Let me know if you need anything else."

Lou ran his hand across his chin. "I need a shave."

"We have communal electric shavers on the shelves over the sinks. Razor blades are forbidden, obviously."

Lou eyed the shavers and made a face. *No way.*

He was pleasantly surprised his shower felt so good. The water was hot, and the soap formed a thick lather. He lifted his face into the hot stream, then turned his back to the spray and rocked side to side, letting hot water fingers massage sore muscles that demanded attention. The first sob escaped him, unbidden and long overdue.

Lou, spiritually dead for years, and locked in a tomb of anger and revenge, longed for the closure he had believed killing Beauregard would have given him. Instead, an aching melancholy had slithered into his soul. Sunshine mocked him. Laughter made his skin crawl. Smiling people looked like gargoyles. He embraced night's dark oblivion.

Feeling impotent, angry, yet relieved, he was furious at these holier-than-thou monks who thought they had the right to play God. He leaned against the stall and slid to the floor, the sound of his crying masked by splashing water.

Fighting his conflicting emotions, Lou used the thick towel like a rough weapon as he dried himself. He slipped the brown robe and cowl over his head and felt the tug of its weight as the folds of material sank to just above his sandal-clad feet. Stepping from the stall, Lou looked for a supply of clean briefs or boxers. Seeing neither, he asked the monk, Cornelius, "Where's the underwear?"

"There is none for residents for security reasons. Someone could hide a crude weapon in their briefs."

"Oh, come on! Even on death row, they allowed us to wear briefs."

The monk shrugged. After glaring at him, Lou turned his back to his guard and walked toward the mirror above the sink. A brown clad monk stared back at him. He leaned to the left, then the right. His image mirrored his actions, proving that, yes, he was indeed alive in a bizarre other world. When he thought of living out his life in this place, Lou gasped and leaned against the sink. He forced himself to stare at his reflection as he pulled in deep breaths and slowly released them. It was as if they condemned him to play the part of a monk in an endless bad play. He passed his fingers over his jaw where a day's beard was sprouting.

Soon I'll look like the mad monk Rasputin.

Lou shuddered. *Get control of yourself. You will find a way out.*

After a few minutes, he pushed away from the sink, squared his shoulders, and cast Cornelius a last glare as he entered the common area.

CHAPTER 16

WINING AND DINING

Lou stood just beyond the lavatory door and scanned the great hall. It had filled more since his shower. The setting sun painted deeper hues on the stained-glass window and drew longer colored reflections on the floor. Even from the distance of ten feet, warmth from the fireplace enveloped him.

Most of the men wore black monks' robes with the red cross sewn on the front. They chatted among themselves or with the brown clad prisoners, many black, and a few Hispanic or white. Lou noticed a bearded prisoner standing alone, his back pressed against the wall. No one approached the lone figure scanning the common area through thick glasses. Lou saw the man's mouth turn down, as if he had just sucked on a lemon. He could feel his disdain from a distance.

As Lou turned his gaze away, another prisoner sitting alone next to a small table caught his eye. Unlike most of the others, he was balding and clean-shaven. His pudgy cheeks and rimless eyeglasses lent him a friendly appearance. He looked engrossed in a book. Lou could not make out the title from where he was standing, but it heartened him the monastery had a library.

From third grade, reading had been his escape from an inebriated, ranting father and from a cleric called "Father," who never missed an opportunity to describe the burning, sulfurous hell awaiting any boy caught in a state of "mortal sin," should death make an unexpected appearance. His mother teased that he would read the side of a milk carton if there were no books in the house. The local library provided a haven for him from dangerous situations and questionable friends. Still, that had not kept him out of jail after all, and now clerics surrounded him and would rule his life.

The prisoner looked up and noticed Lou. Setting the book aside, he rose and walked toward him.

"Hi. My name's Frank Predmore. I guess saying welcome would sound strange, given the circumstances," he said with a weak smile and proffered hand.

"Yep. Lou Skalney." He shook the man's hand and noticed it was soft and well padded.

"I remember my first days here," Predmore said. "I was relieved I hadn't been executed after all, but dreaded what these hulks might do to me."

"How long have you been here?"

"Three years. Dinner will be in a few minutes. We can sit here while we wait."

Lou nodded, relieved to meet someone who shared his dubious resurrection experience.

Frank led him to a small table flanked by two chairs. Once seated, he looked at Lou as if expecting him to say something. *What am I supposed to say?* After an uncomfortable silence, Lou spoke.

"So, the monks in black with the red crosses are the jailers, and the ones in brown are prisoners like us?"

"Right. Counting you, there's twelve of us and fifty-one of them. And they call us residents, not prisoners."

Lou made a brushing motion with his hand. "Can't change a definition just because you want to. What keeps the monks in control? I don't see guns or clubs. What are they like?"

"You must have noticed you're never out of their sight. They watch everything we do like hawks. They don't need to carry weapons either." Predmore leaned toward Lou. "They are the weapons."

"Seriously? A bunch of sadists?"

"Ah, not really. Although if you ask Kurt Niebold over there..." He nodded toward the stone-faced man Lou had noticed before. "He'd say for sure they're not only sadistic, but murderous as well."

"Murderous? Because you say they are weapons?"

"According to Niebold, they're all black belts in Krav Maga. I didn't know what that was, but turns out, it's a self-defense system developed by the Israelis that combines close-combat techniques into one. Israel's Mossad and even our CIA and FBI use it. The monks constantly practice and once they put on a demonstration for us." Predmore whistled and shook his head.

Lou chuckled. "I'll bet that put a damper on things around here for a while."

Frank grinned. "Sure did, for quite a while."

"What...? A ringing bell cut off Lou's next question.

The men strolled through a wide doorway perpendicular to the stained-glass window. Predmore stood and motioned for Lou to follow him. Conversations continued as the men threw their legs over benches to claim their places, brown and black robes intermingling.

Five long trestle tables, polished to a high sheen, reflected shafts of late afternoon sun pouring through a row of windows high on the wall. Lou thought the beams of light resting on the dark wood created a sense of intimacy that contradicted his idea of what a monastery would be like. But then, he never thought he would be in one, much less one populated by monks and murderers.

Predmore led Lou to a table nearest the door, where eight black-clad monks sat. As he took the seat next to Frank, he muttered, "They may make me sit here, but they can't force me to eat."

Frank shot him a quirky smile. As the monks introduced themselves, Lou discovered his trick of connecting a distinct facial feature with a new name would be of little use here. Most wore facial hair, some well-trimmed, but others going for the wild man look. Only their eyes set each one apart; one a wintery blue, others brown, or pale green. After a while, baby-faced Frank Predmore asked Lou the inevitable question.

"So, what brings you to Saint Dismal's?"

Lou made a wry face at Predmore's word play. No one else at the table seemed to notice. "I got justice for my daughter."

"Why? How?" Frank Predmore asked.

"The jury found the man who murdered her innocent. But I know he wasn't. The guy's family is rolling in dough, and for sure they bribed the jury. My daughter got no justice in the court, but I took care of that."

"So you killed him?" Predmore whispered.

"Had to, before he killed more innocent girls."

Lou looked at each of the eight men, daring them to say anything. Predmore turned white and looked away from Lou. The monk seated across from him shook his head and said, "You are in a lot of pain, Lou."

Predmore acknowledged the monk with a nod. "Brother Aaron guards the entrance to the monastery. Well, that would be the exit, too. Same thing, entrance and exit," he babbled, shooting Lou a quick glance.

Lou frowned, puzzled at Frank's anxious behavior.

When Abbot Anselm stood, the room fell silent as he raised his hands in prayer. Lou noticed some prisoners bowed their heads, and others, like him, stared at the walls. After the invocation, all eyes followed a monk, who placed two bottles of wine on each table.

Wine? What kind of prison serves wine while inmates and jailers eat together?

Next, a corpulent monk wheeled in a serving cart full of plates covered with mounds of golden pastry that filled the room with a rich aroma. Lou watched Frank pour a generous portion of wine into each of their glasses. Eyeing the plate placed before him, he could not believe he was looking at Beef Wellington.

"What the…?" Lou directed questioning eyes to Brother Aaron.

The monk smiled, ignoring Predmore, who kept his eyes averted, and explained, "The only escape from here is death and most try starvation at first. We won't force feed you, but we'll sure make it hard for you to refuse to eat. We celebrate and dine like this every Sunday and when there's a new resident."

Lou had considered refusing food or drink. He had faced death on the gurney in Huntsville. He could do it again, but he could not deny he felt relieved to be alive. *How can I feel both ways? What do I do with that?* His eyes locked on the ruby liquid that called to every nerve in his body. Hand trembling, he surrendered and reached for the glass.

"Okay, Professor Niebold, what's this wine?" One of the brown robed men asked the loner prisoner, who was busy spearing his dinner. Niebold stopped eating, sniffed the wine, took a sip, and swirled it in his mouth.

"Fixin Clos Napoleon." He frowned and returned to impaling his beef. Abbot Anselm smiled and raised his glass in tribute to his sullen charge.

Brother Aaron did not wait for Lou to ask. "Niebold is a bit of a wine expert, an oenologist. Abbot Anselm is too. Funny they would share the same interest." Aaron chuckled, "So far, Niebold's 200 and 16."

Lou did some quick math in his head. "That would mean he's been here a little under four years."

I've been here for two days. Four years. Five years. I can't do a lifetime here.

He shuddered. With another sip of his wine, Lou felt his arms grow weak and his head lighter. He stared at the plate of food sitting before him. Small tenderloin pieces smothered in a rich pâté, accompanied by chunks of mushrooms and tender onions, lay in a bed of golden pastry. He moaned. Struggling to come to grips with the thought of living in this insane place had occupied his mind and taken all his energy. Food had been the last thing on his mind since his so-called execution. Now his stomach growled, and he felt his mouth fill with saliva. Lightheaded and weak, he muttered, "I'll starve myself tomorrow," and reached for his fork.

Everyone remained seated after dinner.

"So, what happens next? Why is everyone still sitting here?" Lou asked Frank.

"Kitchen monks gotta count all the silverware and glasses before we can leave because we could use them as weapons. We sat here for a half-hour one time 'till they found a knife that fell off the cart."

"Humm."

Lou felt himself drifting off, as if his full stomach were pulling down his eyelids. He took a deep breath, fighting drowsiness. He blinked, widened his eyes, and turned to Frank.

"Tell me how you came here."

"Kidnapping," Frank whispered, and looked away.

Lou wondered why Predmore sounded so ashamed. It wasn't as if the prisoners got here because they were model citizens.

"I didn't know they executed people for kidnapping," Lou said.

"It was aggravated kidnapping. Someone died."

"Who?" *It's like pulling teeth getting his story.*

Predmore looked at Lou and heaved a sigh. "It was the little girl I kidnapped, all right? I had a small landscaping company that took all my time. No social life to speak of. Never had many friends. Then I got the gambling bug. When I was winning, boy, did I have friends. When I started losing, well, that was a different story. I borrowed money to pay my debts and just got in deeper with the mob. They started threatening me big time. I needed money fast. That's all I knew. I decided I'd borrow a kid, just until the parents coughed up the money. I planned to return the little girl right away. Never meant to hurt her and even got a puppy to keep her company. I thought it would be over in a day, two at the most. All the ways it could go wrong never occurred to me."

Frank snorted and shook his head. Wiping at a tear, he continued.

"I pulled into the park where the father was to leave money for his daughter. When I saw the police cruiser, I panicked and floored it, straight into a tree."

Predmore stared at the table, not looking up.

With a bitter taste in his mouth, Lou imagined the little girl's body crushed between shards of metal, her blood flowing over ripped wires and torn fabric. An innocent life snuffed out, like his Becky's, because some rotten excuse for a man could not control his needs. His hands formed into fists, but he forced them to remain under the table. He noticed Brother Aaron observing him and recalled Predmore describing the monks as weapons.

After the cutlery and glassware count was complete, monks and prisoners rose from their tables. Aaron, Predmore, and Lou remained seated, and in the quiet of the emptying dining hall, Predmore spoke.

"You have to understand. I wouldn't have hurt a hair on her head. How could I have known things would happen like they did? I panicked and now wish I had died instead."

His eyes filled with tears. He faced Lou as if searching for a glimmer of understanding. Lou realized that, in some sick way, Predmore was asking him for sympathy, maybe even forgiveness. *Why me?*

He stood abruptly. He had to get out of there. As he walked away, he heard Predmore call after him, "You're a murderer too, you know."

Lou did not respond. Silently, he stumbled to his cell, and collapsed onto his cot. He thought about reaching for his blanket, but fell asleep instead.

A demanding bladder woke him. He kicked off the blanket, ran his hand over the stubble on his face, and stared at the ceiling. The perpetual dim light from the hall confirmed he was a prisoner inside a so-called monastery, and it was not a dream. He sighed.

Nature called more imperiously, and as Lou stepped out of his cell, he almost bumped into Brother Jerome, sitting in a chair just outside his door.

"How long have you been here?" On his best day, Lou was not a morning person, and this was far from his best day.

"Ever since you fell asleep. Look." Jerome pointed down the hallway. Lou scanned the corridor and saw a monk sitting opposite every prisoner's doorway.

"Why?"

"This is a monastery, and we have no armed guards. We house murderers, rapists, gang members. You name it. Our constant one-on-one observation protects you from harming yourself or others." Jerome added with a smile, "Just part of our care for you."

Lou left a string of profanity in his wake as he walked off to begin the first day of his living death.

CHAPTER 17

KILLER PROFESSOR

Jerome was reading when Lou returned to his cell.

"What time is it?" he asked the monk. "There are no clocks in this prison, and I don't have a watch anymore."

Jerome closed the book over his finger and looked at his glowering charge.

"The waking bell should ring in a few minutes, at five a.m. We rise, wash, and have breakfast. After breakfast, off-duty monks, and others who wish, go to Chapel for Morning Prayer. We call that prayer hour Lauds. After Lauds, the bell will ring again, which signals everyone to report to work, or bed if we have been up all night. Meet me outside the chapel after Lauds, and I'll take you to your work assignment before I turn in."

"Why the weird name for morning prayer?"

"The name goes back centuries. We also pray at noon — that's Sext. Our last prayer is Compline, just before sleep."

"So you pray morning, noon, and night here."

Brother Jerome smiled. "The prayers divide the daily hours, and go back to the ancient church and before that, to Jewish custom. Catholic monks carried on the practice, and although St. Dismas monasteries are nondenominational, we find it's good for our spiritual lives as well. 'Ora et labora' in Latin means to pray and work. That's our life here. Besides, it's best the local community hears our bells at regular intervals, so there's no suspicion we're anything but a cloistered monastery."

Lou grunted and rubbed his stubbly chin. "You mean so no one catches on that this is a glorified prison you have no authority to run?"

"We couldn't fulfill our purpose if we appeared as anything else. May I remind you, without us, you would be dead and buried right now?"

Maybe that would have been better.

Lou opened his mouth to comment, but the tolling bell silenced him.

Like territorial crows, monks and prisoners perched in the same places at the refectory tables they had claimed the evening before. Lou nodded his response to Brother Aaron's "good morning," and moved a little to make room as Predmore pulled his leg over the bench. It was not an effortless task, with the brown robe dragging across the wood. Breakfast was slim pickings for Lou's taste. A large bowl of oatmeal, a small dish of fruit, and a mug of black coffee sat before each place. He raised an eyebrow and shook his head. From Beef Wellington one day to hot slop the next.

Predmore interrupted Lou's musings. "How did you sleep? Were you surprised to see a monk watching you all night? It gave me the heebie-jeebies my first night, but I got used to it."

Predmore looked at him, as if seeking some response other than the glare he received. After a long moment, Lou turned to his oatmeal.

I hate oatmeal! It feels like wet plaster and tastes like it too.

He clenched his spoon and devoted his attention to the glop, hoping it would turn off Predmore's chatter. It did not.

Can't you get the message I don't want to talk to you? I keep seeing that little girl you killed. Just shut up.

Trying to block out Frank's monologue — now some nattering about Gregorian chant — Lou reached for his mug of hot coffee and surrounded it with chilly hands. He savored its warmth and rich aroma as he took a sip. Hot hot hot. Just the way he liked his caffeine infusion. Other than inhaling his first meal and sliding into a wine induced stupor last night, this was the first moment of conscious pleasure he had experienced in a long time. Its unexpected intensity surprised him. He closed his eyes, took another sip, and tuned out the world.

"Going to Chapel this morning?" Predmore asked.

"Don't have to, do I?"

"Nope, but I thought maybe we could…"

"No."

"What's your problem, Lou?" Aaron asked.

"Why should I have a problem?" Lou snapped, hoping his sarcasm would kill further conversation. It worked, and silence reigned until the bell rang for Chapel.

After Frank and Aaron joined the others leaving the refectory, two monks remained to clean the tables. Kurt Niebold approached Lou.

"We have some time while they're at Chapel. Mind if I join you?"

Lou looked at the one they called "professor." He observed sharp, chiseled features poking from the man's beard. Brown eyes, made larger by thick glasses, stared at him. He felt a twinge of unease under the man's gaze.

Lou shrugged. "Suit yourself."

"You'll start working for the man today," Niebold said as he placed his mug on the table and settled across from him. "This place is a throwback to the Middle Ages. We work like dogs just for food and shelter. We keep the place running while they watch us."

Lou eyed the monks wiping the tables while he and the professor lingered over coffee.

"Frank Predmore said you believed the monks were murdering sadists."

Niebold waited a few minutes until a monk pushed a cart of empty mugs and bowls into the kitchen before replying in a stage whisper.

"I've been here over four years and, in that time, at least a dozen prisoners have mysteriously disappeared. They're at dinner one evening and gone the next morning. Now what do you suppose happened to them? That lying Abbot claims they transferred them. Transferred where? And why? Every prisoner here is dead to the world. No one would look for us or question what happened to us. These monks can do whatever they want, with none the wiser. Besides, why would you choose this life, unless you were nuts to begin with?"

Lou considered Niebold's theory. It seemed to make sense on the surface. However, so far, every interaction he had with his keepers, from the Abbot to Brother Aaron, was cordial. Does their outward kindness hide evil intentions?

Niebold could be right. I'm dead as far as the world is concerned. Who would know or care if they murdered me? But what would be their motive?

Kurt stopped talking when a monk re-entered the dining hall. In the lingering silence, Lou asked, "Why does everyone call you 'professor?' Did you teach winemaking?"

Kurt laughed. "No, the study of wine and winemaking was my hobby. I was a physics professor until murder most foul."

"What?"

The professor gave Lou an empty stare before replying. "I was about to have my research on the next super string revolution published when one of my grad students claimed I was stealing the results of her work. That was absurd, of course, but even a hint of something like that and I could have lost the Physics Chair, not to mention a possible Nobel prize and my career. So, I killed her. Burned her body and buried it."

Lou cringed at the gruesome image Niebold summoned. He had expected Kurt to claim the university authorities had framed him and he was innocent. Instead, the man admitted to killing the grad student, burning her corpse, and burying her with as much emotion as if he had confessed to swatting a fly. *I may be a murderer, but this is one sick sociopath.* Lou shivered.

"You don't sound sorry for killing her."

"Why should I be? I'm just sorry I'm here now and my research will never prove the theory of everything."

"There's no right or wrong for you?"

Kurt snorted. "Of course there is. Right is what works for me and wrong is what doesn't. That's all there is to it, no matter what these monks say."

Lou narrowed his eyes and observed the professor. The man appeared totally untroubled by his past. *Can people go through life that way? According to Kurt, they can. Could he, Lou Skalney, make that work as well?*

As if in answer, his mind flashed to the day his daughter was born.

Holding Becky for the first time had changed him forever. He had brushed his forefinger along her cheek that felt like velvet. Lou breathed in her baby scent and lost his heart to her when she first gazed up at him. He would protect her with his life, this beloved child of his. And yet he failed.

How could a God who created such a precious child watch her murder and just stand by? Isn't God supposed to be our Father? What kind of Father is he? Why bother pleasing him? Why not take care of number one, like Kurt?

He ground his fist against his cheek to block gathering tears. Dealing with simple cause and effect was so much easier than dealing with morality, or God. Maybe the professor was on to something.

Niebold abruptly stood and stretched before shuffling away with a dismissive wave over his shoulder. When the bell rang at the end of Lauds, Lou sighed and downed the last of his coffee. It was time to meet Jerome. He rose reluctantly and made his way to the chapel.

CHAPTER 18

LAY OF THE LAND

"I'll show you the monastery grounds before I take you to your workstation," Jerome said when he met Lou outside the chapel. With that, the portly monk set off at a spritely pace. Lou lagged behind, his painful knees slowing him through winding corridors and down the stairs. He was panting by the time he caught up with Jerome, who was waiting for him at a simple wood door.

The monk chuckled. "Little winded? All the prisoners arrive out of shape, but don't worry, life here will take care of that."

"Is that a threat or a promise?"

"Both," he said, opening the door.

Lou followed Jerome outside, astonished to find the door had been unlocked. They walked toward the field that faced the monastery, where Lou saw rows of low, rectangular wooden boxes, each about 20 feet long and three feet wide. Curly kale filled one box, and he watched Frank Predmore pulling a huge zucchini from under a tent of green leaves. High wire fencing surrounded the entire complex of raised beds. The side of a red, two-story barn ran along the right of the crops.

"This is our farm. Brother Malachi runs it and is second in command after Abbot Anselm. We grow only what we consume, so we don't need to plow acres with expensive farm machinery. We prefer to plant our vegetables and herbs in these raised beds. It's easier to rotate crops and add natural compost to enrich the soil. Brother Malachi believes pesticides and chemical fertilizers are concoctions of Satan."

Lou managed his first smile. "Fertilizer hit the ventilation system once too often?"

"Good one, Lou."

Lou noted brown and black-robed figures working together as one monk, wearing a floppy straw hat, moved among them. "Is that Brother Malachi, in the hat?"

"Yes. You'll meet him later," Jerome answered, setting off east, toward another field. Lou glanced over his shoulder before following.

"What's that?" he asked, pointing back to an outbuilding attached to the monastery wall.

"That's where we store equipment and small tools. We can do our own repairs because Brother John is a gifted mechanic. And around the corner are the dog kennels." Jerome grinned. "Come, there's more to see before you start work."

Waving Lou on, the monk set off again. Soon they came to an open field covering about two acres. Lou watched white bundles move slowly within a large circle. Jerome pointed to two Border Collies he said were named Angus and Tipp. The dogs ran and barked, staring down any sheep that may decide to leave the group and wander off. Brother Jerome waved at the monk and his brown-clad partner, who were whistling and making strange sounds to which the collies readily responded.

Moving on to more green acreage, Jerome said, "Our cows graze over there and all the way to the stone border wall."

Between where they were standing and the grazing cows, a flock of chickens pecked away at vegetable scraps within an enclosed pen. Outside the enclosure, various dogs and cats of no breed that Lou could determine roamed freely.

Back at the vegetable beds, Jerome pointed to a field of corn and wheat that lay on the other side of the barn. It stretched to the stone wall at the west end of the monastery property. "And that's the farm," he said.

"I guess Abbot Anselm was telling the truth about raising everything you need here. What is it I'm supposed to do?" Lou asked, dreading the answer.

"Come, I'll introduce you to Brother Malachi and he'll get you started."

Lou groaned.

Up close, the monk wearing the straw hat was older than he appeared from a distance. Tanned and wrinkled, Lou guessed he must be over 70, even though he moved with the ease of a younger man.

"I'm Malachi. I see Brother Jerome showed you the property. It's simple work here on the farm, and we don't hold with formalities. If you need anything or have questions, just ask me. Work hard and we'll get along fine. I'll pair you with Niebold today. You already know him, and he could use help to weed the beds. I'll get you a hat."

Lou looked around and grimaced.

"Don't bother. There are no other tasks in this entire place other than farming? I detest yard work, especially in this heat."

Malachi put his hand on Lou's shoulder and leaned closer to his ear. "Well, a new verdict just came down. You will harvest crops forever."

Lou was about to snap at the elderly monk, but Malachi's wide grin forced a laugh out of him instead.

With that, Brother Malachi handed Lou a trowel and led him to a long bed of carrots. Niebold looked up, and squinted into the sun.

"You want a hat, Kurt. There's several in the barn." Malachi's remark sounded more like a tired reminder than a suggestion. "You already know Lou Skalney, so you can work together." Kurt ignored Malachi but gave Lou a nod.

"How long have you worked the farm?" Lou asked Kurt as he eased his weight onto complaining knees. With great effort, he dug into the soil surrounding a dandelion. Now seeing the carrot crop up close, Lou sighed at the number of weeds. He felt the sun on his neck and beads of perspiration forming around his collar.

These robes are too hot for outdoor work.

He considered grabbing one of those hats from the barn after all, but heaving himself to a standing position seemed far too strenuous. Instead, the new farm hand concentrated on digging and pulling.

"They put me anywhere they want around here. Now that we'll be harvesting soon, they'll torture me on the farm for a while. I like the solitary work," Niebold added with a meaningful look at Lou.

Good. I don't feel like talking either.

After an hour that felt like four, Lou jammed his trowel next to a stubborn weed and lowered his weight onto the handle to lever out its root. The handle broke, leaving the spade portion in the dirt.

Kurt smirked. "Putting your all into this?"

In response to Lou's expletive, Niebold suggested he could find another trowel on the shelf in the back corner of the toolshed.

Once on his feet, Lou trudged to the shed, muttering under his breath as his knees complained all the way. He noticed Brother Malachi in an animated conversation with Abbot Anselm at the far end of the wire fence. Lou remembered Jerome said Malachi was the number two monk here. Engrossed in conversation, neither seemed to notice him.

The small tool shed was dim, with light only from the open door and a window on the far-right. Lou followed the light and found a workbench leaning against the back wall. Sure enough, a pile of hand tools lay scattered upon it. He sighed, sifted through the mess, and stopped rooting around when he heard Anselm and Malachi.

They must have stepped into the shed for privacy. Malachi sounds angry.

"The problem isn't that I can't spare Niebold to lug the wine shipment into the cellar. The problem is you refuse to acknowledge that a St. Dismas monastery is no place for fine wines. We have several residents who struggled with drugs and alcohol all their lives. The last thing they need is wine, much less Fixin Close, or whatever it was last night."

"We've discussed this before." Abbot Anselm's voice sounded tired, as if he were trying to instruct a dull student. "With our surveillance system, the only effective alternative they have is to refuse food and drink. Wine lowers resistance and, coupled with our Sunday and resident- arrival- day menus, no one has successfully starved themselves in the five years I have been Abbot. As for drug and alcohol abuse, they only have a small portion, and no access to more. Or they can choose to drink water. They learn control."

"Control? It must be torture."

"Do you hear them complaining? Perhaps your opposition comes from your Amish background. That would be understandable."

"Mennonite, as you well know," Malachi snapped.

"Of course," Anselm conceded, and added, "As Abbot, the responsibility and consequences fall on me and not you."

As Lou heard their footsteps fade away, he recalled his first meal in the monastery. The Abbot had a point. He had considered starvation, but the wine weakened him, physically and mentally. He realized he ate his breakfast of gruel this morning without a thought of suicide.

They sure broke me fast. Interesting about Malachi, though. He seems like a tough boss, like some supervisors I worked with. I can deal with a guy like that. He takes care of business. But what's this tenderness for winos and druggies? And Malachi's background — what is a Mennonite doing here? Monasteries aren't part of their religion. What else do those two lock horns about?

Lou jumped when he heard his name called.

"Back here," he replied, as he pulled a trowel from the pile.

One of the farm monks appeared. "Niebold said he told you to find another trowel in the shed. He knows better than that. You should have told one of us, and we would have gotten it."

So, your surveillance isn't as perfect as you think. No one knew where I was, except Kurt. I think he wanted to show me something.

"Well then," Lou said as he turned, trowel in hand, to face the monk. "I'll need one of those straw hats."

As the morning wore on, Lou often leaned on his haunches and scanned the monastery grounds. He was interested in the perimeter, and those high stone walls.

What keeps prisoners from climbing over them? Surely someone tried that already. They think their surveillance is so good, but I was off their radar for a while without even trying. Maybe they're playing mind games, saying no one escapes.

By the time the bell rang for Sext, Lou was hot, hungry, and aching all over. He dragged himself into the monastery for lunch, where Frank approached him as he entered the refectory.

"How did your first day go? You look done in."

"I'll live."

He was about to sit when he noticed monks and prisoners lining up at the sideboard. As he moved to join them, Frank stopped him.

"It's beef or chicken sandwiches and salad. Which do you want? I'll bring it to you."

"Never mind. I'll get it myself."

"That's all right. I'll do it."

"It's not all right," Lou said, and strode toward the food. Soon, with hands loaded with a full plate and cutlery, he found a spot next to Niebold.

"Thanks for setting me up with the trowel. I disappeared for a while."

Kurt nodded and smiled without looking at him. "You're welcome."

Lou's first workday on the farm had exhausted him. His muscles screamed for relief as he limped toward the showers before bed. Apparently, he was not alone in his agony since two other prisoners were already filling shower stalls with steaming hot water. Again, Brother Cornelius pointed out the clean supply of towels, washcloths, and robes. Silently, Lou showered until he felt human. After shuffling to his cell, he turned to see Brother Jerome approaching.

"Are you on night watch again?"

"Yes."

"Knock yourself out. I'll sleep like the dead tonight, even with you spying on me."

But it was not to be.

CHAPTER 19

NIGHT TERRORS

Nestled between his mattress and wool blanket, Lou curled up on his left side and closed his eyes, blocking the image of Brother Jerome sitting outside his cell. Exhausted, he soon drifted into sleep, but not for long.

When screams jarred him awake, he bolted up in bed, eyes searching the dark for the source. At first, he thought he was having a nightmare, but then he saw Brother Jerome stand and look down the hall. Lou jumped out of bed and rushed to his cell doorway, where the monk blocked him.

"What's going on?" he said and stepped forward.

Jerome placed a restraining hand on his chest. "A resident is distraught, and his monk is helping him."

Lou heard pounding and yelling.

"Helping or assaulting him?"

He remembered Predmore telling him all the monks held black belts in Krav Maga and Niebold's theory about murder in the dead of night. Would that prisoner disappear from the monastery? Tomorrow will they claim they transferred him?

After a while, subdued sobbing replaced the sounds of the struggle.

"It's all right now, Lou. You can go back to sleep." Jerome sounded reassuring, but Lou was having none of it.

"All right? What did his monk do to him? Beat him to a pulp?" Lou pushed forward. "Get out of my way. I want to see for myself."

Jerome's eyes bored into Lou's. "No, he did not beat him to a pulp. He kept Harold from beating his own head into a pulp against the cell wall. It's not the first time he's had such episodes, and unfortunately, won't be the last."

"Humph. So you say." Lou's voice was bitter with challenge. He leaned forward, his eyes darting between Jerome and the corridor.

Jerome said, "Right now, you have all you can handle, just getting used to the idea of spending the rest of your life here. Everything is new — the people, our way of life."

"What does that have to do with Harold?"

"Like him, in time, your thoughts will haunt you, and you will find nothing to distract you from facing your personal demons. You will question who you are, how you could have done what you did, and who you will become. You have two choices — come face to face with the living God or try to flee from him. There is nothing here other than that, beyond eating, sleeping, and working. Our residents often cry out in the night when their subconscious forces them to face what they could not while awake. Some become desperate to escape in any way possible."

Lou scratched his neck and sighed. "I need to sit and think." He turned from the monk and settled on his cot. Jerome resumed his post at the cell entrance while Lou pondered those two choices — coming face to face with God or fleeing from him.

He remembered the first two lines of a poem he once read with the image of being chased by a relentless God — "The Hound of Heaven" by Thompson-something-or-other. Frederick? Ferdinand? Felix? Francis! That's it. Francis Thompson.

I fled Him, down the nights and down the days.

I fled Him, down the arches of the years.

Lou lay down and pulled up his blanket, imagining running through a dark tunnel with a dog yapping at his heels. After a while, all was silent, as if nothing had happened, and he slept until the morning bell.

The next morning, while Lou ate his scrambled eggs and thick buttered toast, he listened to Brother Aaron and another monk discuss Harold's episode that night.

"He was too quiet," Aaron murmured. "I always wondered what was going on in his mind."

"Mostly kept to himself," the other monk added.

Predmore concentrated on his breakfast, and for once did not make conversation. Lou looked around the refectory. *Where is Harold? Why are the monks talking about him in the past tense?*

He scanned the refectory and pursed his lips. Lou looked at Kurt and found him staring at him, as if waiting for the light to turn on. Kurt's imperceptible nod shouted accusation. Testing the monks, Lou asked what happened to Harold.

"We transferred him," Aaron announced, loud enough to be heard tables away.

Lou caught Kurt Niebold's smirk, and his heart sank.

Before reporting for work, Lou searched for Brother Jerome and found the monk walking toward the cells.

"Hold up, Brother." Lou quickened his pace to catch up to Jerome. *He's fast for such a big guy.* "I want to know what happened to Harold. He wasn't at breakfast."

Jerome turned to his charge and waited for him to catch up.

"You heard Brother Aaron."

"Yes, but I want to hear it from you. Kurt thinks that's the standard line when someone disappears around here. 'Transferred,' you say. Maybe 'murdered' instead."

Jerome sighed and shook his head. "Why would we murder him?"

"Why does anyone murder? Sometimes the reason isn't obvious. For sure, no one would miss any of us. You monks could get away with anything."

Jerome crossed his arms. "That's absurd. Harold has been troubled for a long time and we could not help him. Last night showed he needs a different level of care — one this monastery cannot provide. Another St. Dismas monastery in our chain will be better able to assist him. As for Niebold refusing to believe we transfer, rather than murder people, he has a way of looking at truth and denying it. Now, if you will excuse me, I need some sleep."

Lou watched Brother Jerome's back recede down the corridor. *Which one is telling the truth?*

CHAPTER 20

FOILED!

A month of farm work and healthy meals pared fifteen pounds from a now bearded Lou. He moved quicker, without needing to catch his breath, and his knees ached less. He was in shape, ready, with no reason to put it off.

Lou waited until mid-morning when he knew Brother Malachi would send the monks to the raised beds to pick the vegetables for the day's lunch and dinner.

With everyone busy on that side of the barn, I can slip around the corner and into the wheat field. I'll disappear like I did the day Niebold sent me into the shed. No one knew where I was for a while.

It seemed to take forever until Brother Malachi instructed his workers to gather the vegetables. He was about to step toward the wheat field when Malachi called him. "Lou, bring the wheelbarrow from the barn."

Lou stopped, frozen in mid-step, jaw clenched. After a few seconds, he forced himself to respond.

"Okay."

Lou retrieved the wheelbarrow and brought it to the monks. Hiding his frustration, he helped them load the vegetables and offered to take the produce to the kitchen. Once away from the barn, pushing the wheelbarrow over bumpy ground, and almost spilling its contents at one point, his mind raced to find another way to escape through the wheat field.

Just be bold. There will never be a perfect moment. Maybe now, while they think I'm unloading this stuff.

Lou rang the bell over the door closest to the kitchen and tapped his foot, waiting for someone to come for those blasted vegetables. After what seemed an eternity, Kurt Niebold opened the door.

"Help me carry them in. I'm stuck doing kitchen duty," Niebold said, eyeing zucchinis large enough to be weapons, surrounded by clusters of ripe tomatoes.

Lou looked over his shoulder. "Sorry. I have to get back to the farm."

"Since when? Why are you in such a rush?" Then after a moment, "Ah ha, escaping today?"

"No." Lou kept his face blank as he lied.

Kurt raised an eyebrow and locked eyes with his fellow prisoner. After a few seconds, Lou looked away.

Maybe it will be impossible today, after all. But what if they reassigned me like they did Niebold? Then I'd have to make another plan.

"Hey, far be it from me to discourage you. You must try. Everyone does. Even I tried. You look hyped up. That's how I knew."

Niebold leaned forward and stage whispered, "What's your plan?"

"No plan. Just take the vegetables. They need my help in the gardens. I'll come back for the wheelbarrow later." Without waiting for a reply, Lou walked away.

Instead of turning toward the garden, he veered toward the wheat field until he was far from the kitchen door and nosy Niebold. He fought the impulse to run. Instead, he walked casually into the field, as if on another errand. The back of his neck itched with the urge to look over his shoulder, but that would give him away. Instead, Lou lowered his head as if in deep thought, and concentrated on putting one foot ahead of the other. He expected to hear his name called, but there was silence.

How much farther? After a few minutes that felt like hours, he dared to raise his eyes and saw the stone perimeter. He was getting closer. *Don't look back. Watch your step. Keep going.*

For the first time in months, Lou considered life on the other side of the wall as a real possibility.

Those monks can't go around town asking about me. It would blow their cover. And since I'm supposed to be dead anyway, the authorities won't be looking for me. In this robe, I can pass myself off as a monk begging for money. Isn't that what they do? Vow of poverty and all that? My beard and monk's robe are a perfect disguise. Once I beg enough cash, I can get a hold of Rudy. With his contacts, he can get me a fake ID and I can start a new life.

He grinned and continued wading through the tall golden stalks.

Lou could hardly believe his good fortune when he reached the stone wall. He was going to escape! They said no one ever could, but he, Lou Skalney, was going to prove them wrong, and it was so simple. He looked up to gauge its height; about twenty feet, too high to leap over. *If I can get toeholds, I should be able to scale it.* As he gingerly tried to wedge his toes between two stones, Lou realized the sandals' soles lacked the flexibility he needed. When he bent to remove them, he learned what the term "blood running cold" felt like.

Out of the corner of his eye, he saw a large brown dog racing towards him, and it was not looking for a treat — unless *he* was the treat. *I never even saw that dog! Where'd he come from?* Hearing a loud bark and deep growl behind him, Lou saw another dog, this one, with a white snout, snarling at him. He recognized the breed — Malinois. Father Briscomb had one that guarded the rectory from irate parents and hapless students.

Lou froze and thought of Clint Eastwood's famous line in *Dirty Harry,* because every ounce of those dogs dared him to make their day. He knew the worst thing would be to run and felt like an insect pinned to a pegboard. He barely breathed as he scanned the horizon for one of those blasted monks. They had seen him try to escape after all and just let him make a fool of himself. Lou ground his teeth.

They didn't even bother to catch me, just released their dogs to do the dirty work. Now they'll make me sweat until they're good and ready to call them off.

Lou waited for what seemed forever while the dogs barked and snarled. Eventually, he made out the top of Jerome's head bobbing along the rows of wheat. *Come on! Move it!* The monk did not appear to be in a hurry. When he finally arrived, he softly commanded the dogs to stand down, in what Lou later learned was Flemish.

"Now you know why we have no watchtowers or razor wire on top of the walls," Jerome said before Lou could utter a word. "Just to save you the trouble of more escape attempts, you should know all the monks monitor our residents' locations constantly. No one has escaped yet, and it would save you future aggravation if you believed me, Lou."

The monk looked meaningfully at him, as if to say, "Do you finally understand?" He added, "Brother Malachi released Sargan and Caesar when you were half-way to the wall."

Jerome whistled at the Malinois, who fell in at his heels as they walked back to the monastery buildings.

"So what now? Solitary confinement?" Lou kicked at a loose stone.

"This isn't a prison."

"Oh really? No one ever escapes and you watch us constantly. Sounds like a prison to me. And the head warden, your Abbot — what's his story? You can't tell me he hasn't run a prison somewhere."

Brother Jerome ignored the angry challenge in Lou's voice. "For a while Abbot Anselm lived in a Benedictine monastery, but after a few years, felt called to serve God in the world, and decided he wanted to bring the Gospel to prison inmates. He became a chaplain in a state prison, believing he was doing what God wanted him to do. Abbot hated the executions and said he was depressed for days after. That may be how the St. Dismas people heard about him. They approached him to join their organization. He's been Abbot here for five years. Brother Malachi was Abbot before, but he wanted to run the farm. It's a better fit for him since he was a farmer before."

"What brought Brother Malachi here?

"God's will."

Lou sniffed, remembering that was the answer Jerome had given him when he asked how he came to the monastery.

"Is that it? Just 'God's will?'"

"That's not just it," the monk said, making air quotes around "it." "That's everything."

Lou shook his head. "I don't get you people."

They walked on in silence. As they neared the farm door entrance to the monastery, the bell pealed for lunch and Sext. Lou's stomach rumbled. Nothing like terror to stimulate the appetite.

When he entered the refectory, the prisoners punched their fists into the air and chanted, "Woo! Woo! Go Skalney!" The monks remained silent.

Lou lowered his head, thrust his arm up, holding his fist high, a good-natured acceptance of their mocking. *That's right, I tried. The novice did what every one of you did. I'm now a member of the "tried to escape" club.*

His heart raced, and he ground his teeth.

Predmore joined him in the lunch line. Lou tried to ignore him. *This line's moving as slowly as Jerome's walk through the cornfield.*

Until now, he hoped that, somehow, he would escape from this place. This morning's failure drew his fate in stark, black lines. Lou had wanted to believe that the claim no one escaped from St. Dismas was what they told prisoners to intimidate them. But now, for the first time, he faced the fact that he, Louis Skalney, would die within the confines of a hidden monastery.

I've disappeared like smoke. No one knows or cares. I'm dead now, except my body doesn't know it.

Lou pulled deep breaths through his nose, and he concentrated on breathing to relieve the aching reality of his situation. He detested being powerless, clenched his fists and let out a low moan.

"I'd have loved to have seen the look on your face when you reached the wall and met the dogs. Woo boy!"

Predmore's remark unleashed Lou's anger like a hundred firecrackers going off at once. He whirled on him. Frank's eyes widened, and he stepped back, but not soon enough. With his left hand, Lou grabbed Frank's robe at the neck and twisted the cloth, pulling the shocked little man closer. He had just drawn back his right arm, fist clenched, when a black blur flew at him from the side, and body slammed him to the floor. Strong arms pinned him down. Lou turned his head to see his attacker. The monk's expression showed no emotion, but the glare from his icy blue eyes paralyzed him. The monk spoke with quiet authority. "I highly suggest you join us in the chapel after lunch."

Lou knew it was not a suggestion.

Lou ate his lunch in silence and slipped out of the dining room before the bell rang. He chose a seat in the chapel as far in the back as possible so he could escape unnoticed if he wanted. Alone, except for a solitary monk, Lou looked up at the blue and gold ceiling that rose to a pointed arch above him. An altar holding two burning candles stood on a dais that faced the pews.

Lou watched the monk light rows of votive candles that sat on a platform to the right of the altar. The aroma of smoking wax was pleasant and reminded him of burning incense during the Benediction services years ago. It grew comfortably warm in the chapel and Lou closed his eyes while other prisoners filled the pews.

Then, from a distance, he heard a haunting chant.

"Oh give thanks to the Lord, for he is good."

The lone tenor sang each word on one note until the end, when the melody rose, fell, and returned to the original pitch.

"His mercy endures forever," echoed the other monks in the same plainsong.

Lou turned to see Brother Jerome holding high a large cross, his hood covering the tangle of his white curls, lead a procession of monks down the center aisle. The monks continued their simple call and response chant as they processed to their pews. Then, the melody changed. One melody line became two, sung as a round, like the old *Row, Row, Your Boat*. The dueling melodies of prayer wove the notes into a thick tapestry of sound.

When Jerome arrived at the foot of the altar, he nestled the cross into its platform and retreated to the first pew. Abbot Anselm knelt before the altar.

Lou noticed that Predmore, rather than settling into a pew like everyone else, fell to his knees in the side aisle. With his back to the wall, he extended his arms, making himself into an absurd, short, human cross. Lou shook his head and rolled his eyes. He looked away, determined to ignore the fool.

Abbot Anselm rose and approached the podium. He slowly opened an over-sized Bible and turned the pages until he found the Scripture passage he wanted. The rise and fall of the Abbot's voice, as he read a psalm that sounded more like poetry, mesmerized Lou. Smoke teasing his nose, the reflection of candle flames dancing on the walls, and the image of black cowls covering lines of bowed heads sitting before him, brought a long-forgotten sense of quiet into his soul.

He was about to surrender to the sights, sounds, and smells that surrounded him when he again glimpsed Predmore out of the corner of his eye. The man was not only kneeling with arms outstretched, but now tears streamed down his plump cheeks. Instead of feeling compassion, Lou felt disgust, and he did not know why.

Whatever had brought him those blessed moments of peace disappeared as quietly as it had arrived. He slipped out of the chapel, yet returned the next day, and the days after that. He could not explain what drew him there, the place he once had most dreaded.

PART III

FACING DEMONS

CHAPTER 21

BLOOD TRAIL

Lately, Lou felt his spirit squirming. At first, being in the chapel had lulled his senses. The silence before prayers, the plainchant, even the flickering candlelight, calmed something deep within. But now God had planted himself in his brain, like a persistent earworm.

Niggling questions intruded against his will as he paced slowly around the great hall's perimeter during the social hour. Keeping his head down, he hoped no one would approach him. The Abbot's prayers and messages made him wonder if it was possible God really cared about him after all.

Is there some reason I'm still alive? Does God know I did what I did for justice's sake, and it was good? How can God care about everyone, let alone me? Doesn't look like he cared about Becky. In the end, what does anything matter? You're born, you die. Period.

But this Creator Abbot Anselm reads about from the Bible seems like a person, not a mindless or angry force that needs constant appeasement. He seems disappointed in his creatures yet continues to reach out to them.

Lost in thought, he failed to see Niebold stride into the hall. When they collided, the usual "Sorry" and "Watch where you're going" passed in seconds before the professor grabbed Lou's arm and pulled him aside.

"Another one has disappeared," he hissed.

"Another what?"

"Prisoner. I told you that people just disappear. Now Bob Kettering is gone. Check it out at dinner. You won't see him."

"Maybe he's in the infirmary. Did you look? How long has he been missing?"

Niebold sighed and rolled his eyes. "Of course I checked the infirmary and his cell. No one has seen him since last night. I asked the monk who was shadowing me where Bob was."

"And?"

"Transferred. Same old story. I wonder where they buried him." Niebold glared and scanned the hall. "Only now I found something. Follow me."

As they turned to leave, Brother Jerome approached them.

"You seem upset, Kurt," he said.

"Upset? I seem upset?" Niebold's voice grew louder. "You monks think you can do whatever you want to us because we technically don't exist. Where do you people transfer us, as you claim? Our graves?"

Jerome shook his head. "This is not the only St. Dismas monastery in Texas. Abbot Anselm has his reasons for moving some residents to other monasteries and for selecting others for here. I don't know why you insist there's more to it."

"Well, explain this, if you can." Kurt spun away and marched out of the hall, leaving Lou and Jerome to follow. He led them to the door leading to the monastery farm, the door so familiar to Lou in his daily work.

"Look." Niebold pointed to red spots on the floor. Lou and Jerome bent for a closer look and their eyes followed the blood trail along the hall's floor.

Lou's heart skipped a beat. He had thought Niebold was overly suspicious, even paranoid, since he had never witnessed brutality by the monks, other than his takedown in the refectory. And in hindsight, he had to admit he had it coming.

Had the monks beaten Kettering into submission and dragged him away? Dragged him out the door to his death and buried him somewhere on the farm? Could there be other bodies out there, like Niebold thinks?

He shivered and turned to Jerome. "Well?" he asked the monk.

Lou observed Brother Jerome while he waited for a response. Either the man was an excellent actor or genuinely puzzled. The monk inhaled deeply and shook his head. "Let's see where this leads," he said and set off along the red trail.

"Oh, I know where it leads," Niebold snapped, as they followed Jerome.

Eventually, they arrived in the corridor that held the prisoners' cells. Jerome named each cell by the prisoner's name as the trio moved down the line. Finally, they neared the end.

"Predmore and Kettering. It ends at Predmore's cell, not Kettering's."

"So?" Niebold folded his arms. "A monk beat him and dragged him out of his cell. Any fool can see that."

"I wonder," Jerome said as he walked into Predmore's cell. Without hesitation, he lifted the prisoner's mattress and studied the floor between the cot's slats. He ran his hand under the wooden frame and did the same to all sides of the rudimentary desk and chair. Satisfied there was nothing in the room other than the cot, sheets which he flung apart, the desk and the chair, he returned to the corridor.

"What was that about? What were you looking for?" Lou said.

Brother Jerome turned to him. "Frank has difficulty believing God will forgive him for causing the girl's death. That's why he is so quick to confess what he did to anyone who will listen. It's his way of washing his conscience again and again. But it's never enough. He's engaged in self-flagellation because he believes if he hurts himself enough, God will be merciful and love him again. Over the years, he's been creative in inflicting self-injury. We thought he was beginning to understand that it's only through Jesus' death on the cross that we are forgiven, and not through self-torture. God hears our cries of sorrow and contrition, no matter the sin."

"So what set him off now?" Kurt asked, skepticism written on his face.

Jerome looked at Lou. "You did."

"What? How did I set him off?" Lou stepped back and did not mention that he simply disliked the man.

"Frank's action caused the death of a child, a father's daughter. Another man, like Frank, killed *your* daughter. In his mind, if you can accept him, maybe God will accept him again. You are the personification of his victim's father, and by extension, the path to divine forgiveness."

"That's just sick," Lou said, folding his arms and glaring at Jerome.

"What about your projection, Lou?" the monk said.

Lou stiffened. *What is he talking about? What am I projecting? The guy killed a little girl. What does he want—a medal now that he's sorry? Won't bring her back.*

Jerome continued. "I see Frank trying to ingratiate himself with you and, yes, that can be irritating. But I believe your rejection of him goes deeper. In your heart, Frank represents the man who killed your daughter, even if you don't see it."

Lou remembered the evening he met Predmore and told him how he had assassinated Becky's killer.

That's why Frank suddenly was so jittery. He was afraid of what I would think of him. I hated him the moment I learned about the little girl he killed. I still don't like him, but it's his problem, not mine.

Lou challenged the monk's assessment. "So how is he worse now?"

"He's resumed kneeling on the chapel floor with arms outstretched. If you ever tried to do that, you'd know how painful it can be to hold your arms up for ten minutes, let alone an hour. Even Moses had people support his upraised arms while the Israelites were defeating the Amalekites in battle. It's Frank's public form of confession and penance that we thought he'd gotten over. It returned when he met you."

"Who says? Don't lay it on me, Brother."

Niebold pronounced his diagnosis as the trio walked toward the hall. "Textbook projection."

"What would you know about it?" Lou snapped. "You're a physicist, not a shrink."

"Don't have to be a shrink to know how guilt messes with your mind."

"Did you hear about Kettering?" Predmore asked Lou as he slid next to him on the bench at dinner. Lou looked around the room and saw another prisoner sitting in Kettering's spot. It was like he never existed.

Lou turned his attention to Predmore, keeping the information about the blood spots to himself. What was Predmore's take on Kettering's disappearance? "What do you know about Kettering?"

"They say they transferred him," Predmore said.

"Why secretly?"

Predmore shrugged and looked away. Lou was not about to let Predmore off the hook that easily, but the Abbot rose, silencing all conversation. Lou studied the Abbot for any sign showing something was different in their controlled world. Would he mention Kettering, offer a warning about breaking rules, or asking too many questions? Would his prayer give a clue?

Anselm intoned the usual invocation, with monks responding in the same manner. The prisoners remained silent, as if in unanimous protest.

Lou pushed his potatoes into his green beans and moved a few pieces of chicken aside. He considered the two scenarios and neither comforted him.

If Niebold is right, why would the monks kill a prisoner who isn't causing a problem for anyone, who kept mostly to himself? Niebold is more of a troublemaker than Kettering ever was. If they're a bunch of sick sadists who like to torture and kill for pleasure, wouldn't it show somehow? But then, this business about transferring someone in the middle of the night doesn't make sense either, despite what Jerome said.

Lou did not like Jerome's guilt theory either.

I'm not taking the blame if Predmore wants to beat himself up. It's not my job to forgive him. Anyway, Jerome found nothing in his cell that could hurt him.

Frustrated by his circling thoughts, Lou stabbed a chunk of chicken and took a bite. It was no use. The food was cold, and his stomach churned. Sighing, he parked his fork and took a sip of water.

Perhaps Niebold is right. Maybe these monks get away with murder because they put on a good show of piety, while their hearts are full of more evil than the prisoners they control. Will I be next? It surprised him to realize he cared.

More to silence his swirling thoughts than to pray, he opted to join the monks for Compline. *At least the chanting and candles will take my mind off today.*

As Lou entered the chapel, he watched Predmore take his usual place on the side aisle, back to the wall, arms outstretched. Not my fault! Lou looked away, slid into the last pew, and inhaled the smoke from the burning tapers. He tried to empty his mind and focus on the monks' plainchant. Watching their slow procession down the aisle calmed him. With hoods covering their heads, black robes, red crosses emblazoned on their chests, they looked and sounded like monks, not Niebold's murderers. Surely the professor was wrong. Lou surrendered to the mesmerizing rituals and commanded himself to relax.

When Abbot Anselm mounted the podium for the evening's devotional topic, and announced he would "unpack the Lord's Prayer," Lou smiled. It seemed a strange way to describe digging into a subject. He imagined Anselm emptying the contents of an enormous trunk and holding up each object for closer investigation.

Go ahead, unpack the Lord's Prayer. I'll just snooze. He closed his eyes and settled deeper into the pew. That was the one prayer he remembered. He knew it word for word and didn't need it unpacked. The Abbot's words floated in the atmosphere, a monotonous drone to accompany Lou's drooping eyelids.

Anselm's words, "Forgive us our trespasses, as we forgive those who trespass against us," pierced the white noise playing in his head. Lou startled, eyes opening wide. His heart sank. Jerome's remarks about Predmore seeking his forgiveness flooded back. *No! I'm not ready to forgive.*

But God had parked himself in his head and was getting ruthless.

CHAPTER 22

TRAIL'S HEAD

"**A**re you coming to bed? It's Midnight."

Kathy sounded irritable as she poked her head into Rudy's home office, where the computer screen lit the dim room. Rudy sighed and logged off.

"I can't find anything about St. Dismas Monastery, Dismas monasteries, or even any monastery near Huntsville. It's like it doesn't exist. I think I'll meet with the Bishop and ask if he knows anything."

A grinning Bishop Keenan greeted Rudy just outside his office. "Are you hot on the trail of another story? I liked your series on genetically modified organisms in our food supply. What's next? And how are my niece Kathleen and the children? Giving you a teen-age run for your money?"

"Not anything I can't handle — yet." Rudy shot his uncle-in-law a rueful smile.

"Give them time, my boy. Give them time. You're raising them well, so they won't stray far. Maybe test the limits, but they'll be fine. Call me if you need reinforcements." He grinned and winked.

His Excellency Patrick Joseph Keenan ushered Rudy into his office. "Hold my calls, will you, Mary?" he said over his shoulder before he closed the door.

He offered Rudy a chair and settled behind his desk. "What can I help you with?"

"Do you recall I mentioned my friend Lou Skalney?"

"Of course. The fellow who killed Beauregard Abbington. Terrible business." He shook his head, not a silver hair out of place.

"Lou asked me to handle his funeral arrangements. You know his wife left him? Well, anyway, I put it off too long. It was hard to face the fact they really would execute him. We go way back. You know I used to stutter when I was a kid, and one day Lou beat the stuffing out of the school bully who was picking on me. I had trouble dealing with Lou's death, put things off, and when they executed him, I was tied up in traffic, coming back from a story in Austin. Got there just in time to follow the hearse to the funeral home."

"I'm sure your friend would have understood." Bishop Keenan's voice was soft.

Rudy shook his head. "That's not what's bothering me. The hearse first went to a St. Dismas Monastery, on the edge of Trinity County. It drove into the monastery, like it was dropping something off, and then drove out. I trailed it to the funeral home, and by the time I met with the funeral director, he said they had taken Lou to the monastery for cremation. Something isn't right. The monastery has no license for cremations. What monastery does cremations, anyway?"

Keenan frowned. "None. That's absurd."

"Do you know anything about this monastery? I found nothing about it online."

The Bishop shook his head. "I agree with you. That seems unusual in this day of the internet. The monastery would be in Bishop Haggerty's diocese, and it's strange he never mentioned it. It may not be a Catholic monastery, but perhaps Anglican or Eastern Orthodox, or even non-denominational like the Taizé community in Burgundy, France. I'll ask Bishop Haggarty what he knows about this St. Dismas community."

"Thank you. I look forward to what you discover."

Rudy rose, and with a blessing from the Bishop, left to do the only thing he could think of.

After giving the bell's rope a good yank, Rudy studied the stone walls surrounding the monastery. With some rope and the right shoes, it could be possible to scale the wall, but that was the last thing he wanted to do. He was about to ring the bell again when he heard the clink of the lock and quickly reviewed his cover story. Rudy's face had assumed the expression of a sincere penitent by the time the gate creaked open. The same monk who had let in the hearse waited for him to speak.

Rudy cleared his throat and looked into the man's eyes; they seemed friendly and kind. "Father, I was wondering if you take people in for retreats and such."

"We're monks, not priests, and, no, we don't offer retreats. This is a cloistered monastery and there are no guests."

"I was driving by and saw someone drive in." Rudy thought it best not to tip his hand and mention that the someone was driving a hearse.

"We have occasional deliveries and outside contacts for monastery business, but that is all."

Rudy shoved his foot in the way as the monk tried to close the gate.

"Is this a Catholic monastery?"

"Our monks are Christian men who take perpetual vows. We follow many Catholic disciplines because they are spiritually beneficial, but we are non-denominational and independent."

Rudy pulled his foot out of harm's way just before the gate closed.

Once back in his car, he drummed his fingers on the steering wheel and considered what the monk had told him. As Bishop

Keenan suspected, St. Dismas was not a Catholic community, which would explain why Bishop Haggarty never mentioned it.

Since he was investigating this so-called monastery on his own time, he did not want to waste his Saturday.

Someone in this town knows something, and I'm going to find out what. It's time for lunch.

Rudy rolled down the main drag, looking for that every-town's-diner, where the waitress knows everybody, calls them "Sweetie," and sucks up gossip like strands of spaghetti. He passed the miniscule post-office, a small hardware store, and a gas station. Other than the H-E-B grocery store and Larry's Liquor Emporium he had passed on the way to the monastery, the town looked like a forgotten corner in Texas Development and Planning.

And there it was. "The Ranchero" looked busy, and Rudy nabbed the last parking spot on the block. Once inside, he scanned the diner while the bell hanging over the door announced his presence. Ladies "doing lunch," as Kathy would say, filled the tables to his right.

Rudy turned to his left and looked at the generous backsides of half a dozen men sitting on stools along the counter, eating lunch, and softly talking. He took the last stool on the right and watched the waitress walk toward him, pulling out her order pad. She smiled and called him "sweetie" as she handed him a menu. Rudy pretended to study the fare while he grabbed quick glances at the man sitting next to him.

He was gray-haired, heavyset, and wore thick jeans, a plaid shirt, and a leather vest. Rudy typecast him as a retired cowboy, but realized he could be so far off base, the guy could be a banker on vacation. Time to get banker/cowboy talking. Rudy cleared his throat and asked him, "What's good here?"

The man turned to him, and without hesitation said, "Chicken fried steak dinner. Comes with corn on the cob and mashed potatoes and gravy. Top it off with Franny's apple pie à la mode and you got yourself one fine meal." He grinned and patted his stomach.

"Thanks, I'll try that." Rudy offered his hand with a smile, all the while bemoaning his soon-to- rise cholesterol level. "Name's Rudy."

"Hank Campbell." He shook Rudy's hand. "What brings you here? You lost or something?"

Rudy noticed the fellow sitting next to Hank, looking at him and smiling at the question. It was time to do a little digging.

"Yeah, I am kind of lost. Must have taken the wrong exit, but it is pretty country around here. What is it? Farms and ranches?"

"Mostly," Hank said, and flicked his thumb toward the man on his left. "My brother Steve and I run a small cattle ranch just outside of town. Just a few hundred head, but they keep us busy enough. We grew up on the Lazy Q Ranch, and after our parents passed, why we just kept it going. What about you?"

Rudy shrugged. "I'm a writer. I guess you would say being nosy comes with the territory. Like, what's with that St. Dismas Monastery in the middle of nowhere? I drove by and noticed it looks like a fortress or something."

"What do you write?" Steve asked, leaning toward his brother.

"I'm a reporter," Rudy said briefly, trying to move the conversation back to his question.

Hank grinned. "You going to write about the monastery?"

"Depends if it's worth writing about."

By now, the other men at the counter were listening to the conversation.

A man at the end joined in. "Heck! They're a strange bunch. They say they're closeted."

"Cloistered," Hank corrected. "Means no one goes in or out, except for deliveries for their farm and the wine, of course."

"Sacramental wine?"

Rudy wondered why everyone laughed.

"No Sweetie — good wine. Larry said he delivers some pricey stuff every few months," Franny said.

"Has Larry been inside the gates?" Rudy asked before he ordered his chicken fried steak dinner.

"Just inside. Larry said the monks come and unload his truck. They pay him cash and he leaves." Franny suspended her carafe. "Coffee?"

"No thanks. So, is that all you noticed? Just occasional deliveries?"

Hank pulled in a deep breath. "Well, I'll tell you, I noticed more than once — I double as the local coroner, so I'm sometimes out and about at all hours — cars driving out of the monastery in the middle of the night. Now, where would those monks be going at three a.m.?"

"Did you ever ask?" Rudy found the upfront approach worked best.

"Tell him about the hearses," Steve said.

"Oh yeah, we've seen hearses come and go from there," Hank added before Rudy could ask a quesstion. "Told the Sherriff, but he said that wasn't a crime, and as long as there were no missing person reports, he had no reason to ask for a search warrant."

"Weird." Rudy pulled his wallet from his back pocket. "Here's my card in case anything interesting turns up," he said, handing it to Hank.

"Yeah, maybe you should investigate the place."

Rudy nodded before tucking into his lunch. "Who knows? Maybe I will."

CHAPTER 23

MOSES AND MACKEY

Lou salivated when Abbot Anselm announced at breakfast a new resident would arrive today. He imagined what feast might be in the works for dinner. *Cripe, I've turned into Pavlov's dog.* Fondly recalling every bite of the Beef Wellington they had served the evening he had arrived, Lou's thoughts ran wild.

Perhaps Lobster Newburg? Maybe not so much here in Texas. A nice veal scaloppini with oven roasted potatoes and the asparagus we yanked out of the garden yesterday? Would Niebold name the wine correctly?

Seeing the grins around the refectory assured him he was not the only one anticipating the evening meal. Never mind that some unknown schmuck had shriveled in terror as a needle poked into his vein to let flow a concoction he believed would kill him and leave family and friends to grieve. No indeed, it would be good eating tonight. Woof Woof.

Lou reported for work after breakfast and Lauds. He tried to concentrate on harvesting the green beans Malachi had set him to, but unwelcome thoughts intruded on his task. He could no longer bask in the mesmerizing music and ritual of Chapel and continue to ignore the Bible verses and Anselm's remarks. They had begun to haunt him. Lou shook his head as if to cast his uninvited thoughts into the dirt.

But they would not budge, and he recalled Anselm's comments this morning about Moses' life. He could understand Moses killing the Egyptian who beat that Hebrew. *Moses was taking care of business, like I killed Beauregard Abbington, so a few less of his fellow Hebrews would suffer the same fate. Did God punish Moses for murder? He did not.*

Lou yanked a handful of beans, furious at the unfairness of it all.

Old Moses gets to escape into Midian, where he tends sheep, marries, and raises a family for forty years. As if that wasn't a sweet enough deal, God calls him back to become a leader of his people. We both killed for revenge, but I get executed and buried alive in a monastery for the rest of my life. Moses got a soft life tending sheep and a family to boot. How is that fair, God?

He assumed his question had been rhetorical, so when an answer came to mind, he stopped his work, surprised. He was no theologian, but the thought was so clear, so obvious. God had not let Moses off the hook at all. Instead, he pulled him away from his life in the royal household to mold him while he served his future father-in-law. Eventually, Moses would grow to become the man to lead God's people. He humbled Moses big time. If Moses had resumed life as usual after killing the Egyptian, his sin remained a secret, he would have been no use to God. It took forty years.

Lou groaned. *Forty years. A lifetime at my age. When God steps into someone's life, he sure plays hardball.*

He imagined that burning bush with a voice whooshing out of it, giving Moses his marching orders. *Does God still work like that?* In a way, he hoped the answer was yes. Then he would have at least a glimmer of hope his life could be salvaged, as Moses' was. But then, wouldn't it be far simpler and safer knowing what to expect and handling things himself without some meddling deity?

He grabbed a fistful of beans, flung them into the pail, and looked up. Lou often scanned the farm while doing chores, seeing if he could identify the monk assigned to watch him. Occasionally, he would flush one of them out by leaving his assigned post and heading in another direction. He never got far, and soon tired of the exercise. *Do those jailers double or triple team each of the prisoners? What does it matter? I'm going nowhere fast.*

He thought he would visit the library after lunch, rather than attend Sext. He would probably gain a new black shadow, but did not care. Enough of God and his ways for a while. Besides, Niebold had told him there were history books in there.

Lou stopped abruptly in the library doorway. *What was Predmore doing here? Why wasn't he in Chapel doing his pathetic imitation of a human cross?* As he turned to leave, Lou bumped into Brother Jerome.

He frowned. "Don't you have a procession to lead?"

Jerome responded with a cherubic smile and shooed him into the library. Lou complied with one step. "Where are the history books?" he challenged.

"Well, that depends. Do you want to read copies of the works of the historian Josephus who wrote during the first century? We have books on church history, on the history of theology, on the history of the Reformation. Do you want to read about church councils or about the Early Fathers? Do you want...?"

"Just point me in the right direction."

Sally would have described the monastery library as "cozy," but in Lou's eyes, it was too small and dark. Wall to wall shelves rose floor to ceiling, jammed with books of all sizes in various stages of wear. With nothing to do but eat, sleep, pray, or work, reading provided an escape from his daily tedium. He closed his eyes and savored the musty smell of old paper and hints of ink.

I should have come here sooner.

But that would have implied he had given up and accepted his fate. Lou still mentally ran possible escape plans, but they all came to a dead end. Sometimes, in his imagination, he came to a dead end, too.

He sighed and ran his index finger across the book spines of authors whose names began with the letter A. Not too many A's, but there were quite a few books by Augustine. Lou remembered the nuns called him a "church father," whatever that meant. He lived over a thousand years ago and started an order of monks. Lou snorted and pulled *Augustine's Confessions* from the shelf. *What did he have to confess? Perhaps the church father was not so saintly after all.* Lou decided to find out and looked for a chair.

Jerome had settled himself at a table with one lamp that barely squeezed out 40 watts. Predmore sat across from Jerome, right foot thrust out from under the library table, his book propped to catch the meager lamplight. Lou noticed a corner with an empty chair next to a floor lamp. As he sidestepped to avoid tripping over Frank's foot, he noticed the bandage marred by a dark brown stain just above the sole of his sandal. The blood trail. Of course — it had been Frank. He remembered Jerome's explanation about Predmore seeking his friendship as a sign that God could forgive him, and how Frank would try to hurt himself with self-inflicted punishment.

"What did you do to torture yourself, Predmore?"

"Nothing. Just got a stone in my sandal is all, and it got infected."

Lou sighed and looked at Jerome. The monk said nothing, silently observing them.

"One little stone wouldn't do that. Why did you leave it in your sandal?"

Before Frank could respond, a verse from the Bible came unbidden to Lou — "and He was pierced for our sins." Imagining Christ's pierced hands and feet, Lou groaned and closed his eyes.

I don't need forgiving, he mentally shouted at whatever brain cells were running amuck in his head. *I took care of business and got justice for my daughter. Abbington is the one who needs forgiving.*

He looked again at Predmore's foot, more to refocus his mind than out of pity. It looked sore, and he felt a first twinge of sympathy for Frank.

"Tough break, man," he said, not unkindly as he walked to the chair. Predmore coughed and buried his face in his book. Jerome smiled.

By the time his mind nestled into Augustine's fourth century, the bell to return to chores rang. Lou sniffed. He did not want to leave this newfound world for the daily grind that had become his existence, but at least he had some fine dining ahead this evening. He was curious about this new prisoner, too.

A twinge of disappointment surprised Lou when Predmore sat at another table for dinner. *Can't blame him. Maybe I embarrassed him.* He looked up as Niebold and a younger fellow took their seats across from him.

"This is their newest victim, Colin Mackey," Niebold said. "Colin, meet Lou Skalney."

Thin, with a buzz cut, the new prisoner had one of those forever-young boyish faces, making him look too innocent to be a prisoner at St. Dismas.

Lou was surprised that Niebold, of all people, would be the one to welcome this Mackey person. That was not like him, since usually Kurt stood aloof, studying everyone through his thick glasses as if they were bugs under a microscope. He wondered if Niebold had noticed Predmore's foot.

"Hey Mackey," was all Lou could come up with.

"Yeah man," Mackey replied, a grin spreading across his thin face as he watched the monk placing bottles of wine on the tables. "What's the deal with the booze? You guys drink here?" His voice rose, sounding giddy. When the kitchen monk slid the chicken cordon bleu with asparagus and a golden risotto before him, Colin looked up, amazed.

"What the…? You gotta be kidding!"

The question was rhetorical as he bent over his plate, ready to demolish his food. Niebold placed a restraining hand on his arm and whispered, "Wait." Mackey looked up with a puzzled expression as Abbot Anselm stood and intoned the prayer before dinner. At "Amen," Colin clutched his fork. Niebold stopped him again.

"What now?"

Kurt did not answer, but sniffed his wine, took a sip, and rolled it around in his mouth. Looking at Anselm, he announced, "A lively Sancerre. Excellent choice." Abbot lifted his glass in a silent salute, and the monks followed suit. Niebold turned to Colin. "Now you may eat."

"Sheesh. About time," Mackey replied and polished off his meal as if afraid someone would pull it away any second. During dinner, he replied to the few questions directed at him with only one or two words, a few grunts, and as little eye contact as possible.

After Mackey downed the last morsel and drop of wine, Kurt said to him, "It's about time you told people why the State executed you. They'll find out, anyway."

As if he were describing a science experiment that had earned him an A, Colin announced, "I killed three women and two men. Cops only knew about the women. Would have killed more if they hadn't caught up with me."

Lou studied Mackey's face, searching for remorse, but he found only self-satisfaction. He may as well have announced he had cooked five hot dogs for a picnic, he thought. In the silence following Colin's admission, Lou asked, "Why?"

Mackey shrugged. "That was a great meal. You guys eat like this all the time?"

"Only on Sundays and when there is a new prisoner—like you. The rest of the time, they work us like dogs and eliminate anyone they want," Niebold replied.

Guess Predmore's bloody foot wasn't enough to change his mind.

Lou studied Kurt, who apparently already knew what Mackey had done.

Why does he treat the death of five people, as if they were of no consequence? But then, that's how Niebold sounded when he confessed he had killed his graduate assistant — no remorse whatsoever.

CHAPTER 24

STEALTH

The next morning, Lou looked up from his scrambled eggs. He could hear Mackey and Niebold's conversation from a table away. The professor was interrogating the newest prisoner, while Mackey wore an expectant expression, as if hoping his answers were meeting with approval.

"Are your parents living?" Niebold asked.

"Don't know. They left me to the foster system. Probably too drunk to care what happened to me." Mackey stabbed a slice of ham and ripped it off his fork with his teeth, his angry tone causing several monks to turn and listen.

"Been in a lot of homes? How did they treat you?" Kurt asked.

"I got hit a lot, picked on, and–oh yeah, in one, the so-called mother locked the cupboards and fridge, so we were hungry all the time." Mackey eyed Niebold's plate. "You gonna eat that toast?"

Kurt handed him his toast and watched him devour every crumb.

Weird relationship between those two, Lou thought. *Must be a birds-of-a-feather thing, since both killed without a qualm. At least I killed to protect others. Did the foster care system make Mackey a murderer? Not every kid that goes through the system ends up like him. What else happened to him? I can almost understand Niebold because at least he had a motive. Not a good one, but a motive just the same. He said he believed whatever worked for him was good and what didn't work was bad. He doesn't seem to share most peoples' understanding of wrong and right, let alone good and evil. But what possessed Mackey to kill five people for no reason and not care? The two of them look like best friends, or even a father and son. The father Mackey never had?*

Lou studied the smug faces of what he realized were two sociopathic, cold-blooded killers. Yet he found Kurt's conversation interesting and occasionally helpful — of course, when it suited him. Other than being paranoid, Niebold was a good source of information.

With the close surveillance around here, what can he do to me? Lou shifted uncomfortably on his bench. Probably whatever he wanted. The guy is brilliant. No doubt he could kill me, and I'd never see it coming, and neither would the monks.

As the refectory emptied for Lauds, Lou skipped going to the chapel to observe these new best friends while he nursed a second cup of coffee. With everyone off to pray, the room was quiet enough to hear every word of their conversation.

"So, you never attended one school for more than a year?" Niebold sounded surprised.

Mackey shook his head. "Never been with a foster family longer than a year. Guess they all hated me like my folks did."

Kurt opened his mouth as if to respond when Brother Jerome approached Mackey. Lou guessed he was about to give him the same instructions he had given him on his first day. *How long has it been? Can it be only six months? Seems like a lifetime.*

"You're welcome to join us in Chapel, or you can meet me outside Chapel after Lauds, and I'll get you set up for your work detail."

Mackey sneered at Jerome. "You can't make me pray or work, fat man," he said, and cast a quick smile to Niebold, who opened his hands as if to show he was innocent of influencing the boy. A smirk played at the corner of the professor's mouth while he waited for Jerome's response, which was swift.

Jerome bent and leaned close to Mackey, so they were nose-to-nose. "If you wish to eat, you will work. It's that simple."

Mackey mocked him with a grin. "You wouldn't dare starve me to death. That would be murder and you're holy good guys."

Jerome straightened, his voice so soft Lou strained to hear his words.

"As your new mentor ceaselessly points out, you prisoners are already dead. You have no one to help you because no one knows you exist. You have one choice. Work, eat, and live. Or refuse to work, starve, and die. It is your action, not ours, that will determine your fate. I expect you will come to the correct conclusion within the next forty-five minutes."

Lou watched the monk walk, unruffled, out of the refectory. *I would have knocked the little creep's block off if he had spoken to me like that.* He let out a long breath.

"Wait up, Brother." Lou sprang to his feet and caught up with the monk in the hall. "Why didn't you deck the guy?"

Jerome shrugged. "I'm not in a battle with him personally. I'm in a battle against the forces of darkness that drive him. There's a big difference."

"Forces of darkness," Lou repeated, his voice derisive. "That sounds like something from science fiction. You really believe in invisible forces of good and evil? Demons and angels dueling it out? Next you'll be saying Satan wears a red suit and carries a pitchfork."

"In 1988, the U. S military unveiled the B2 stealth bomber. Why would that bomber be an asset in warfare?" Jerome said.

"That's obvious. If it's a stealth aircraft, the enemy wouldn't see it coming and wouldn't try to shoot it down."

"So, if an enemy can make its target believe its bomber does not exist, how effective would it be?"

"Totally effective."

"Think about that in terms of the spiritual battle between good and evil, between God and the Satan some don't believe exists."

Lou was silent a moment while he considered the deeper implications of Jerome's remark. "Hmmm, interesting. Where'd you come up with that?"

"The concept is in the Bible. You should read it sometime."

That evening in his cell, Lou opened the Bible that had been sitting on his desk for months, and wondered why he had waited so long. He could not claim other diversions like TV, radio, or the newspaper.

Lou started at Genesis, but soon flipped to the New Testament. He was more familiar with those stories and began with the Book of John.

"In the beginning was the Word, and the Word was with God, and the Word was God. He was with God in the beginning. Through him all things were made; without him nothing was made that has been made. In him was life, and that life was the light of all mankind. The light shines in the darkness, and the darkness has not overcome it."

Lou recognized the reading from his distant Sunday school days, and wondered why it seemed so clear to him now that the "Word" was Jesus. And there was that force of darkness stuff Jerome had talked about.

"I see you're reading the Bible," Jerome said from his chair in the corridor. "Feel free to ask questions."

Lou returned the Bible to his desk and grabbed his blanket, not ready to give his jailer the satisfaction of answering questions. He closed his eyes and was drifting off to sleep when a scream jolted him awake. Heart pounding, he threw off his blanket, leapt to his feet and rushed to his cell doorway. Jerome stood, blocking his exit. Craning his neck to look past the monk and down the hall, he accused Jerome, "Who is that? Are you monks torturing someone again?"

Jerome's gaze followed Lou's.

"Most likely it's Colin Mackey. Sometimes first nights here can be upsetting."

"Upsetting? Ya think? Second nights aren't so easy either. Maybe Niebold has been right all along. You monks can do anything to us, and no one would know or care."

"That's technically true, but we don't. Sometimes a damaged soul cries out in anguish when stripped of all defenses and distractions. Here in the monastery there is nothing blocking man from God. His monk will help him. Now go back to sleep."

"Likely story." *A replay of the last midnight torture around here? Will Mackey disappear by morning, too?*

"Yeah, I'm sure I'll sleep, Brother Jerome."

Lou returned to his cot, clenched his fists, and stared at the ceiling, mind whirling until dawn.

I'll get to the bottom of this or die trying.

CHAPTER 25

POOR IMITATION

Lou opened his eyes when the five a.m. bell tolled.
Between Mackey's screams last night and Harold's the other night, who can sleep in this hellhole? So tired. I'll just stay in bed. What can they do?

Decision made, he turned on his side, but his traitorous bladder objected. Muttering, he threw off his blanket and staggered toward the lavatory, consoling himself with thoughts of hot coffee.

"I wonder if Mackey will show up," Predmore said as he slid next to Lou and put his plate of sliced ham, eggs, and toast on the table. "Wasn't that quite a performance last night?" He eyed Lou's skimpy breakfast of toast and coffee. "You're not hungry today?"

Frank was full of questions, none of which Lou wanted to answer. He shoved his slice of toast away, too tired to chew, and sipped his coffee. Where is Mackey, anyway, he wondered. The so-called transfer?

He noticed Niebold looking around the room. *How will he react if they claim they transferred Mackey? Probably like a wizard of doom whose prize apprentice was kidnapped.* A shiver ran up Lou's spine.

When Jerome entered the refectory, Niebold shouted, "Where's Mackey?"

"Sleeping in this morning. He had a difficult night." The monk loaded his plate and walked toward Brother Aaron, who shifted to his right to make room.

"Not transferred, as you all like to say?" Kurt sounded wary, but a bit relieved.

"No, Kurt, just sleeping in. You'll see him this afternoon at lunch."

Lou's suspicions short-circuited his relief. *What did they do to Mackey during the night? Why had they transferred Harold after his screaming fit and not Mackey? What happens when someone acts up? We can't see what the monks do to them in their cells.*

Later, while Lou sat in a back pew, waiting for the monks to enter the chapel after breakfast, he thumbed through the first two chapters of Luke. It was hard keeping his eyes open. Between dozing and thinking of the night before, he barely heard the Abbot's sermon.

By the time Chapel ended, Lou decided he would find his answer tonight.

Fresh air and weed pulling brought Lou somewhat back to life. When the bell rang for Sext, he was awake and hungry for lunch. Upon entering the refectory, he immediately sensed excitement among the monks and curiosity from the prisoners. While relieved to see Mackey, he doubted the guy's presence accounted for the jovial atmosphere. Even Abbot Anselm was smiling.

After everyone took their places with plates piled high, Anselm rose for the invocation.

"Let us praise God for his bounty of food and his constant mercy poured upon us sinners. We especially thank you, Lord of the Harvest, for our newest monk, Brother Timothy. Bless his life here and may he be a blessing to all of us. In Jesus' name. Amen."

The monks smiled and murmured greetings, while the prisoners looked around to see this new monk. Predmore was the first to spot him.

He poked Lou in the ribs. "There he is, just in front of the head table. Looks as young as Mackey."

Lou studied the new monk. He did look as young as Mackey, hardly old enough to have taken final vows.

He must have, though, because he's wearing the black robe and red cross. I wonder what he's like.

From what Lou could see, Brother Timothy seemed to fit right in, with laughter and smiles all around. *Maybe life will return to what passes for normal around here now, but not yet.* Lou was determined to make this night anything but normal.

After a gourmet dinner in honor of Brother Timothy, Lou devoted the hour of Compline to plan what he would say and do during his four-star performance tonight. He knew it needed to be noisy with some violent show of mental anguish. Lou nixed banging his head against the cell's stone walls as way too painful. That left shouting and overturning his chair — anything to get Jerome, or his replacement, into his cell. There may be some wrestling, but he planned on losing. He needed to see what they do to their prisoners who act up.

Will they transfer me? Maybe that wouldn't be good; I could end up in a worse place. Murder me? Whatever happens, I've got to know. He shuddered.

Once in bed, with Jerome settled in his chair, Lou tossed and turned for two hours, striking down second thoughts like carnival whack-a-moles.

If I want to find out, there's only one way—unless I accept what they say. It's now or never.

Lou threw himself out of bed and onto the floor. "Aaaagh! No!"

Crawling to his desk, a growl formed deep in his chest and rumbled through lips pulled away from bared teeth. Out of the corner of his eye, he saw Jerome walk to his doorway and stop. *He needs more?* Lou grabbed the leg of his chair and tossed it across his cell, while swearing he wanted nothing to do with a God who let his daughter down in her moment of desperation. Surprised he was sobbing actual tears, Lou shouted that he, and he alone, got justice for Becky, and saved other daughters as well. At the top of his voice, he shouted, "Beauregard Abbington deserved to die. I did it and I'd do it again, and again." With each word, he pulled his desk further from the corner of his cell until it teetered on two legs just above his head.

Jerome rushed to him and caught the desk in mid-topple, setting it upright. Lou briefly thought of pulling on the monk's leg, so close to his hand, but feared Jerome's considerable weight landing on him — as if he could really bring down a black belt in Krav Maga, anyway. In his moment of hesitation, Jerome lifted him from the floor and spun him around. They stood face to face.

"What do you think you are doing?" Jerome sounded unperturbed by his prisoner's outburst.

Lou grabbed Jerome's arms and tried to shake the monolith, who did not budge. Out of tricks, Lou gave up. He should have known he had no idea how to act out convincingly, so his theatrical debut had been miserable. His father would have knocked such behavior out of him in a second. Living the mantra the old man had instilled in him, "a man takes care of business," makes no room for temper tantrums. Yet in his frustration and emotional return to Becky's death, Lou Skalney had cried for the first time. A part of him heard his wracking sobs with a stranger's detachment. They welled from the depth of his soul. The dam had broken. Jerome led a weeping man from his cell and down the corridor.

Lou knew Brother Jerome was taking him somewhere, but a deep sorrow overrode concern. He was only mildly curious about what would happen next, and did not care.

It was no surprise when Jerome opened the door to the chapel and guided him into a pew. A large candle burning in its holder on the altar, along with lit sconces along the walls, defeated the darkness and won perpetual twilight for the chapel. Jerome settled next to him and said nothing until Lou's sobs subsided.

"What happens next?" Lou tensed, waiting to hear his sentence.

"What do you think will happen?"

"I get sent away, punished somehow, or killed."

"So that's the reason for your performance. You couldn't take my word for it and had to find out for yourself." Jerome shook his curly white head. "We will sit here until morning. I will pray and turn you over to Jesus."

Lou shrugged. *Big deal.* The day had exhausted him and now he was enduring an absurd, anti-climactic ending. He closed his eyes and hoped for sleep.

CHAPTER 26

CRUMBLING DEFENSES

Lou's head nodded as he dozed beside Brother Jerome. After a while, back aching from the unyielding wooden pew, he leaned forward with elbows balanced on his knees. He stretched stiff muscles, and glancing at Jerome, wondered if the man was sleeping or meditating. He looked like a snow topped black mountain. His eyes were closed, face relaxed, his breathing slow. Just to check, Lou rose, and immediately felt a restraining hand on his thigh. When the monk shook his head, Lou sat and closed his eyes. He was drifting off to sleep again when a question startled him awake.

If Beauregard Abbington were innocent of Becky's death, what would that make me?

His eyes flew open, and his heart skipped a beat. Did I think that, or was it Jerome?

"What did you say?" he asked the monk.

Jerome opened his eyes and turned to him.

"I said nothing. What do you think I said?"

"Come on, now. I'm too tired to play games. You asked what it makes me if Beauregard were innocent of my daughter's death."

"I did no such thing, but that is a good question. What does it make you?"

They stared at each other for a moment until Lou mentioned he had been having weird thoughts lately.

"Such as?"

Lou looked away, searching for examples. After a long hesitation, he said, "I was working on the farm and thinking about Abbot

Anselm's talk on Moses and his life as a fugitive killer. I thought he got a good deal while I'm stuck here. And then it hit me. The years he spent working for his father-in-law could have been God's way to prepare him to lead the Jews out of Egypt and stuff. I never would have thought of that before. Maybe it's because of all this Bible reading around here."

He searched Jerome's face for an answer, but the monk's expression offered no clue. Lou sighed and continued. "Then there was the time I noticed Predmore's bandaged foot in the library and recalled somewhere reading about Jesus' hands and feet being pierced for us. Frank's sore foot reminded me of that. You monks and your Bibles are messing with my mind." This time, he did not wait for Jerome's reply and added, "Or I must be losing it."

"Are you resigned about that or hopeful?" Jerome raised an eyebrow and offered a slight smile.

Lou bristled. "That's not funny. Now tonight I get this question. If Beauregard was innocent, what would that make me? Why am I getting these thoughts? Is there no end to them?"

Jerome studied him for a long moment and nodded.

"I apologize. I wasn't mocking you."

Lou nodded at the monk's sincerity.

"I would consider the content of these thoughts, Lou. The first one about Moses was Biblically correct. Moses spent 40 years working for his father-in-law until he returned to take on Pharaoh — and reluctantly at that. As for the second, Jesus could have called on an angel army to deliver him from execution, but instead, he obeyed his Father and paid the price we, you and I, could not pay for our sins. As for your question tonight, I think it is worth answering. What would killing an innocent Beauregard make you?"

"He was guilty!" Lou clenched his fists. His heart pounded, and he struggled to catch his breath.

"So you say. But you haven't answered my hypothetical question."

Jerome rode out a long silence while Lou stared at the altar, where candlelight flickered over its surface. Minutes passed. Eventually, Lou shuddered and whispered, "If, and it's only if, Beauregard were innocent, I would be a murderer."

"Innocent or not, you did murder him. You *are* a murderer. That's why you're here. Do better than that. What would it make you?"

"What do you mean? I just told you."

Jerome shook his head. "All these months I've known you, you claimed Beauregard killed your innocent child and God did nothing to protect her. But if you killed Beauregard, and he had not murdered your daughter, you killed another man's child. You would be the very Beauregard you judged and hated. And, according to your theory, God did nothing to protect him from you, either."

Lou slumped. He felt a thickness in his throat while something in him broke open. His heart? Mind? Soul? Just allowing the concept of an innocent Beauregard to take root in his mind buried him in a mountain of guilt. Its weight choked the breath out of him. *It can't be true, but dear God, what if it is?*

Jerome continued. "As for those thoughts — in each incidence, they sound Biblically correct and logical. They may rise to your mind now because you can no longer keep them buried."

"How do you know? You're a monk, not a shrink."

Jerome smiled. "You know that before I joined the monastery, I owned a bookstore, and read just about everything in stock. I found the psychology books especially interesting."

Lou grunted and looked away. "Well, okay then. If I'm not crazy, and if God's not sending me crazy thoughts, then is my subconscious trying to tell me something?"

Jerome nodded. "God doesn't communicate through burning bushes so much anymore. Our Creator uses any means to communicate with us, even our minds, which he fashioned. I don't believe you will find peace until you face your issues. I think God will pursue you until you turn to him and confess. Whether Beauregard killed your daughter is not your problem now. Your problem is you are guilty of murder."

Jerome looked into Lou's eyes and continued.

"No one, ever, is beyond God's love or mercy, no matter what he may have done. You do not have to carry this burden of hate for Beauregard, and guilt for killing him for the rest of your life. Lou, Satan is fighting to keep you shackled by hate, denial of your guilt, and rationalizations. He does not want you to repent and become God's child again."

Lou's eyes filled with tears. *Could God love me that much? Don't I need to make up for what I did?* He shook his head, overwhelmed.

"It's too much for me," he said to Jerome. "I'm so tired. Now I can't trust my own thoughts. Are they mine, or is God playing with my brain cells?"

The monk put his arm around Lou and helped him to his feet. "Reading the Bible will help answer that question. Meanwhile, let's get you to bed for a few hours of sleep. You need them."

Lou slipped into dreamless sleep. When he opened his eyes, Brother Timothy had replaced Jerome. He studied the younger man, nose buried in a book, and never looking up to check on his charge.

That's okay. I'm too washed out to try anything. Keep reading, I need to think.

Lou pondered Jerome's description of Satan trying to keep him shackled to his guilt so he could not turn to God for mercy and forgiveness. *It's like God and Satan are dueling over me, like I'm a prize. Me, a prize? Hardly.*

Truth was, he did long for a Father God to embrace him. His own father never did, no matter how much he needed a hug, or even a grunt of approval. Instead, Hank Skalney taught his son to take care of business. And where had that gotten him? Waves of guilt washed over him as he considered the chilling question. What would killing an innocent Beauregard make him?

"Forgive us our trespasses as we forgive those who trespass against us."

Do I have to forgive Beauregard first? I'm still not convinced Beauregard was innocent. In God's name, how do I forgive? I've traded one prison for another.

Uneasy in his own skin, Lou shoved his feet into his sandals and walked out of his cell. Only when he passed Timothy did the young monk raise his head.

"I'm washing up," Lou said. "What time is it?"

Timothy smiled. "Almost time for Sext. You slept through breakfast. You'll just make lunch."

Lou nodded. He dreaded entering the refectory, knowing his absence at breakfast after his pathetic performance last night would be the major topic among the prisoners.

Niebold probably announced my demise by now. Too bad I'll disappoint him. And Predmore — Oh Lord, could I have misjudged him, like I may have misjudged Beauregard?

Relieved only some prisoners glanced his way when he entered the refectory, he walked to the end of the line snaking its way to the serving buffet.

The stage whisper behind him was raspy. "What did they do to you?"

Lou jumped and turned to face his inquisitor, who apparently had been lying in wait for him.

"Niebold, where did you come from?"

The professor looked at him expectantly. "So?"

"They did nothing, Kurt. Brother Jerome took me into the chapel so I would calm down. I sat. He prayed."

"That's it? Why did you lose it in the first place? I wouldn't have thought you, of all people, would have had a screaming fit." A slow grin spread across his face. "You faked it, didn't you? You sly dog, you wanted to know."

Lou shrugged. "I wanted to find out what happens to prisoners when they act up at night. Obviously, they didn't kill me, Kurt."

"So, Jerome sat there and prayed. And you just sat there too? That's all?"

Lou shrugged. He was not ready to share the details of his conversation with Brother Jerome. Still, he knew Kurt would not give up until he got answers. To buy time, Lou slowly piled his plate with a ham and cheese sandwich, sliced tomatoes, and pasta salad. His stomach growled, and he realized he was famished. Niebold trailed him to the table where Predmore and Mackey were already eating.

"Hi Frank. Can we join you?"

Lou would not have blamed the man if he told them to take a hike, but after a few blinks of surprise, Predmore shifted to the left to make room. He said nothing until Lou and Niebold got situated, then asked, "You okay?"

"Yeah, I'm okay, Frank." He wanted to add, "I'm sorry I treated you the way I did," but the words stuck somewhere between his brain and mouth. Instead, he asked Frank if his foot was healed.

"Yes."

"Good, I'm glad," Lou said with sincerity.

Niebold snorted and rolled his eyes. Predmore offered Lou a weak smile.

After the four of them devoured their lunch, Kurt returned to Lou's nocturnal performance, as if it were a knot that still needed untying.

"No way you and the monk just sat in the chapel all night. There's something you're not telling. Did he try to scare you with the fire and brimstone shtick? Lay guilt on you? They do that, you know. Make you believe you owe some fake god good deeds, so you spend the rest of your life at their beck and call."

Lou stiffened. *Why do I listen to this miserable sociopath? What does he know about love or forgiveness? Is logic and looking out for yourself all there is? If something stands in your way, get rid of it?*

The possibility of a real God reaching out to him in love had warmed his heart — a heart he thought had shriveled but continued to beat.

His recollection of the words of the 23rd Psalm echoed in his mind.

"Even though I walk through the darkest valley, I will fear no evil, for you are with me; your rod and staff, they comfort me."

He smiled and cupped his hands around his mug.

CHAPTER 27

SARGAN AND CAESAR

When Lou returned to the farm the next morning, he hoped hard labor would drive those intrusive thoughts from his mind.

Brother Malachi squinted in the bright morning light and adjusted his wide-brimmed hat. "Lou, I need you to unload the chicken feed from our supplier."

To Lou, the old monk looked like a weathered farmer who had long ago traded blue overalls for a black robe. He imitated his boss and angled his own hat to block the sun's rays.

Malachi continued his instructions as they walked toward Brother Aaron at the monastery entrance. "We load deliveries onto that platform near the gate, and from there, transport them to where they're needed."

Malachi nodded his greeting to Aaron, who was pulling a wheelbarrow from the edge of a loaded platform. Lou guessed its wooden base held about a hundred large sacks. Eyeing the heap and the distance to the barn, he shot Malachi a quizzical look.

"I'm supposed to wheel those sacks all the way to the barn and then unload them without help?"

Malachi gave Lou a mischievous grin. "You got a better way to get them there?"

"What, you don't boss angel armies around too?"

Brother Aaron interrupted their banter. "Abbot Anselm is sending you Mackey, although I don't know how much help he'll be, given his reluctance to work."

"Colin Mackey." Malachi pronounced the name as if he were identifying something he had just fished out of a cesspool. Without another word, he marched toward the entrance to the monastery's main building. Lou and Aaron watched wide-eyed as the elderly monk flung open the thick wooden door and disappeared inside.

"What was that about?" Lou said, turning to Brother Aaron, who was staring at the slowly closing door. When the monk did not answer, Lou reviewed what he knew of the latest prisoner and Brother Malachi.

Mackey is young, in his late twenties. A serial killer. Most likely a sociopath. Weird relationship with Niebold. Not afraid to test the limits. What beef does Malachi have with this one in particular? We're all killers. Malachi disagreed with the Abbot about serving wine, and now this. Must be hard watching your replacement make decisions you would not. Maybe that set him off. Does Malachi prefer running the farm to running the monastery? Was that switch his idea, or someone else's?

Lou sighed and rolled the wheelbarrow parallel to the loading platform. Aaron joined him, and together they loaded the first sacks. "I can help you load, Lou, but can't leave my post." The monk sounded apologetic, and Lou smiled his appreciation for the sympathy.

Just then, Abbot Anselm, Brother Malachi, with Mackey in tow, strode from the monastery door toward the pile. The three stood in silence, the monks looking like they were still considering whatever they had said to each other. Mackey stared at the ground. Abruptly, the Abbot turned to Malachi.

"Release Caesar and Sargan for security," he ordered and walked away, head high, robe swaying with each step.

Lou remembered the snarling Malinois that had instantly obeyed Jerome's command to stand down, and trotted beside them as they returned to the monastery. Working these months with Malachi had shown Lou the monk was a man of strength and kindness. By now, he trusted and respected him, and knew under his watch the dogs would

keep Mackey in line. Besides, he was curious to see the kid's response
to the sweet little pooches.

Malachi and the two prisoners walked back to the farm and
around the corner of the toolshed to the kennel. Lou saw each dog
lived in a separate unit that held a blanket, water bowl, and a doggie
door leading to an enclosed yard. A few of the twelve units stood
empty because the dogs were working or napping in the sun.

We live in open cells surrounded by a prison, just like the dogs.

When they approached two neighboring units, Sargan and Caesar
leapt to their feet. Colin's eyes widened at the sight of the dogs, and
he stepped back. He flashed a terrified look at Lou.

"I remember these boys," Lou said. "I met them when I tried
to climb the stone wall in an escape attempt. Brother Jerome later
told me they breed Malinois for police and military work, but are
obedient, so they won't tear you apart unless commanded." He
grinned at Mackey. "Stay close to Brother Malachi because they only
respond to the monks who command them — in Flemish."

"Sheesh." Colin blinked and licked his lips, eyes darting from
one dog to the other. Sargan, at least sixty pounds of muscle covered
in brown fur with a black pointed snout, bolted to his cage door,
and Caesar imitated him. Both dogs resembled German Shepherds,
but were leaner, with larger, more pointed ears. Malachi bent to
open each cage, and without looking at the prisoners, explained
that the dogs would not harm them if they did not run or move
suddenly.

"Caesar will stay alongside you as you transfer the grain bags from
the loading platform to the barn, Lou. Mackey and I will keep Sargan
with us at the barn."

Lou's earlier bravado flagged as Caesar dogged his heels, but they
soon reached an agreement. *You don't try to escape, I won't remove
your leg.*

When he brought the first sack-laden wheelbarrow to the barn,
Malachi directed Lou to a huge plastic crate in the rear storage area.

Shafts of sunlight pouring through two windows lit his way, along with the help of several cracks between aging walls.

On one side, Lou noted bales of straw, and on the opposite, shelves holding farm implements and baskets of organic compost. He glimpsed the edge of a portable gas tank hiding in the corner. Once Lou parked the wheelbarrow next to the crate, Mackey unloaded it, tossing the sacks carelessly into the container. While he worked, Mackey's only acknowledgment of Sargan was to throw it frequent, menacing looks. Never did he speak or make eye contact with Lou or Malachi. Mackey's attitude surrounded him like a thick miasma, and he worked as if he had a vendetta against each bag. Sargan did not look interested in a truce. His body quivered, and his tail constantly wagged, as if primed for the command to attack. He must sense Mackey's hostility, Lou thought.

Intimidated by the dogs, the young man's furtive glances unsettled Lou. By the time the bell pealed for lunch and Sext, Lou sensed it would not take much for the newest prisoner to explode. Constantly observed, and without pockets in their robes to hide weapons, he wondered just how and when.

Lunch was predictable. Vegetable soup—again. "Eternal harvest," Lou muttered, dipping his spoon into his bowl of broth filled with carrots, kale, potatoes, tomatoes, and red beans. The morning's workout with grain sacks had given him enough appetite to drain two bowls. Despite his earlier complaint, Lou savored the flavors that danced on his palate.

When he eventually looked up from his lunch, he observed the two sitting across from him. Niebold nodded his head as Mackey alternated between shoveling soup into his mouth and describing his morning. Vicious, heavy, mean, dogs, and kill, played heavily in Mackey's narrative, until he concluded, "I hate animals!"

"Any reason?" Niebold sounded only mildly interested in the answer.

"Yeah, one of my foster homes had a pit bull. Almost chewed my leg off."

Colin yanked his foot onto the bench and pulled his robe up to show six inches of raised scar tissue running along the side of his calf. "See?"

After studying it, Niebold whistled. "Impressive," he said, before resuming his lunch. Lou rose a few inches and leaned over the table to view the evidence. He wondered how much abuse Collin Mackey had endured before he was old enough to live on his own.

"How many foster homes did you live in?"

"Eight or nine. I lost count after a while. They were all in it for the money."

Lou persisted. "There wasn't even one family that treated you okay?"

"Well, one. But the guy got a job out of state, so they moved, and I got put back in the system. But by then I was almost 18, so it didn't matter. Pass the butter."

Lou doubted it did not matter. *What could it have been like living in a foster care system that treated Mackey like a commodity to be tossed aside when no longer wanted? But then, he couldn't have been easy to live with. I don't have to read all the shrink books Brother Jerome did to know this kid's a time bomb. Maybe that's why Brother Malachi and Abbot seem to disagree about him.*

"Listen, kid," Niebold said, "the dogs run by instinct and training. They're predictable. Just do nothing to set them off. It's people you need to learn about — what are their motivations, their fears, their hopes? Know that and you have control. Depends on what you want to do."

Lou turned to Kurt. "Professor, if you're so smart, why are you here?"

CHAPTER 28

SAVAGE ATTACK

Lou had grown used to Mackey's sullen disposition, but his growing edginess worried him. This morning he noticed Mackey seemed more restless, his eyes darting around their work area. Lou suspected Malachi observed Mackey's behavior too, since he assigned Brother Timothy to work with him and Mackey. They were to check the barrier fences surrounding the vegetable beds for breaks or underground burrows, since apparently, some critters were dining as well as the monks.

"Brother Malachi is sure there's a break somewhere, but I can't see it," Timothy muttered, pulling weeds away from the fence to find any openings or holes in the ground. He worked, bent over, a few feet behind Mackey. Lou followed with a weed-whacker and double checked for hidden openings.

A sudden, high-pitched cry brought Brother Timothy's head up from the grasses. He straightened his back and stretched. "Sounds like a red-tailed hawk," he said, scanning the sky for the bird of prey.

Taking advantage of the monk's distraction, Colin moved with lightning speed. Mackey attacked before the little clover nibbling rabbit could register the presence of nearby humans. He clutched it with his left hand, and with his right, yanked its rear leg from its socket, twisting it viciously. The rabbit's scream as it writhed in Colin's grasp pierced Lou's heart. He grabbed the poor animal from Mackey while Brother Timothy slammed Colin onto the ground. Other monks rushed to the fence and surrounded Mackey, who now lay spread-eagled in the grass.

Lou felt the rabbit's heart racing as he clasped the squirming creature close to his chest. He raced toward the monastery clinic, the rabbit's screams heralding his arrival.

Brother Luke whirled from the counter where he had been loading surgical instruments into a small autoclave. Another monk lay on a bed, his bandaged ankle covered with an ice pack. They both stared at the distraught resident holding the writhing rabbit. Lou ran to Brother Luke.

"Mackey broke its leg. He yanked and twisted it. Do something!"

He thrust the rabbit toward the doctor, who looked from the rabbit to Lou and shook his head.

"I'm not a vet, Lou. The poor animal is in pain and the best thing I could do is put it out of its misery. It's a wild varmint, after all."

Lou shook his head. Clutching the pitiful creature, and determined to save this rabbit, he did not notice Brother Luke's glance toward the doorway.

"Brother Malachi, I was telling Lou…"

"I know, and you're right. But in this case, I don't think it's about the rabbit." Malachi entered the clinic, eyes locked on his fellow monk.

It looked to Lou as if the old farmer were sending the doctor a hidden message, but in that moment, he did not care what it was, if it would save the rabbit. Lou cradled the quivering animal. He would protect it, no matter what.

"They eat your crops, Malachi, and you know Abbot Anselm would have a problem with this. No pets allowed," was Brother Luke's last salvo.

"Won't be the first time he's had a problem with my decisions," Malachi muttered.

Luke made a wry smile and sighed. "Best I can do is re-align the leg, and I don't want to know anything more."

Conversation at supper that evening centered on Collin Mackey's violent outburst. Mostly, the monks had little to say about the incident, other than to assure the residents that they had segregated Mackey from the monastery population for safety reasons, and Abbot Anselm was dealing with him.

"I knew there was something off about that guy," one prisoner declared.

"There's something weird about him and he always seems like he's ready to blow up," another chimed in.

Niebold bounded to his feet and glared at the men. "None of you know anything about him!"

Lou thought he was about to say something else, but instead, Niebold marched out of the refectory, leaving a river of silence behind him.

When the low murmur of conversation resumed, Lou returned to his dinner. Grateful Brother Malachi had agreed to let him care for the rabbit, he thought about the small crate they had filled with straw and tucked into the far corner of the barn. He imagined "Pete" nibbling on the carrot they left him and decided he would check on the rabbit's water supply before turning in for the night.

While Lou found an island of peace in the barn over the next few days, Niebold's paranoia grew daily, as Mackey failed to reappear.

"They killed him," he said at breakfast a week later. He slammed his dish of oatmeal next to his coffee mug and settled across from Lou and Predmore. Staring at his fellow prisoners, Niebold laid out his case.

"One: They dragged him off to the Abbot right away. Two: He never returned to his cell. Three: No one has seen or heard from him since. There's no monk guarding any other cell that I can see. Just disappeared. Poof! Like all the others. Here one day, gone the next. Well, they're not getting away with it this time."

Lou challenged Niebold. "Really. And what are you going to do about it?"

"You don't want to know," the professor said, enunciating each word. Lou looked into Kurt's eyes, and sensed the man's wrath, wrath that bordered on madness. Lou crossed his arms, as if to protect himself from Kurt's palpable fury. After a moment, he leaned toward Niebold.

"Kurt, can't you see Mackey was in pain? Looking back on that day he attacked the rabbit, he was so anxious, even distraught, that I think nothing could have calmed him, except maybe a big dose of some knock-out drug. No one can live with that kind of tension. I saw it building in him every day."

"So that's probably why they transferred him," Predmore concluded for Lou.

Lou nodded his head. He wondered at the depth of dislike he once held for Frank.

"He wasn't in pain when he was around me," Niebold said. "If those monks were so smart, they should have assigned him to work with *me*, not you. I know how to handle him. They brought this on themselves, and they will pay."

CHAPTER 29

OMINOUS CLOUDS

"Kowalski, in my office." Bertrand Norris, managing editor of The Lone Star Daily, stage whispered to Rudy as he walked by his desk. Bert favored few words, both in speech and copy.

Rudy dropped his pencil and trailed his boss, trying to block the worst-case scenarios his imagination was busy creating.

This doesn't bode well.

He remembered his first days as a new reporter when Bert sat in his office, his teeth clamped on a fat cigar emitting a smoky stench. He looked up from the copy Rudy proudly handed him and thrust it back to the cub reporter after just a glance.

"Give me a first sentence that makes me want to read the second sentence," he said, and returned to slashing another manuscript with streaks of red ink.

Now twenty-one years later, with the cigar banished by anti-smoking regulations, Bert admired Rudy's first sentences that had become well-honed hooks, impaling the readers' interest. Since then, Bert had morphed from terrifying editor to mentor to peer, and Rudy loved his job, which he wore like an old shoe.

Norris dropped his well-padded body onto a chair that had seen better days and slammed his hands on his desk. Rudy sat across from him and waited while Bert rummaged through a pile of papers until he yanked the memo he was looking for. Thrusting it at Rudy, he said, "Read this for yourself," then leaned back, folded his hands over his paunch, and waited for his star reporter's response. It was not long in coming.

"Four-day work weeks! I work like a dog now. How am I supposed to cover all my assignments and write decent copy by deadline if I have only four days to arrange interviews, go to news sites or do background research? Are they nuts?"

"It's that or layoffs, Rudy. They'll start with senior workers who earn more, like you and me. Readership is down for print media everywhere. Sign of the times with the internet and all. We're dinosaurs, my friend. Some papers send someone who can barely string a coherent sentence together, give them an iPhone and call it reporting. But hey, it costs less." Bert threw up his hands and shook his head.

Rudy could not argue with his boss, since only an hour ago he had informed a younger reporter that the broken windowpane from a botched robbery was not a "windowpain," even though broken glass can hurt. "I thought it was a good play on words," the reporter had responded with a shrug.

"When does this take effect?"

"Monday next week. I'll announce it at our morning session tomorrow. Just wanted to let you know first. Geez, Rudy, this stinks. If I can hang in here for six months, I'll be able to retire, but you'd better make plans."

"What plans? Another sinking newspaper?"

"You're good, Rudy. Few can make it freelance, but you stand a chance. I'd get some articles ready to pitch to the national market." He grinned. "Maybe you got a novel cooking?"

"Who has time?" Rudy was about to stand when Bert's next sentence caught him in mid-lift.

"Didn't you tell me a while back you were suspicious about your friend Lou Skalney's execution? Did you discover anything else? Maybe that would make a good story."

Rudy resumed his seat and blew out a long breath.

"Interesting you should ask. Remember I said the hearse carrying Lou went first to a monastery?"

Bert nodded.

"Turns out it's a cloistered monastery and no one in town knows much about it, except cars, and sometimes hearses, go in and out at all hours. The funeral director told me they run a crematorium there, and that's why they took Lou's body to the monastery. I checked the county records, and the monastery doesn't have a license to run a crematorium. In fact, the clerk in the county office looked at me like I was crazy when I mentioned it to her. It raises even more questions."

"No webpage, nothing?"

"Nope. I checked with Kathy's uncle, Bishop Keenan. He said he'd ask the Bishop in the monastery's diocese but thought Bishop Haggarty would have mentioned it if he had a Catholic cloistered monastery on his turf."

When Rudy stood to leave his office, Bert said, "I'd follow up if I were you."

Rudy grinned.

Kathy took Rudy's news far more calmly than he had expected. He thought she would fume in righteous anger at the drop to a four-day workweek, and panic at the looming possibility the paper would lay Rudy off. Instead, she stopped peeling potatoes and reheated a cold half-cup of coffee. Settling at the table, she shoved Rudy's chair leg out with her foot. He slowly accepted her invitation, an unspoken question furrowing his brow. She barely waited until he sat.

"Actually, this brings up an idea I've wanted to discuss with you. With Gabe starting his Junior year and Lisa in middle grade, I've been thinking it's time I return to work." She raised her hand to stop Rudy's response and continued. "I can earn enough money as a teacher to pay for his college tuition each year. And you can go on supporting the family. I don't think they'll really lay you off. You're too good, and they know it. We can get by on only four days a week, and pay Gabe's tuition, if I get a job starting in the Fall."

Rudy frowned. They had met in college. He was a struggling journalism major, while Kathy sailed through her education courses, a young woman sure of her purpose, a born teacher. She once told him playing school had been her favorite pastime since childhood. She would line her dolls in neat rows, silent students hanging on her every word.

"I hate to see you work outside the home. Motherhood is the most important job in the world and–"

"I'll still be a mother, and it's easier for teachers." She grinned. "We have the same schedule as our kids."

Rudy knew he was going to lose this one. His father had raised him to be a provider because that's what a man did. But somewhere along the line, the rules changed. Now women want fulfillment, whatever that meant. He knew he was lucky Kathy had been content being a homemaker until now, and her logic was irrefutable. Her salary could cover Gabe's tuition, especially if they had a year's head start.

Rudy sighed. "You're right. I can't argue with you, but I still don't like the idea."

"I know." She covered his hand with hers.

Rudy gave her a half-smile. "At least there's a silver lining. I'll have time to investigate what happened to Lou after the execution."

"Are you still harping on that? For Pete's sake, we went to his funeral and saw him buried."

Rudy sniffed. "We saw an urn buried."

"Oh, come on."

"Look, Bert said I should plan on writing for the national market as a freelancer, just in case. What if this is the tip of a huge iceberg? One big exposé and I'd have an entrée to a market that Stephen King would have envied in his earlier years."

"Maybe you could look for a regular paying job, if it comes to that." Kathy frowned and removed her hand.

He grinned. "Of course. No family of mine will starve on my watch."

Rudy hoped his confidence was not misplaced.

CHAPTER 30

FEVER AND FRIENDSHIP

Every day, Pete, nose quivering, scurried to the crate door when Lou arrived to feed him, change his water, and replace the straw.

"Looks like we can take that splint off soon, little guy," Lou said to Pete one afternoon as he sat on the barn floor, his back against the wall. A tear rolled down one cheek as he pulled his knees up to make a cradle for Pete. Petting the rabbit's head with his forefinger, Lou remembered those nights he held baby Becky close to his heart and rocked her back to sleep after she woke crying. He smiled, gazing at the cute face with the big eyes, long ears, and twitching nose.

At least I can comfort this little guy.

Something about holding Pete close thawed Lou's heart. Precious memories of caring for Becky flooded him and released long pent-up tears. Sighing, he closed his eyes. After a moment, he spoke, voice thick with emotion. "I wish I had kept something of Becky's, anything that could bring her back to me, even a little."

Both so innocent, so vulnerable. At least he could comfort this animal now, if not his daughter. As for his estranged wife, Sally—she had ached for his comfort, but he withdrew into his own world of pain, building walls of silence between them. He cried for his failed marriage, for Sally, who had put up with so little from him.

I murdered and called it justice, and wreaked revenge on someone who may have been innocent. I am guilty of ruining our lives, and for what?

His wife and child gone, Lou considered his future in this medieval style monastery. He wondered at the choices he had made that brought him here. Sitting with Pete in the afternoon's growing dusk, his memory reached far into the past. He hummed a fragment of Becky's favorite lullaby.

After three weeks in the crate, Pete's lop-sided hop had grown stronger. Soon he would be ready for the open field. But lately the rabbit seemed off his feed and listless, and even fresh carrots failed to entice him. Lou told himself that maybe he just needs to be free again.

The rabbit surprised Lou the next morning when he nipped his finger. The skin appeared broken, but there was no bleeding. He patted Pete and left the barn, pruning shears balanced against his shoulder. He nodded at his assigned monk- shadow-for-the-day as he walked toward the bushes.

That evening, he found the rabbit curled into a little ball, its back against the crate's corner. He barely looked up at his keeper as Lou scooped the old straw and replaced it with new. The rabbit did not move despite the activity around him.

"Come on, fella, let's get you onto the clean straw."

Pete hung limply from Lou's hand as he transferred him onto his new bed. Rather than scratch out a nest for itself, the rabbit staggered a few steps and plopped down. Lou frowned, absentmindedly sucking his sore index finger. *I'll ask Malachi or Luke what could be wrong with Pete if he doesn't look any better soon.*

During Compline five days later, Lou felt the first jolt of pain bolt from the base of his skull to his forehead. It felt like his head was in a vise, and it hurt to keep his eyes open. Behind closed lids, he tried to will the pain away, to focus on the chanting, or prayer, but nothing worked. The pain held his skull in a merciless grip while a wave of nausea washed over him. Fearing he would vomit, he rose to leave the chapel, but dizziness forced him back onto the pew. He tried to focus on the large cross, nestled in its stand, hoping it would anchor his spinning world. When his stomach threatened again, Lou grabbed the back of the pew in front of him, preparing once more to stand. Just as he tried to rise, and realized it was no use, he felt powerful arms encircle and lift him. He turned and, through squinted eyes, recognized Frank Predmore.

"Come on, Lou. I'll get you out of here."

Slowly, the two of them walked out of chapel and into the lavatory where Lou vomited.

Later in the clinic, with his temperature registering 102, Lou shivered and moaned while Brother Luke drew blood, swabbed the sore on his finger, and started an intravenous drip.

"Headache, the worst headache—" Lou moaned before drifting into a terrifying landscape where twisted trees loomed, and devilish creatures scurried between his feet as he tried to navigate a gnarled forest floor.

In his delirium, terror drove Lou to find Becky. Believing he heard her calling for him, he stopped and listened, trying to determine from which direction came her cries. Once he thought he found her, but when he bent to take her hand, she turned into a rabbit. Doggedly, he plowed through the dark forest of his dreams, searching for his daughter. Sometimes he was searching for Pete. They both needed him, and somehow, he believed finding one would save the other.

Was it his curse always to hunt and never find? He grieved in the surreal twilight for his daughter. Wavering between delirium and consciousness, he yielded to overwhelming sorrow. His old defenses lay useless at his feet. He moaned, cried, shivered, while holding his aching head as still as possible. His soul writhed, and his body slipped deeper into shock. Words and phrases barely registered as he drifted in and out—gentamicin, streptomycin, dehydrated, system failure, tularemia, and rabbit fever.

Four days later, his brain no longer pounding in pain, Lou opened one eye. He saw Brother Luke speaking with Malachi in the clinic's doorway. Things snapped into place. He was not dreaming. He turned his head and saw Predmore at his bedside.

"How long have you been here?" Lou's voice sounded scratchy. He cleared his throat and started again, but Frank stopped him.

"I kept you company during the nights."

"Every night," Brother Luke said as he approached Lou's bed. "He mopped your forehead, gave you water, and never left your side. You had a serious bout of tularemia from handling an infected rabbit."

Lou felt exhausted, as if he had run a marathon, but it was a good tired. There was relief too, for he felt his fever burned away the last shred of anger that had colored his encounters with Frank. Now he looked into the eyes of a friend and asked, "Pete?"

"He's okay too. Got over it by himself."

Lou smiled. "Thank you. I didn't deserve all you did for me, especially after the way I treated you." He swallowed and continued in a soft voice. "I'm so sorry. I don't deserve your forgiveness."

Frank shrugged and coughed. Waving his hand, he said, "None of us deserves forgiveness, but we all get forgiven anyway, if we're sorry."

"Do you really believe that?" Lou asked, recalling the stone Frank had tucked into his sandal, and how guilt had turned him into a crying, kneeling, human cross during Chapel services.

Predmore offered a weak smile. "I'm beginning to."

That night, Lou tossed and turned. Alone in the clinic, but for his assigned monk-guard, the phrase "as we forgive those who trespass against us," ran through his mind like a shred of melody caught in a tangle of twisted neurons. He tried to focus on Frank's forgiveness, but his thoughts returned to his great sin. Surely, God can't forgive me for what I did. Yet Jesus forgave Dismas, while he hung on a cross next to him. I remember Abbot Anselm saying that's why this monastery is called St. Dismas.

In the dark hours of that long night, only two words danced in his mind. Murder. Forgiveness. The guarding monk watched Lou stare into the darkness. After a while, Lou whispered, "It's gone. Burned out of me."

The monk leaned forward. "What is?"

"The fury and hate I felt for Beauregard Abbington all these years. Could a fever melt a heart of stone? Or am I too weak to carry that load anymore? I think of him now and there are no feelings, except I'm sorry I killed him. Is that possible?"

"What do you think?"

Lou looked at this monk, who was not about to let him off the hook, and recognized Brother Timothy.

"I suppose it's possible, but I don't know how that could be, and so I doubt it."

"Must you understand before you can believe?"

"Makes sense, yeah."

"Then that's knowledge, not belief."

Lou tossed his head from side to side. "It's all too much right now. Can I have some water?"

Timothy handed him a glass and lifted Lou's head. After Lou drank, the monk whispered, "Go back to sleep."

He imagined Jesus saying, "All things are possible with me, even forgiveness for murder."

Lou drifted off.

PART IV

ARMAGEDDON

CHAPTER 31

PARANOIA

Lou tried to catch floating snippets of conversation in the refectory the morning Brother Luke released him from the clinic. Surprised he found comfort in surroundings he once loathed, he savored the cinnamon sprinkled on his hot cereal.

Darn if I'm not liking this slop.

A shadow fell across his bowl as a sullen Niebold settled onto the bench across from Lou. He slammed his cup of coffee onto the table, spilling most of it.

Lou noticed the professor's eyes appeared larger behind his thick glasses and his cheeks more sunken.

Could he have lost that much weight while I was in the clinic? Where was his breakfast?

"You're not eating today, Kurt?"

"Not hungry." Niebold sipped in silence, trailing his forefinger through the coffee puddles. After a long moment, he stared at Lou and said, "Enough of this. Something has to be done."

"About what? Mackey? What did you expect, after what he did?"

"They didn't have to kill him!" Kurt made a fist. "They must be stopped."

Lou shuddered. He had been right when he thought Mackey was about to erupt, and now his gut was sending more warning flares.

Lou tried to sound reassuring. "Kurt, I don't believe the monks murder people. Mackey's family and the system damaged him, and it wasn't his fault. Still, he is dangerous. This wasn't the right place for him. Can't you accept they sent him where he would be less likely to hurt himself or others?"

"You bought into their lies?" Kurt hissed. "I thought you were on my side. People keep disappearing. Doesn't that scare you, or at least raise questions? Am I the only one with a brain around here? They claim this is the wrong monastery for someone who tortures animals. Come on. We're here because we murdered people. Torturing animals is the least of our so-called sins. Bogus excuse, and I say those monks kill with impunity."

"I believe you liked him, or at least understood him more than anyone else. But you're torturing yourself, thinking the monks killed him."

Kurt glared at Lou, and after a long moment, bolted to his feet and stormed out of the refectory. Lou noticed Brother Timothy's head shoot up from his breakfast after a jab in the ribs from seatmate, Brother Aaron. Timothy dropped his spoon and set out after Niebold.

Silence followed in the wake of their exits. Lou let out a sigh when the bell for Lauds tolled. By the time he settled into his usual seat in the chapel, he had to catch his breath, and hoped he could get through the day.

When the chanting began, Lou closed his eyes and let it wash over him. Simple notes, the rising and falling of the sparse melody, released his spirit to flow where it would, like warm fudge oozing down a scoop of ice cream. Lou relaxed his muscles, took a deep breath, and released the tension from his encounter with Kurt.

After chapel, Brother Jerome approached him before he could rise from the pew.

"You will work with me in the library today," he said, before exiting with the other monks. Relieved, Lou waited until the chapel was empty but for one lone monk extinguishing the candles. Quietly, he left, leaving the monk to his silent task.

When Lou entered the library, he saw Brother Jerome light the last of the reading lamps that sat on each table. He wondered what work there could be in a small library that serves less than 100 people and features only one topic. Still, he found the book-lined room a comforting, windowless cave into which he liked to crawl. It calmed him.

Lou imagined a monk, quill in hand, bent over a slanted desk, illuminated by candlelight. He could almost hear the quill's scratch on parchment as it formed each letter. "Do you want me to transcribe a Bible or two?"

"You can start with Genesis and quit for lunch when you get to Numbers. Or you can rewrite the catalog cards. They've gotten smudged and dog-eared."

"All of them?"

"So you want Genesis to Numbers instead?"

Lou made a face. "Ah no. Cards it is."

Jerome grinned. "See? Everything's relative. Use this pen and here's a stack of fresh cards. Enjoy."

Jerome settled into the chair behind the librarian's desk and opened his Bible, while Lou set up his workstation on a nearby table and formed a neat pile of "A" cards. Soon he came to the card for a book about St. Anselm. He read the brief description of this Abbot of a Benedictine monastery who became the ArchBishop of Canterbury. *Well well, and then there's Abbot Anselm of Saint Dismal.* He snorted and returned to work.

After an hour of tedium, Lou parked his pen next to his pile of re-written index cards and arched his aching back. Rubbing the kinks out of his shoulders, he observed Brother Jerome still engrossed in his Bible.

Lou cleared his throat and said, "I've started reading the Bible, but after a while it gets too confusing with all the smiting, kings running amok, and prophets talking about things I don't understand. How can you read it for hours?"

Jerome looked at Lou and waited a few seconds before responding.

"You're a reader. What's your fascination with books? Why do you like to read?"

Lou frowned and rubbed his forehead. He expected an answer, not another question.

"I like to learn about things, like what happened in the past, how the world works, about nature, about, well, everything. Especially since I have no life here." Lou emphasized the last three words.

Jerome ignored the bait. "The Bible tells me about God and his relationship with us. It gives me wisdom and assures me of a Savior whose existence prophets had foretold hundreds of years before. If I'm troubled, I find peace in the Psalms. I find wisdom in Proverbs. I find hope in the Gospels. Sometimes, it feels like God uses this book to speak directly to me."

"How long did it take you to find that peace and so called wisdom? Is the Bible always right?"

"I admit the Bible can be confusing. That's why people have written commentaries based on the original Greek, Hebrew, and Aramaic languages, and the historical context." Jerome grinned. "You'll find them when you get to the 'C' cards."

"How about the Reader's Digest version?"

Jerome chuckled. "How about reading the Bible with others and learning with them? We have a few small groups that gather to do just that. I suspect Frank Predmore would join a group if you were in it."

"What do you do in a group?"

"We read selected chapters, or just a few verses, and discuss what we read. Each group has a monk to guide the discussion and explain the commentaries that make the verses clearer. It gives us the opportunity to debate and sometimes question and challenge what we think the verses mean.

Lou thought for a moment. Well, why not? "It might be interesting, and I'd like some answers. I'll try it."

Jerome grinned. "As the Bible says, 'Ask and it will be given to you; seek, and you will find; knock, and the door will be opened to you.'"

"Yeah, right. We'll see."

In the Abbot's office, Anselm and Malachi stood facing each other like two aging lions. Anselm spoke first.

"You know why we don't allow pets anywhere in the monastery."

"Pet food is too expensive?"

Anselm frowned. "I don't appreciate your sense of humor, Malachi."

"Maybe God will send you one if you ask."

"I did. He sent me you instead."

"Even God has a sense of humor."

The Abbot sighed and returned to the subject. "Pets create problems. Yet you ignored the rule, and over-rode what would have been my decision, if you had asked. A resident could have died, and you endangered the health of everyone on the monastery farm, keeping an infected animal on the grounds."

Malachi's jaw tightened. "It wasn't about an injured rabbit, it was about Lou Skalney's state of mind. Your latest resident's cruelty broke through Lou's defenses, and I believed tending the injured rabbit would help him start to heal. I had no way of knowing the animal would contract rabbit fever." He spoke softly, but could not hide the tension in his voice.

"Where is the rabbit now?"

"He got well, and we released him. You finally transferred Colin Mackey, so everything is back to normal." Malachi folded his arms and flashed his Abbot a quick smile.

Anselm challenged him. "Tell me what you would have done about Mackey."

"I wouldn't have accepted him in the first place. I don't believe this monastery has the resources to handle this sociopath safely."

"We manage Niebold."

"He's older, more intelligent, and less compulsive. Mackey was a loose cannon."

Anselm took a deep breath. "You were Abbot before I arrived, and I appreciate your insights. But we differ in certain areas. Until now, I've felt I could rely on you as second in command, but it's troubling you did not approach me about keeping the rabbit."

"I'm not trying to usurp your authority, Abbot. When you arrived to run the monastery, I was relieved. I'm a farmer, always was, always will be. Even though I left my Mennonite community to marry an Englisher, I never stopped farming and, well, you know my story. But I think I know more about animals than a former prison chaplain, although I admit the rabbit fever stumped me."

"The question is, Brother Malachi, do you trust me?" Abbot Anselm rubbed his face, his index finger trailing his scar.

When Malachi did not respond, Anselm sighed and extended his hand, palm up. "I must ask you to surrender your phone."

For five years, they had shared the monastery's two cell phones with their daily-changing access codes. Now Malachi would become like his fellow monks, and only Anselm would have access to the outside.

What if something happens to him? Should I refuse to surrender my phone?

Malachi thought of the farm, of his monks who labored with him under the scorching sun of summer and the cold of winter. He had formed a bond with the farm brothers and residents like Lou Skalney. He closed his eyes. No longer being second in command was one thing, but Anselm could reassign him anywhere. All Malachi knew was farming, and it was all he wanted to do.

Fearful of pushing Anselm to another level of discipline, Malachi reached into his pocket. His hand closed over the phone, caressing it for the last time. Slowly, he withdrew it and placed it on Anselm's palm.

CHAPTER 32

RELEASED

Bert shook his head. "Rudy, they're crazy to lay you off. Dumb decision. I'll probably be next."

The editor yanked open the bottom drawer on his right and plopped a couple of juice glasses and a bottle of Jack Daniels between the mounds of papers cluttering his desk. He poured two drinks and handed one to Rudy.

Rudy looked at the golden liquid sloshing in the thick glass and then at Bert. The last thing he wanted at ten in the morning was to be laid off. The second last thing was whiskey. He did not even like whiskey at ten in the evening. Rudy took the glass so the man could put down his arm.

So Bert's prediction came true.

"Start again from the beginning, okay?"

Bert sighed. "Like I said, the paper's losing money. Between the internet and twenty-four-hour news feeds on TV, the morning paper has become a relic. Who has time to read it? Even *I* don't have time, and I'm the editor. They can't charge the subscribers enough to pay the staff a decent wage, and that's why they're laying off people like you. They're increasing the rates for obituaries and selling more ads just to stay afloat, but that leaves less white space for news. Besides, you cost too much because of your seniority. I'm sure I'll be next after I do their hatchet work. Getting rid of old-timers like us saves them pension costs too. You will get severance pay, so stop in HR for the paperwork. I'm sorry, Rudy."

The finality of it left Rudy speechless. They stared at each other, and after a while, Rudy stood and turned toward the door. When he saw a security guard standing next to his desk and holding an empty box, Rudy looked back at Bert. But his editor, his friend, his mentor, did not look up from an open folder.

"One day I'll get an exclusive and this paper will grovel to pay me a fortune for a story only I could have gotten," Rudy informed Bert's bent head.

The editor looked up and gave him a thumbs up. "You do that."

Rudy emptied his desk, careful to pack every scrap of contact information, resources, and articles in progress. Pictures of Kathy and the kids and a few choice mementos made it into the box. He left scraps, broken pencils, torn envelopes, and every other piece of trash for his former employer. Other reporters stopped to offer condolences and wish him well. Rudy shook hands, accepted hugs and goodwill punches. He walked to the elevator, box in hand, and did not look back.

After driving a few miles toward home, Rudy realized he was not ready to walk into the kitchen, holding the contents of his work-life in a box. *What will I say? Guess what, guys? Daddy doesn't have a job anymore.*

He needed time to think, to deal with his new reality. True, Bert had warned him, but it was still a shock. He knew Kathy would have no difficulty finding that teaching job she wanted, so they wouldn't starve. Forget college tuition; her wages were supposed to cover that. Now he hoped they would cover the essentials. Rudy thought of their savings account and prayed they would not drain it before he started earning again.

He headed away from the suburbs and out into the country. After a half hour, he turned onto a dirt road and pulled to a stop. He cut the engine and closed his eyes.

Couldn't happen at a worse time. Kathy will cheerfully work until retirement, but our lives will change even if I find work. It might mean moving unless I can make it as a freelancer and can stay here. At least I now have time to investigate Lou's execution. Too many questions don't add up.

He recalled his parting words to Bert. Rudy's suspicion that the monastery was up to something suspicious had grown. What if the truth morphed into an expose' of national interest? He drummed his fingers on the steering wheel while reviewing what he knew so far about St. Dismas.

It did not fall under the auspices of any traditional religious group he knew. What went on behind those cloistered walls? Why did the hearse carrying Lou's body stop there before going to the funeral home? His research had ruled out cremation. The monastery does business with certain townspeople, buying wine from the liquor store and probably grain to feed whatever animals they have on the farm. Yet Rudy could not find a miniscule electronic footprint that led anywhere.

There's a story here, and it's big.

After the initial shock, Kathy stepped toward him as he sat at the kitchen table.

"We're a team, and now I'm up to bat. You'll find something soon, honey. It's just temporary." She walked behind his chair and hugged him. Rudy patted her hand.

"This is the perfect time to take a break so I can follow up on Lou's execution."

"So you're really going to pursue this full-time now?" Kathy frowned. "What about looking for another job instead?"

"Give me six months. If I don't have this wrapped up by then, I will take any legal paying job I can find." He forced a smile. "My severance package should cover us until then, and we won't need to touch our savings."

Kathy released Rudy and sat opposite him. After looking at each other in silence, she ran her hand over her mouth, then cradled her chin. "You're determined to follow this, this–hunch?"

"I have to know, Kathy. If Lou wasn't executed and taken to that monastery instead, who could have pulled that off? And why? It would have to be the work of powerful people. Besides, a story like that could launch my career as a freelancer."

Kathy frowned. "And this is what you want to spend six months pursuing?"

Rudy took her hand. "I have to. What if he's alive? I know it's one chance in a million, but I've followed slimmer leads that made headlines."

"We saw him buried, Rudy."

"I know we attended a funeral for a container full of someone's ashes."

He waited. Kathy did not take her eyes off Rudy. The sound of the clock's ticking filled the room. Finally, she whispered, "All right. Six months. Not a minute more. Make no mistake, I'll hold you to that. And then if nothing comes of it, this ends."

Rudy grinned and kissed her. "You're a good woman Kathleen Margaret Mary Keenan Kowalski."

Lisa frowned at the plate Rudy placed before her.

"Um, Dad. The toast is like, black, and I hate runny eggs. Eeew."

"Eggs are full of protein and the burned toast will give you pink cheeks. Eat."

Lisa looked at her father with his uncombed hair standing on end and a beard awaiting a shave. "Pink cheeks? Who says?"

Rudy tried to look serious. "That's what my grandmother used to tell me."

"So she couldn't cook, either, huh?"

"Not breakfast, anyway."

Rudy's confession brought a chuckle from Kathy, and he challenged his wife. "Et tu?"

Kathy raised her hand in a gesture of peace.

"Just that I remember your grandmother's cooking. At least your eggs aren't runny. You're a sweetie making breakfast, and I appreciate being waited on before my interview. Don't get discouraged. You'll be turning out culinary masterpieces in no time."

"Yeah, I'll stick to cereal, thank you." Gabe's deepening voice rumbled his opinion.

Rudy threw his hands up in mock surrender. "I raised a pair of ingrates. Eat, be thankful, and get out of here. I have work to do."

A half hour later, he sighed as the door closed behind the last of his beloved family.

Did Kathy feel this relief when the kids and I left every day?

He rubbed his hands in anticipation.

Rudy turned onto the highway leading to Trinity County, home of a certain cloistered monastery. At ten in the morning, the county clerk's office was quiet, and he settled at a table, grateful he finally had time to plow through public records going back several years. Eventually, he discovered one Misericordia Consortium had purchased St. Dismas Monastery from the Benedictines in 2008 for four point three million dollars cash. After jotting down all the information available from the record, and making photocopies as well, Rudy decided to re-visit the Ranchero for lunch before heading home to his computer.

He scanned the restaurant when he entered. The place was quiet except for two occupied tables and one lone diner at the lunch counter. Rudy recognized the waitress behind the counter, but could not remember her name, other than she had called him "Sweetie."

He took a seat at the counter and pulled the menu from its slot between the napkin holder and the ketchup bottle sitting in front of him. As he scanned the fare, he noticed out of the corner of his eye his counter-mate dropping money next to his empty plate and leaving.

"Know what you want, Sweetie? Special today is the barbequed chicken. Coffee?"

Rudy looked up to see her welcoming smile and coffee carafe held high.

"I'll have the vegetable soup, chef's salad, and tea, please." After a moment, he added, "Quiet here, isn't it?"

"Oh yeah. The quiet before the storm. Lunch crowd should be in soon."

"I was here a while ago and met a rancher, Hank Campbell. Would he be part of the regular lunch crowd?"

She shrugged. "Comes in once in a while when he has business in town. Other than that, he and his brother keep to themselves."

"What's their ranch called, again? Is it far from town?"

"The Lazy Q. It's just down the road. Turn right on Benson Street, go straight for about nine miles and it's on your right. Big sign next to the gate."

After leaving a generous tip, he found her directions were spot on. Rudy drove slowly down the long dirt road that would end, he assumed, at the main house. Along the way, he admired the black and white cows ambling behind the fencing and wondered what breed they might be. Some grazed while others rested on the ground. The contented cattle under the cloud-dotted blue sky brought a smile, and he thought Andrew Wyeth could not paint a more bucolic scene.

Rudy stopped to savor the moment. He rolled his window down and took a slow, deep breath, filled with the smells of earth, grass, and more than a hint of manure. Scanning the horizon, he noticed the corner of a red roof. *That must be the house.*

He felt relief when Hank opened the door. After explaining again who he was, Hank nodded. Rudy quickly got to the point.

"I'm still interested in that St. Dismas Monastery. Could I ask you what you know about it?"

"Don't know all that much, but come in. I'll answer whatever questions I can."

After an hour's conversation, Rudy realized he already knew as much about the monastery as Hank, and feared he had reached another dead-end. He had one last question.

"Have you ever been inside the monastery?"

"Well, yeah. We've been servicing their cows for a few years now. In fact, I suspect they'll be calling us soon. That monk, Malachi, runs everything on the farm, but my brother and I have seen only the cattle barn and pasture. They're kind of secretive if you ask me. But that's okay. They pay on time and that's all I care about." Hank grinned and added, "Got us a great new bull this year — Buster. So far, he's one of the best, but headstrong."

"Any chance I could tag along if they call for Buster's excellent services?"

"And do what? Know anything about bulls, cows, or mating cattle?"

"Not a thing. But I'll stay out of your way and do whatever you say. I just need to get inside."

Hank thought for a moment, then drawled, "Well, I guess it can't hurt. An extra pair of hands might be useful. Buster can be a bit contrary."

Rudy wondered how a contrary bull might behave and decided not to ask. After handing Hank his new business card, he left the ranch, feeling a sliver of hope.

CHAPTER 33

SUCCESS?

It had been a month since Abbot Anselm had requested Brother Malachi's phone, and its absence still rankled the old farmer. This morning, having supervised the unloading of alfalfa, Malachi looked forward to lunch and a hot cup of coffee. He shivered and sneezed, despite the warm Spring morning. Out of habit, he tapped his pocket to check for the phone that was no longer there. Malachi added a prayer for patience and good health.

"Getting a cold?" Brother Aaron sounded concerned as they stood next to the now empty loading platform.

"Hope not," Malachi said with a weak smile.

"I hate to add to your burdens, Malachi, but I need to discuss Brother Timothy with you. He approached the gate the other day, alone. I asked him where his assigned resident was, and he just grinned and said, 'on the farm.' When I asked him for specifics, he shrugged and said it was all right, since there were a lot of monks there. He added he was only running a quick errand."

Malachi shook his head. "That's not good. Thanks for telling me. I'll speak with Abbot about him."

True to his word, Malachi lingered near the chapel door after Sext. When Anselm approached, Malachi stepped forward.

"A word, Abbot?"

Anselm nodded. "Walk with me to my office."

The two senior monks ambled through the corridors, talking about generalities, testing the strained terrain of their five-year relationship. Their cordial conversation made Malachi wonder if he should raise the subject of his phone.

When they entered his office, Anselm walked behind the desk, and for the first time in Malachi's memory, brought his chair around to the front, next to the visitor's chair. After taking their seats, Anselm leaned back, thrust out his legs, and crossed his ankles. Malachi followed suit, like two old friends settling in for a long talk.

"I have some concerns about our new monk, Brother Timothy." When he finished sharing Aaron's observations, Anselm nodded.

"This is serious, Malachi. Our monks must be vigilant. Perhaps our training was not sufficient for Timothy. We will have Brother Joseph work with him when he's next assigned a resident. We must see improvement soon."

Malachi sighed with relief.

"How is the farm doing, by the way?"

"Crops are doing well, but we're still fighting critter incursions." Malachi chuckled and described the monks' recent encounter with a hedgehog in the tomato bed. "That reminds me. We need to get Bessie and Harriet serviced for calving. Will you call the Lazy Q Ranch and talk to Hank Campbell? Their bulls are good breeding stock, and we've used them for years now."

Anselm reached into his pocket and pulled out Malachi's phone. He smiled, handed it back to the older monk, and said, "Call him yourself. We will use the alphabet code this month."

"All right!" Rudy set the phone down and pumped his fist. "That was Hank Campbell, the rancher I told you about." Rudy grabbed a carrot from the counter where Kathy was chopping vegetables for dinner.

"And?"

"And tomorrow I'm going with him and his brother, Steve, when they bring their bull for stud to that monastery. This will get me inside the gate. I don't plan to leave without answers."

Kathy smiled as she dumped onions, carrots, and peppers into the simmering broth at the bottom of her soup pot. "Good. Maybe then you can move on."

Rudy gently grasped her hands and turned her toward himself, his expression firm.

"I'm getting onto those grounds posing as a ranch hand. When they're done, I will have to find some way to stay. I suspect there is something going on they don't want made public, and it may take me a while to find out what it is. If I'm not home, even for a week, don't panic. I've worked undercover before, and you know the drill. Promise you won't worry. You know I can handle myself." He grinned and added, "Maybe I'll need to sign up to join the order to get answers, but I promise not to take any vows of celibacy."

Kathy's eyes glistened. "I always hated it when you went undercover, and now hoped I was done worrying about you."

Rudy enfolded her in his arms.

Hank Campbell was leaning against the cattle trailer when Rudy pulled to a stop near the barn on The Lazy Q. As he approached, carrying his overnight bag, the cattle rancher pushed away from the trailer and extended his hand in greeting. He chuckled when he eyed the reporter's overnight bag. "This won't take all night. It's not like Buster has to woo them with dinner and a movie."

Rudy grinned. "I know, but if I can get them to let me stay a few days once I'm on the property, maybe I can get the story — if there is one. Meanwhile, what do I do? How do I help?"

After some bribery with alfalfa, Hank, Steve, and Rudy loaded Buster into the trailer. Before climbing into their two-seater truck, the brothers briefly explained the mating procedure. Ultimately, it would be Buster's gig. Rudy followed the ranchers in his Mustang.

He recognized the monk who opened the monastery gates to them. This time, he was cordial as Hank introduced Rudy as his ranch hand. Brother Aaron shook Rudy's hand.

"Pleased to meet you," Rudy said.

For a second, Rudy thought he saw a flicker of recollection on the gatekeeper's face. *Does he remember meeting me that one time?*

After Aaron closed the monastery gate, Rudy perched on the edge of the truck bed, and Hank carefully steered toward the cow barn.

Rudy scanned the monastery grounds. The two-story stone monastery rose long and massive on his right. Straight ahead, he saw a sagging red barn surrounded by raised beds, overflowing with green leaves, red, and orange vegetables. He noticed what looked like a shed attached to the side of the monastery that faced the barn.

"I don't see any cows," he shouted over the motor, craning his neck toward the pasture behind the red barn.

"It's down this way. You'll see a gray wooden barn coming up soon," Hank called back as he dodged holes along the rutted path. Clutching the side of the truck bed, Rudy spotted a pair of Border Collies patrolling a small cluster of sheep.

After Hank stopped the truck and turned off the motor, the three stood next to the trailer.

"What else do they have here besides cows, sheep, and vegetables?" Rudy said.

Hank laughed. "You name it: chickens, goats, even a wheat field beyond the red barn."

"Do they sell this stuff?"

"Not that I know of, but you can bet their grocery bill is about zero."

"Other than the wine."

Hank laughed. "Oh yeah, other than the wine. Here comes Malachi. He runs the farm," he said, pointing to a tall, lean monk in a black robe with a red cross sewn on the front. Another monk, in a simple brown robe, hurried to keep up with the old farmer-monk's long strides. *A novice?* He watched Malachi turn and speak briefly to his companion, who then changed direction and headed toward the monastery shed. As Malachi approached them, Rudy recalled his uncle Leo, whose face, like Malachi's, told of hard-won battles with Mother Nature.

After introductions, the elderly monk led the men to an enclosed pasture where Harriet and Bessie awaited their suitor.

"The vet assured me they were ready to mate. Did you bring the same bull as last year?"

"No, Brother. This year it's Buster. We bought him a few months ago, and according to his breeding record, he's sired some fine calves."

Malachi nodded.

"That went fast," Rudy whispered to the Campbell brothers after Buster added to his reputation as an enthusiastic stud.

"We didn't have to do anything, once we got Buster in the pasture," Steve said.

Hank chuckled. "Let's hope we can get him into the trailer as easily."

The rancher did not get his wish. Malachi smiled. "He'll come around soon. No rush."

Rudy took advantage of the distraction. "Brother Malachi, is there any way I could spend some time in your monastery? I'm a free-lance writer and I know there would be interest in an article about life in a monastery like yours. I promise I would cause little disruption for a day or so while I get the feel of the rhythm of life at St. Dismas and talk to some of your monks."

"This is a cloistered monastery. That means closed to the world."

"I know, but there are only a few cloistered religious orders in the south. That's what makes St. Dismas unique, and maybe with publicity, you will get more novices."

Malachi frowned and folded his arms. "It appears you used subterfuge to get onto our property. You aren't a ranch hand, are you? You're a reporter."

Rudy forced himself to maintain eye contact with Malachi, despite the old monk's glare.

"Guilty as charged. I confess I do whatever I need to get a story."

"Why are you determined there is a story here? Cloistered monasteries do not interest most people."

"On the contrary, life in such a monastery is so far removed from people's every-day lives, it's shrouded in mystery. Readers would find it fascinating."

Rudy saw his argument was making no headway with the old farmer.

I can't tell him I think my friend may have been brought here after his execution. If I'm way off base, the monks will think I'm nuts and throw me out of here. But then, they could hide Lou anywhere in that monastery and I'd never find him. What secrets are they hiding? I'll give this monk just enough facts to make him think I know more than I do and see what I can flush out.

Rudy considered his next words while staring at the Campbell brothers, who were trying to coax Buster back into the trailer.

"People in town said they've seen hearses coming and going from here, and cars leaving in the middle of the night. I'm sure you agree that kind of activity is not common to cloistered monasteries. Your monastery does not belong to any Christian denomination or eastern religion I can find. I discovered St. Dismas is owned by a conglomerate called Misericordia and it paid the Benedictines four point three million in cash for the property. Now, I suspect the monastery would prefer to discuss the Misericordia Conglomerate with me, rather than leave me to dig further without your input."

Rudy stepped closer to Malachi and added, "I will find what I'm looking for. It's what I do."

He expected a sharp response from Brother Malachi, but the old monk looked down at him for a long moment, his expression sympathetic. "You do not know what you are asking. Wait here," he said and walked toward the monastery's entrance.

Rudy approached Steve and Hank. "I can't thank you enough for this opportunity."

"You getting that interview?"

"Looks that way. Thanks again for letting me tag along. Appreciate it."

"Nice going." Hank gave him a high five.

Rudy watched the truck and trailer rock its way toward the gate.

Malachi returned after several minutes. "Abbot Anselm has agreed to speak with you. The Campbells left?"

"Thank you, Brother Malachi, and yes, they did."

"Don't thank me yet. Brother Aaron seems to recall you once asked about coming here for a retreat," Malachi said as they walked along the path to the monastery.

Rudy shrugged, and they continued in silence, his shorter legs pumping to keep up with Malachi's strides. When they arrived at the monastery's main entrance, Brother Aaron and Abbot Anselm awaited them.

The Abbot approached Rudy. "I am Abbot Anselm. Brother Malachi informs me you are interested in writing about St. Dismas and Misericordia. I can assure you, you will find nothing worth writing about." He frowned. "Brother Aaron remembered you once approached him about retreats. We choose to remove ourselves from the world so we can better live and worship our Lord. I'm sure you can understand how publicity would interfere with that. I hope, after a brief tour, you will be on your way to write a more interesting article on another topic."

Turning to Malachi, Anselm said, "Perhaps you can ask Brother Timothy to bring the farm novices into the monastery for their lunch."

The two old monks locked eyes before Malachi strode away.

What was that about? Rudy wondered.

Abbot Anselm folded his arms and studied Rudy.

If he thinks I'm going to flinch, it's not going to happen. And what's the story behind his scar? Tough guy? I can be just as tough. Rudy locked into a face-off with the Abbot until Anselm finally spoke.

"Misericordia is a not-for-profit financial organization with substantial resources. It supports various religious endeavors that align with its philosophy of redemption and keeps a low profile. I would not entertain sinister motives if I were you. Misericordia, which is Latin for 'mercy' by the way, underwrote the purchase of this monastery so we could fulfill our purpose. That's all there is to it."

"Who belongs to the organization?"

"I will compile a list and send it to you. Be sure to give us your mailing address before you leave."

After twenty minutes of questions and answers, Anselm said, "We'll continue our conversation as we walk. You've seen the area where we keep our few cattle. I'll show you our sheep herd and then the farm."

As they walked, Rudy admired the rolling fields and white streaked sky. The aroma of rich earth reminded him of the way soil smelled when he was a boy digging in his backyard, determined to reach China. They stopped to watch a Border Collie run beside a cluster of puffy white sheep, while a black-clad monk whistled commands.

Rudy smiled. "It looks almost choreographed."

Anselm nodded. "In a way, it is. Man and beast communicating as God created them to. It is a sight I enjoy every day. Now, on to our farm. Brother Malachi was a farmer before joining the monastery, and he avoided chemicals or pesticides long before the term 'organic' became popular. We believe God made every plant, animal, and insect for a purpose. Even the humble weed serves us."

"Neighbors complain much?"

Anselm ignored Rudy's quip. After a leisurely walk and dissertation on the attributes of dandelions, they reached Malachi at the first of the raised beds. As the monk opened the wire gate to show Rudy a crop of summer squash, a voice called, "Brother Malachi!"

Rudy froze and stopped breathing. He knew that voice. He had known it all his life. It can't be, but, dear God, didn't I always suspect this?

Three heads swiveled toward the speaker.

"Didn't I ask you…?" Anselm said to Malachi.

"Yes, yes, I told Timothy. I don't know why this one is not inside having lunch with the other novices."

Unsuspecting, Lou drew closer to the three men and said, "Brother Joseph said to tell you the log splitter…" He stopped in his tracks and stared at Rudy.

"Didn't Brother Timothy tell you to go in for lunch?" Malachi asked.

Lou said nothing.

"Well?" Malachi sounded inpatient.

Lou, red faced, kept his gaze on Rudy as if fearing he would disappear if he looked away. He cleared his throat. "Brother Joseph and I were in the back of the tool shed, working on the log splitter. I guess we didn't hear Brother Timothy announce that."

Rudy exhaled and studied the novice standing before him. Now bearded and lean, his friend could have disappeared in plain sight had he escaped from prison in that get-up. Yet here he stood.

You aren't dead! How and why did you get here? Dear God, what have they done to you? I was right all along, and so help me, I'll get to the truth now.

Rudy rushed to the statue-like novice, ignoring the man's barely perceptible headshake, and gave his raised-from-the-dead friend a giant bear hug.

Lou whispered, "You're in danger. Leave now."

CHAPTER 34

TRAPPED

Rudy whispered back, "Not on your life. Think I'm new at this?" Neither noticed Abbot Anselm's initial reaction to their reunion. By the time Lou and Rudy turned to him, the Abbot was wearing a composed a smile that did not reach his icy blue eyes.

"Perhaps you would like to be our guest while you get reacquainted with your friend," Anselm said.

Suddenly, I'm welcome, but according to Lou, I'm in danger. It could be a trap, but I've gotten out of worse situations. I didn't get this far to leave without answers, no matter what it takes.

"Thank you, Abbot. I appreciate that." Rudy gave Anselm a wide grin and ignored Lou's soft groan.

He told himself he would call Kathy later and tell her he had gotten in.

"Brother Malachi will escort you to your room. We would ask you to honor our dress code and wear a brown robe while a guest here. After he has gotten you settled, you can wait in the great hall where we gather for socialization before dining." The Abbot turned to Lou. "If you will accompany me to my office."

After they left, Rudy said to Malachi, "Your Abbot Anselm changed his mind rather suddenly, didn't he? Not that I don't appreciate the invitation," he quickly added.

"I expect Abbot Anselm empathized with your joy at seeing each other again. Reunions like that are unheard of here, so that may be why he changed his mind. We will assign you a monk should you need anything. That is the least we can do, because you will discover our lifestyle is quite different, and I'm sure you will have questions. We observe the canonical hours — times set aside for prayer during the day. Your monk will help you join us in our simple life while you are here."

Rudy's mind raced with a million questions as he made appropriate comments. Soon, the two arrived at the Monastery's front door.

Rudy found the entrance foyer imposing. Thick stone walls rose to a high ceiling, from which a sturdy metal chandelier hung from a long cable. Made for a dozen candles, it now held tapering light bulbs. Malachi told him the portraits of black-clad clerics that lined the wall on the right, where of previous Abbots. But the corridor opposite the wall intrigued Rudy, and he smiled when Malachi led in that direction.

By the time Malachi invited him to enter a cell with no door, Rudy had given up mapping the winding corridors that led to the living quarters.

If I hadn't accidentally met Lou, I never would have found him in this labyrinth, even if I stayed here for a month.

Rudy made a face. "Is this cell my room?"

"We don't have guest rooms. Everyone sleeps in similar cells."

Rudy eyed the windowless space and the robe and sandals sitting atop a cot. A simple desk and chair completed the furnishings.

"What about privacy?"

The old monk shrugged. "At least the walls separate us. We use the lavatory just off the great hall because people come and go freely here."

Rudy bit his tongue. *If it's so free, why hasn't Lou freely left? I can't believe he'd choose to stay here. He could live anywhere with his beard, and no one would recognize him, or even be looking for him. What in blazes is going on?*

Brother Malachi interrupted his thoughts. "I see a brother already brought your robe and sandals. Do you want to freshen up in the lavatory and change there? Just follow this corridor to the great hall.

You will see the lavatory opposite the entrance. Our dining room, we call the refectory, is also on that side."

Malachi's suggestion seemed innocuous enough until Rudy finished his shower, only to discover his clothing, cell phone, and car keys were missing. He grabbed the towel with a growl, rapidly scraped it against his skin, and pulled the robe down over his naked body. He jammed his feet into the sandals and grabbed the lavatory door in a death grip. Before he could fling it open, a monk appeared at his side.

Rudy jumped and turned on him. "What did you do with my clothes, cell phone, and car keys?"

"We stored them until you are ready to leave."

"You have no right to store anything of mine. I want them returned to my room immediately." Rudy glared at the monk, who returned his scowl with a smile.

"I apologize. I'm Brother Cornelius, and I should have introduced myself and explained how we do things. No one has access to telephones or computers except the Abbot and Brother Malachi. We observe canonical hours, communal dining, share a common library, and have daily tasks. Since there is no need to communicate with the outside world, surely you can live without your cell phone for a few days." Cornelius deadpanned. "Let us know if you need anything else, and we'll teach you how to live without it."

Rudy ignored the monk's attempt at humor.

I don't care if you're the Angel Gabriel. I already caught you in a lie. If dining is communal, why did the Abbot order that Brother Timothy take the novices in to their lunch? Are Lou and the others in brown robes novices, or something else? I still can't imagine Lou voluntarily entering a monastery. He would take his chances on the outside.

Seeing he was getting nowhere with Cornelius, Rudy yanked open the door and reentered the great hall. He scrutinized the giant fireplace, large enough to hold three standing men, and stared amazed at the artistry of the opposite stained-glass wall. He began mentally drafting his description of the enormous space. The stone walls rising to a high ceiling, the adjoining refectory with its benches and rough-hewn tables, created the perfect backdrop for what a monastery should look like.

If only I had my iPhone for photos.

Rudy pulled a chair from a nearby end table and sat. *Now what happens?*

He focused on his immediate impressions. A few novices and black clad monks, with the same medieval red crosses sewn on the upper half of their robes, trickled into the room. Rudy looked and listened for hints that would shed light on his growing list of questions. He searched for signs of discipline or rank, but found none. One solitary novice, his nose buried in a book, leaned against a wall.

They behave like guys gathering for a Rotary Club luncheon. It seems too casual for a monastery.

Rudy sat, his right leg jiggling impatiently as he waited for Lou. A few monks looked his way and nodded silent greetings, while others stared boldly at him. One monk approached and welcomed him to the monastery just before Rudy saw his friend enter the great hall. He leapt to his feet and waved him over.

Before Rudy could speak, Lou embraced him in a bear hug.

"I don't want you to think I'm not happy to see you. Oh man, I'm overjoyed! But you are in danger here."

"What in tarnation happened, Lou?" Rudy demanded when they disengaged. "You're supposed to be dead. We buried your ashes."

Lou raised an eyebrow. "'Tarnation,' Rudy? You can do better than that."

"Yea, but not here. And they took my clothes, cell phone, and the keys to my Mustang."

"I know." Lou nodded and said, "I thought I was going straight to hell from the execution chamber. Instead, I woke up here. At first, I felt relieved, until the Abbot told me I could not leave, and this was my last stop in life. He called it my last pilgrimage — to heaven or hell. The destination was my choice."

"You believed him? Lou, there's no prison wire or alligator infested moats surrounding this place. No armed guards. You must have tried to escape."

"Me and every other prisoner. They constantly watch you. I thought I had it made once I reached the stone border wall. Little did I know they released the dogs when they saw me walking in that direction. And if the dogs wouldn't take me down, they would. Every one of these pious looking monks is a black belt. And there's no communication with the outside. No phones, TV, computers. Just a library full of religious books and a chapel. We work inside or outside, along with the monks."

"Do you know a conglomerate called Misericordia runs the place?" Rudy said.

"I assumed there was something or somebody overseeing these monasteries, but I didn't have a clue who or what."

Rudy frowned. "'These monasteries?' There are more than one?"

I'd give my left arm for a tape recorder about now, he thought.

"Apparently a string of them and all are under the radar like this one. You're a threat, my reporter friend. You could blow the whole thing wide open."

"So you guys in brown are all prisoners? Were they all supposedly executed?"

When Lou nodded, Rudy jammed his right fist into his left palm. "I knew you wouldn't join a monastery by choice. You must hate it here."

The dinner bell covered Lou's silence. "Right?" Rudy prodded, but did not get an answer.

"Let's go into the refectory. I'll introduce you to some friends and other monks. They'll explain more."

Lou found two spaces across from Predmore, Niebold, and Brother Aaron. Rudy was acutely aware of the eyes resting on him and Lou. No one spoke until Aaron said, "Welcome, Rudy."

Lou said, "I'd like you to meet my oldest friend, Rudy Kowalski. Rudy is one heck of a reporter. He suspected I may still be alive and somehow got onto the monastery grounds. He was with Abbot Anselm and Brother Malachi when I accidentally walked up to them, and when Abbot Anselm saw we knew each other, he invited Rudy to stay for a visit."

Niebold barked a laugh. "A reporter, you say? Is there no end to where the media won't go for a good story?" He shook his head and turned to Rudy. "You and Lou suddenly meeting in front of the Abbot must have been quite a scene. I suppose you think you will have a pleasant reunion with your friend and then go home and write about it."

"That's my plan."

Niebold turned to Lou. "You haven't told him?" He pulled his lips into a sinister sneer. "Oh, let me do the honors."

"No need," Lou said. "I already told Rudy he was a threat to the entire monastery system." Turning to Rudy, he continued. "When I spoke with Abbot Anselm in his office after our reunion, he said he had hoped to give you a brief interview and send you on your way. Everything changed when we recognized each other. Even if you weren't a reporter, you would be a threat to the entire system. He said since you already know too much, there is no reason to hide anything. When I asked him what he planned to do with you, he said he needed to confer with his superior to see if there was a contingency plan that will allow you to leave."

Rudy's jaw dropped. "Allow me to leave? So I'm a prisoner like you?"

Predmore chuckled. "Our bad luck you aren't a female reporter."

Rudy ignored Predmore's remark and watched as a monk placed a plate of golden chicken breast, baked potato, and sesame coated broccoli before him. Lou waited for his friend to process the information.

Aaron said, "Abbot Anselm has given us permission to speak freely with you. Yes, St. Dismas is one of several monasteries established to take in felons the state believes it executed. To do this, the conglomerate you unfortunately discovered has inserted physicians into the penal system dedicated to our mission."

Aaron described the Dismas modus operandi Anselm had explained to Lou on his first day. "Obviously, certain funeral homes work with the organization as well."

Predmore gave a mirthless laugh. "You could say we're the walking undead. We're still prisoners, and no one knows or cares that we exist, and we'll never leave here alive."

Rudy stared, looking from one to the other. When he finally found his voice, he could barely whisper.

"Why would you do such a thing?" he asked Aaron.

"We do not believe in the death penalty, but that there is a better way," Aaron said. "Your friend and the others share our simple lifestyle until our Father calls them home. God willing, by then they will know his love and forgiveness, and have found a peace they never knew before. There is nothing to distract them from encountering God. We simply work, pray, study, and worship together."

Rudy stared at the monk. He shook his head, struggling to find his voice.

"Do you know how many laws your Misericordia is breaking? Kidnapping, for starters."

"Yes, we do," Aaron said. "But your friend would be dead right now if not for us. Instead, you are having dinner with him. There are enough deaths in America."

Niebold interrupted Aaron. "Got it, Reporter Rudy? You're one of us now. They can't let you out because you'll blow their entire operation." He threw his head back and laughed.

Rudy glared at Niebold. "It's easy to make a dead man disappear, not so much a living member of society. Make no mistake, I'll get out."

CHAPTER 35

NO WAY OUT

"Thank you for seeing me," Rudy said as he settled into the chair across from Abbot Anselm's desk. He smiled at the old monk, thinking to start on a friendly footing.

Anselm leaned forward and formed a steeple with his fingers. "Did you and Lou have a pleasant evening? It appears you are close friends. How long have you known each other?"

"Ever since grade school. He's the closest thing to a brother I have, and I can't tell you what it felt like to see him alive."

"You seemed happy to see him, but not surprised. Lou appeared more shocked than you."

"I had some suspicions that he might be alive."

Rudy told how he had watched the hearse carrying Lou's body first stop at St. Dismas and how he discovered the funeral director had lied about cremation services at the monastery.

"Those were the first suspicions I had about Lou's execution and St. Dismas. Lou and the others told me you would keep me from leaving. That's ridiculous, of course."

He set his jaw and looked into the monk's eyes. As the seconds ticked by, Rudy felt his heart rate speed up.

This can't be real. No Abbot in the 21st century can keep me a prisoner.

He imagined how frantic Kathy would be, and his stomach sank at the thought of Gabe and Lisa growing up without him. No way!

Abbot Anselm spoke, his words measured.

"You had no right to lie your way into this monastery. Yes, I understand you have a life and a family you love, and you want to return to them. Frankly, I would like to be rid of you, but I have a problem. I allowed you to visit with Lou because when you recognized each other, I knew you would soon have enough information to put the remaining pieces of your puzzle together. Therefore, there was no reason to keep you and Lou separate, but you are a threat to our existence, and we cannot allow that. So here is the truth for which you foolishly risked so much."

Abbot Anselm's explanation about the Dismas system confirmed what others told Rudy.

"If you made our operations public, we could no longer carry out our mission. I am in contact with the Misericordia Board of Directors, and until we know what to do with you, you will remain on the grounds. I assume Lou told you about our constant surveillance and the impossibility of escaping. We will inform you of the Board's decision as soon as we receive it. Meanwhile, because of our constant observation, you may go where you wish and enjoy what little comforts we have."

Rudy sat wide-eyed, blood draining from his face. *Surely, the board will confirm the Abbot can't keep me here forever.*

He took a deep breath and forced himself into his reporter mode.

"How long has this system been running?"

"I believe for the last fifteen years."

"And there has never been a breach?"

"Not that I know of."

"No one ever leaked anything? Where do your monks come from? How do you recruit them?"

"They are men of strong faith to begin with and are pre-selected based on rigorous standards before we approach them to be monks in the Dismas system. I'm told once approached, no one refused to enter or pledge their silence."

"They actually agree to this?"

"Compared to some ways of living, it's a good life."

Rudy shook his head at the Abbot's vague answer and pressed his lips into a fine line. After a moment's silence, he tried another approach.

"You claim to be vested in bringing sinners to repentance and redemption. You believe you are serving God, so I ask you, does serving a holy God involve kidnapping? And when my wife pounds on your gate, demanding to know where I am, are you going to add lies to your list of sins? If you keep me a prisoner, you will deny the very Scripture you read every day. Here's a challenge to your faith. I return to my family, write my article, and you trust God to direct the outcome. Do you have enough faith for that, Abbot?"

Rudy noticed Anselm's posture stiffen and his eyes widen. *Never thought of it that way, did you. Tell that to your Misericordia bunch.*

Rudy abruptly stood, shoving his chair back. "I expect to leave these grounds by day after tomorrow at the latest. See that you make that clear to your organization's board."

After meeting with the Abbot, Rudy's day flowed with the slow, steady rhythm of monastic life. He and Lou worked side by side on the farm and conversed with the monks and other prisoners during breakfast and lunch. He hoped his memory would serve him well, since he lacked a recorder or writing material to capture his impressions.

The so-called "residents'" peaceful demeanors struck Rudy as odd. Except for the one called Niebold, these prisoners appeared to care about each other. He saw no conflict or jockeying for power or status. Rudy struggled to understand the dynamics in this bizarre place. *Could the monks be what the Abbot claimed?*

"In any other circumstance, I would have enjoyed that service. I haven't heard Gregorian chant since second grade," Rudy said as he and Lou exited the chapel that evening after Compline.

Lou gave Rudy a rueful smile. "Seems like a lifetime ago, my friend."

Suddenly, he grasped Rudy's arm and suggested they return to the chapel. "I've been thinking. Let's talk for a moment."

Once settled in the back pew, they ignored the monk kneeling opposite them, head lowered, and apparently engrossed in prayer.

"Listen, Rudy. I believe them when they say the only reason they're keeping you here is because you could blow this thing wide open. Think about it. If it all came out, the authorities would execute us prisoners for real now. You don't know what it feels like to be strapped down, helpless, while they run a lethal drug into your body. It terrified me, Rudy. Going through that again would kill me." He smiled at his own pun. "Besides, the monks would face charges of kidnapping. It's true that at first I hated them for locking me up for the rest of my life, but I must admit, they've done me no harm. I'm finding some peace for the first time since Becky died. This God I've given lip service to all my life is becoming real to me. I owe it to these monks, and I don't want to see them serving time in jail."

"Are you telling me you prefer to remain a captive behind this heap of stones? To work like a peasant all your life? Most of all, you can't mean I should remain locked up, too. Are you nuts, Lou?"

"Of course not. I'd like to live free if I could. And if, by some miracle, I had the chance, I'd jump at it. But I think you could get out of here if you promise you will keep St. Dismas' secret. I believe the Abbot would grab at any chance to let you out if he could trust your silence. Even to him, it's obvious you don't belong here."

Rudy closed his eyes and thought about his friend's suggestion. *If I remain silent, I will be an accomplice to kidnapping. This is the biggest scoop of my life. If I hang tough, I will get out and have an article to skyrocket my career. I'll escape somehow, even if it takes Kathy raising a ruckus.* He smiled at the image of his determined wife on a rescue rampage.

"Kathy, her uncle Bishop Keenan, heck, even the police, will knock down the gates. I can get out without selling my soul."

"Good. Then you can write about my actual execution," Lou said.

"Aw Lou, that's a low blow. I don't want you, or anybody, executed. Maybe I can strike a deal with the courts for my information — my evidence for commuted or reduced sentencing, a kinder justice."

"Justice? Let me tell you about justice. In my determination to find justice for Becky, I ignored Sally's pain and torpedoed a marriage that needed tending. I was so bent on punishing Beauregard Abbington, I couldn't mourn Becky's death. I failed to trust God, to love my wife, and won nothing for the sake of justice. Don't make the same mistake I did. Your family is too important.

"Besides, Abbot Anselm knows that Kathy, even the entire town by now, is aware you entered here for an interview. He'll just lie and tell them you left, and he doesn't know where you went from here. They can search the place all they want. This is a rabbit's warren of corridors, cells, rooms, towers, sheds, and barns. They'll move you and your car like chess pieces, one step ahead or behind where the authorities check. No one will find you, Rudy. For Kathy's sake, promise to keep your mouth shut, get out of here, and let God sort it out."

Rudy studied his friend. *Where did this person come from? When did he start trusting God for anything?*

"Oh Lou," Rudy moaned. He ached to enfold Kathy in his arms, to hold his children close to his heart.

CHAPTER 36

INFERNO

When he noticed Malachi standing in the doorway to his office the next morning, Abbot Anselm raised his hands and thrust his palms forward as if to stop him. The monk entered anyway.

"Don't bother, Malachi. I know what you're going to say. However, the situation is untenable. Knowing what he does, we cannot release the man right now. God knows I want him out of here, and I'm hoping the Board of Directors finds a solution."

Malachi saw beyond the raised hands to the Abbot's face and read the pain etched around his eyes and mouth. Gingerly, he approached.

"I understand what's at stake. But they must realize we cannot hold a man against his will. He's innocent."

"Not so much. Not that we're so innocent, mind you, but he lied his way in here, and now he must deal with the consequences, just as *we* must. By the way, did we destroy his cell phone?"

"Yes, Brother Cornelius drowned the thing in water, so his GPS can't give away his location."

"Be sure that Mustang is hidden as well."

Malachi nodded and stepped closer. "I think Rudy's feelings interfered with his professionalism, clouding his judgment. Apparently, he never accepted Lou's death, and what little he discovered about Misericordia was enough to rouse his curiosity. Finding his friend alive, and discovering what we do, is overwhelming right now. I believe, in time, we will neutralize the potential damage. The Board of Directors has enough influence with the media to kill any article he may write. It will never see the light of day."

Anselm sighed. "You're probably right, but we can't afford to risk it."

He pointed Malachi to the chair opposite his desk and continued after the monk settled across from him.

"We need to proceed cautiously. What will buy his silence? What can I offer the directors so they will approve his release?"

Malachi raised his index finger. "Brother Joseph remained in chapel after Compline last evening. He said Rudy and Lou returned to the chapel after everyone had left. He told me he overheard Lou advising Rudy to keep the monastery's secret for the sake of his family, and surprisingly, for our sakes."

Anselm leaned forward. "Lou Skalney advocated for us? Unbelievable. What did he say?"

"Evidently, he warned Rudy that the state would successfully execute him and the other prisoners this time, and we monks could face kidnapping charges for holding Rudy and our residents against their will. Apparently, he's developed enough regard for us that he'd like to spare us that."

Anselm shook his head in astonishment. "Well, well. I hope so. Kidnapping charges would be the least of our worries if Rudy's story ran."

Malachi continued, "I'm hoping we can convince Rudy to agree to kill the story for his release."

Anselm frowned. "When I spoke with the Board of Directors yesterday, they were adamant we couldn't release him. I begged them to reconsider, and they agreed to delay their final decision for a few days. Now I may have a bargaining chip. Can you work fast?"

"With God's help. The man is stubborn. I'm told he said he thought he could manage some sort of deal so he could publish the story and get mercy for us from the courts at the same time."

Anselm grunted. "He's too cocky by half. Pride goeth before the fall. His fall is one thing. Our fall is another. Do your best."

As the prisoners assigned to the farm gathered after morning chapel, Malachi pulled Lou and Rudy aside.

"We three will lunch outside today, privately. I want to discuss something with you. Meanwhile, we have much to harvest, so Niebold will join us in our labors."

"What's Niebold's deal?" Rudy asked Lou as they knelt before a bed of prolific bean plants. Lou shared Niebold's story while they ferreted out each ripe bean. He wished he could bottle the moment. Sharing work with Rudy under the hot Texas sun took him back to their school days when anything they were doing was more fun because they were doing it together. Rudy's next comment brought Lou back to the present.

"I know a lawyer, big name guy, used to clerk for a Supreme Court justice. He owes me a favor or two and I'm sure he has enough clout to get you guys a deal. Then I can write my story."

Lou opened his mouth to respond when Brother Malachi approached with a pair of empty pails. They had been so absorbed in their conversation and work, they failed to notice their buckets were almost full. Just as the old monk was about to exchange them, he looked up and frowned. Lou noticed Brother Malachi's gesture and turned to see what had caught his eye.

He had heard Malachi assign Brother Timothy to Niebold that morning. What was Timothy doing, walking alone toward the shed?

"Brother Timothy, where is Niebold?" Malachi called out to him.

Timothy turned and walked toward them.

"It's all right. Niebold's in the barn on his knees. He said he wanted to pray. Can you imagine? Kurt Niebold finally praying."

Lou shot a look at Malachi and the two of them raced to the barn, leaving Timothy and Rudy behind.

Lou grasped the barn's door frame to stop his forward momentum. Brother Malachi almost ran into him before he too stopped. The overwhelming stench of gas fumes poured from the entrance.

Inside, Niebold stood before a pile of gasoline soaked straw as it burst into flame. "How?" Lou shouted.

Niebold turned to them. His head, without his glasses, looked like a skull with cavernous eye sockets.

Lou saw where Niebold had flung the gasoline on the walls and floor. The barn would be engulfed in flames within minutes. Malachi stepped forward to grab Niebold, but Lou shot a restraining arm against him.

Suddenly, flames from the straw whooshed up the wall and tickled the roof with orange fingers. Another line of fire snaked its way from the flaming straw to where Niebold stood. In a flash, he became a human torch. Nothing would erase Lou's memory of Kurt Niebold shrieking in agony as fire consumed him.

Instantly, the barn was an inferno. They were helpless. Lou and Malachi fled toward the monastery. Breathless, Malachi pulled the cell phone from his pocket and called 911.

Monks and prisoners ran toward the barn, keeping a wary distance. They watched as the conflagration engulfed the old structure. One monk attached a hose to the faucet near the monastery door, but its weak stream of water disappeared impotently into the blaze.

Everything after that happened at lightning speed. Abbot Anselm appeared beside Malachi and Lou.

"I saw the flames from my office and called 911. What happened?"

"I called too," Malachi replied. "Niebold must have used his glasses and a ray of sunlight through the barn window to ignite the straw. We apparently had a container of gasoline left there from months ago. I thought we removed them all, but I wouldn't put it past Niebold to have squirreled one away. He splashed gasoline all over the barn."

"Who did you assign to him today?"

"Brother Timothy."

Anselm shook his head and heaved a sigh. Quickly, the Abbot took control.

"Malachi, gather each resident and Rudy into my office. Have a brother guard them to keep them far from the fire. Where did you hide Rudy's car?"

"In the abandoned shed on the far edge of the monastery's grounds."

"Good. Are there dogs in the kennel?"

Malachi sucked in his breath. "Probably a few. Caesar and Sargan for sure."

"They should be safe for a while, as long as the fire keeps to the barn. If it travels to the monastery …" Anselm let his sentence trail. "We'll need to release them, just in case. Assign monks to herd the other animals where they will be safe."

Malachi raced to carry out his orders, giving lie to his age. Lou followed.

The fire's roar grew louder. Acrid smoke filled the bystanders' nostrils. When the wind changed and drove the gray cloud closer, some began to cough. Brothers Joseph and Cornelius took off after Malachi, shouting orders to the others. Aaron ran toward the gate in time to fling it open to a police cruiser and an ambulance. Lou heard more sirens wailing and tapped Malachi's shoulder.

Lou shouted to Malachi. "The dogs!"

"What?" Malachi cupped his ear with his hand.

"The dogs!" Lou repeated over the sirens and crackling fire. "I'll let them out."

"No, you go into Abbot's office with the other residents. I'll assign…" But Lou turned and ran toward the kennels. When he briefly glanced back, he saw Malachi watching him, but the old monk soon turned away.

Lou gave the barn a wide berth, heading toward the perimeter of the field surrounding it, and worked his way to the land that lay on its far side. He felt heat pouring from the flames, even from this distance. He coughed and struggled to catch his breath. Panting, he bent, hands on knees, and pulled in great gasps of air. It was sizzling hot. Sweat poured from his forehead and into his eyes. He wiped his face best as he could with the sleeve of his robe.

By now, more sirens added to the cacophony. Lou saw three fire trucks pull up to the inferno. He knew he should keep running to the kennels, but the fire looked limited to the barn and the kennels were situated around the monastery's far corner. Lou had a few seconds to watch one firefighter jump down from the ladder truck and approach Abbot Anselm. He could see the Abbot speaking and pointing to the gathered monks and the barn. The firefighter, whom Lou assumed was the Fire Chief, spoke into a box on his shoulder. Anselm walked toward the gathered monks.

I'll bet the Chief's calling for mutual aid. Three trucks aren't enough for this fire.

Lou knew firefighters called the long metal arm protruding from the second truck's roof a deck gun monitor. It immediately pumped water onto the flaming barn. Then, what looked like a huge inflatable swimming pool appeared between the truck pumping water and the third truck, which filled the pool with water. Firefighters pulled hoses from the side of the truck that sucked up the pooled water and pumped it through the hoses and the deck gun monitor. They used the hoses to pour a constant stream onto the monastery's roof, shed, and walls.

Barn's a loss. Save the monastery. Get to the kennels and free the hounds.

He found the dogs out of their cages, frantically barking and running back and forth within the yard's enclosure. To get them farther away from the building, he threw the gate open and tried to herd them toward the sheep's grazing area. They formed a pack and ran away from the fire and toward the far perimeter, ignoring Lou's shouts and arm gestures. He shrugged, not having a clue how to herd dogs, anyway.

They'll have to take care of themselves.

As he re-traced his steps, Lou stopped short. More trucks, like the one that deposited water into that pool, were pulling up. *Tenders, that's what they're called. More tenders for the pumper truck. Mutual aid has arrived.*

Controlled bedlam reigned. Police left their cruisers, emergency lights still flashing. Monks clustered at the edge of the sheep-grazing field. An officer was speaking with Abbot Anselm, while others formed a protective barrier between the monks and the barn area. EMTs at the ready leaned against their ambulance with nothing to do. Niebold was now a charred hulk.

Without warning, the east wall of the barn collapsed inward, shooting fireworks into the sky. The deck gun monitor swerved over the gaping hole the fallen wall had created and doused the area. The fire was getting its last licks from what was once a barn.

Firefighters shouted orders over the fire's roar as they fought the blaze while protecting the monastery and its outbuildings. Lou tried to stay out of people's way while keeping his distance from the fire. He knew he was supposed to go to Abbot's office with the rest of the prisoners, but the tenders, now shuttling back and forth from the street and the barn, fascinated him. He drew closer to the fire trucks, curious as a ten-year-old.

"Watch out!" a firefighter shouted to Lou, who barely jumped out of the way in time to avoid an on-coming tender. Suddenly, he found himself sandwiched between what he thought of as a tender shuttle. As he walked toward the front entrance to the monastery, he saw tenders entering the monastery grounds on his left, and on his right, others were exiting to refill at the fire hydrant a mile down the road. Walking hidden between the massive trucks coming and going, an astounding thought struck him.

I think I can walk out of here, right under Aaron's nose. He'd never see me between these trucks if I pace myself exactly right. Maybe I can help Rudy if I can get out of here. God help me, and help Rudy.

Feeling as if he were in a dream, Lou put one foot ahead of another, expecting Aaron to stop him at any moment. Nothing happened. Doubting the possibility of success, yet still moving forward, he prayed for freedom and for his friend. He even prayed for the monastery and its monks. His mind was never more focused.

He walked through the gate. Amazed, he tentatively took his first step into freedom.

After a last look at St. Dismas Monastery, Lou Skalney disappeared into a thicket of trees across the street.

PART V

METAMORPHOSIS

CHAPTER 37

GOD AND THE GOOD SAMARITAN

Lou moved on autopilot, fueled by adrenaline. He tore through foliage and ran along the edges of farmers' fields to distance himself from the monastery, pumping his legs until muscle fatigue overcame him. He needed to rest and think.

Dear God, what am I doing? Didn't plan this. Don't know what to do next. Can't stop now. Please help me!

Knowing his robe would draw attention, he slowed as he walked along the two-lane road, as if ambling along on a holy errand. Lou looked at the sky to gage the time of day. How long had he been on the run since the fire started? It was before lunch when Niebold set everything off. So maybe it was about one or two?

"Need a lift, Padre?"

Lou startled. He had not heard the truck that pulled to a stop beside him. The driver looked to be well past his prime, with tanned, wrinkled skin covering a face shaded by his stained and crumpled Stetson. A blue-beaded Rosary hung from the rear-view mirror. Lou considered his options while the truck idled. He could continue walking to God-knows-where for how many hours or accept a ride to civilization. His body told him it was a no-brainer.

"Thanks. I'd appreciate it," he said, opening the passenger door and climbing up and into the cab. He flashed what he hoped was a smile at the driver. "It's way too hot for a long walk," Lou said, wiping his forehead.

"Well, that robe can't help. Name's Jeb."

"Physical mortification is good for the soul, Jeb."

"You believe that?"

"Could fool me, today."

"Got that right, Padre. Where you off to?"

"Where are you headed?"

"Going to pick up the interstate just outside of Arkdale. It's about fifty miles east. I can let you off anywhere between here and there."

"Then I'm going to Arkdale, if that's okay with you."

When Jeb shot him a quizzical look, Lou realized his error. I must sound aimless to him, and an aimless monk won't square with a Catholic. Not wanting to raise questions, he realized he'd better come up with a plausible story, and fast.

"I belong to a mendicant order," he said, assuming Jeb would know the church's term for monks who beg for a living while they do good works and pray. "I trust the Lord to lead me to where he wants me to labor. Like the early Apostles, we travel only with the clothes on our backs, trusting in God's provision. It seems the good Lord has Arkdale in mind for me. What kind of town is it?"

Jeb smiled.

Good, he bought it.

"Well, Padre, it's a large town trying to be a city. There's a plant that makes air conditioners, an outlet for farm equipment, and they've got a factory making those new solar panels. Good shopping and some nice restaurants. Up and coming for a big town. Getting more itinerants now, and those poor devils hooked on drugs." He snorted. "You'll have your work cut out for you if you stay there."

Lou turned to gaze out the passenger window and considered his options. Putting fifty miles between him and the monastery was good.

Would the Abbot send someone to silence me permanently? Someone from Misericordia who would not have the scruples a monk would? The mendicant monk story worked with Jeb, but what I don't know about real Catholic monks could fill a book.

"Like music?" Jeb's question interrupted Lou's thoughts. Before he could answer, Johnny Cash's *Folsom Prison Blues* filled the cab.

Lou smiled. "Perfect selection, Jeb."

Grateful Jeb was a man of few words, Lou gazed out the passenger window as the truck rolled through the Texas landscape. He pulled a deep breath into his lungs and slowly released it, breathing freely at last. Free from the monastery, free from the guilt and death wish he had carried for so long. Seeing houses, fields, stores, and everyday life filled him with so much joy he felt lighter, although he knew he faced roadblocks. He had no idea where he would sleep, how he would find food, how he would keep from being discovered. But for now, Lou Skalney savored this longed-for moment. But it was short lived.

A lone monk suddenly turning up in the middle of town will surely raise questions. I'd better come up with a cover story pronto. But I never could lie well.

Rudy used to tease him. "It's because you lack imagination, Lou. Just think up a story and go with it."

"Easy for you to say."

"Hey, I don't lie." Rudy had grinned at him. "I just spin yarns."

Rudy was a writer in the making, even back then. I'll say as little as I can get away with, but first, I need clothes and food. I stick out like a sore thumb in this robe.

He startled out of his reverie when Jeb announced they had arrived in Arkdale.

"Already?"

Lou studied the street. It was typical Americana. Norman Rockwell style two-story homes, girded by white-railed porches holding either rockers or a bounty of toys, lined the main drag.

It seemed a lifetime ago since he had seen something as pedestrian, and satisfying, as a home. He yearned to walk into one place that held his world together, where everything in it reflected his choices, not those of an authority figure. He had not realized how much he missed his past.

Lou stifled a moan. After Becky's death, he had looked down on Sally's faith, on her friends, who had cried and prayed with her. Oh, he knew it all. He would take care of the business God had not. Focused on obtaining justice, he ignored Sally, and now he had nothing.

If only I could go back and re-live those days. I swear things would be different. If she did what she said, Sally's living in Dallas. What if I go there and find her? The authorities aren't looking for me because I'm dead to them, and the monastery erased my history. Maybe she would keep my secret and we could begin again. I could get a fake identity. Impossible. Or is it?

Jeb brought Skalney back to reality when he pulled into the Shell gas station just before the interstate.

"I can't thank you enough, Jeb. I wish I could give you something for your gas at least, but…" He let the sentence trail off and shrugged. Lou extended his hand in thanks before opening the passenger door.

Instead of shaking it, Jeb reached into his pocket and tucked a rolled bill into his passenger's palm. Lou looked down and blinked away tears of gratitude.

"You don't have to. I just appreciate the lift."

"No, take it, Padre. And pray for me, will you?"

"Certainly. And thank you. God speed."

It was not until the truck's taillights disappeared into the distance that Lou opened his hand. Fifty dollars. "Thank you, God," he said, not caring who heard him.

Ignoring quizzical glances from the other two drivers working the pumps, he began the walk toward the heart of what appeared to be Arkdale's business section. Lou noted McDonald's arches, fast food being all he could afford. Feeling the late afternoon heat boring through his robe, his greatest need right now was civilian clothes. He scanned the street and saw only small specialty shops and businesses, but several blocks later, he came to a busy intersection. If the increased traffic was from nearby parking lots, he hoped that meant shopping malls. He turned right off the main thoroughfare and grinned.

"Ah, Wal-Mart, 'where America shops,' as they say," directing his remark to no one.

Soon, a man past middle age, in dire need of a shave and wearing jeans and a plaid shirt, strode out of the store. He carried a large bag filled with a thick brown monk's robe. Lou savored the feel of cotton brushing against his skin, the caress of fabric along his legs. It had been a long time since he wore that universal American outfit, and it felt good.

Now for a Big Mac and greasy fries. I wonder if they'll taste as good as I remember.

An hour later, he turned the paper that had held his hamburger into a ball and dropped it into the empty French-fry container. It tasted even better than he expected, and he fought the urge to buy another. Instead, he took a sip of cold coffee and gazed at the twilight gathering outside the brightly lit dining area. Lou had exactly five dollars and twenty-three cents left and no idea what to do next. He knew he could not stay in McDonalds all night and shuddered. He had no choice but to find somewhere under that rising moon where he could spend the night without being attacked or arrested.

Carrying his robe-filled bag, Lou stepped into the semi-darkness. He headed toward the intersection that had led him to Wal-Mart, but after a half-hour realized he must have missed a turn. Now he saw larger homes, windows glowing with welcoming yellow lights. They sat recessed from the street, some surrounded by privacy fences. Others sat on property dotted with trees, bushes, and flower beds. He toyed with the idea to nestle into a remote corner of one of these high-priced lots.

It beats sleeping on the street. But what will I do if I'm discovered? They would call the police for sure.

Lou prayed as he continued his solitary walk. He reminded God how he parted the Red Sea so his people could escape Pharaoh, and how Jesus said a bird does not fall from the sky without the Father knowing it. People were more important than birds.

I need you now, Lord. I need a place to sleep and help to decide what to do next. You know I didn't plan this escape. I can't go back and don't know how to go forward. God, help me. And Rudy. Please help us.

Lou decided to trust God heard his prayer and there would be some sort of answer. His confidence remained even after walking another half-hour. He was determined to hang in there until God made his move. As the houses grew sparse, the business district long behind him, he realized if he did not retrace his steps, he would soon be in the country again. *Perhaps I would be better off in the woods or a field, away from prying eyes.*

Then, on his left, he saw a church steeple poking the night sky. As he drew closer to the white clapboard church, he laughed aloud as he read the lit sign on the front lawn.

Saint Louis Roman Catholic Church

Daily Mass 8 AM

Sunday Masses 9 AM and 11 AM

Confessions Saturday 4 PM—6 PM

You have got to be kidding. This kind of stuff doesn't happen. My name? Okay, God, if it's really you, the front door will be unlocked. Fat chance.

His heart raced. Looking around to be sure no one was about, Lou kept to the shadows as he made his way to the front door.

Will it count as God's action if the front is locked, but I get in through a side door or a window?

By now, he was so caught up in the scenario of God taking over, Lou felt as if he were in one of those out-of-body-experiences, except he was very much in his body.

I can walk away, but no way am I going to.

Right now, knowing was more important than sleeping. With a last glance to reassure himself that he was alone, he sprinted up the steps, grabbed the door handle and pulled so hard he almost fell backward when it swung open. Regaining his balance, he quickly slipped inside. Lou leaned against the closed door while his eyes acclimated to the dim vestibule.

Did God do this? The name of the church, the unlocked door, can't all be coincidences.

He closed his eyes and whispered, "Thank you."

A moment later, he noticed a rack holding bulletins and various booklets — "Christian Marriage," "Overcoming Habits and Addictions," — standing to his right. Steps leading to what he assumed was the choir loft rose on his left. He walked toward the closed double doors that faced him. Finding them locked, he returned to the steps and climbed.

He guessed right. The floor at the top of the stairs creaked with each step as he walked toward the organ. He looked down at the altar bathed in dim lights glowing from the vaulted ceiling above it. To the right of the altar, extinguished vigil lights awaited re-lighting by hopeful parishioners. The stocky little candles stood in tiers within a metal stand, which Lou knew from his childhood, held an opening for coins from the faithful.

Don't even think it.

The choir could sit when not singing, because there were four rows of padded benches. He smiled and stretched out on the lowest one, using his folded robe as a pillow. Lou crossed his arms and thanked God for taking over and asked him to continue at the helm because he had not a clue about what to do in the morning.

Pretty impressive how...

He fell asleep.

CHAPTER 38

MOVING FORWARD

W hen Lou rolled over in his sleep, the fall from the narrow bench smashed his face onto the choir loft's hardwood floor, jammed his shoulder against the bench leg and knocked the wind out of him. Now wide-eyed, in pain, and stifling a curse, he fixated on the wad of pink gum attached to the bench's underside until the aching subsided. Lou pulled himself to a kneeling position and looked up at the small window on the loft's back wall to see that night had surrendered to bright morning. He gingerly tested his right arm's range of motion, and thankfully, it was normal. Lou crawled to the loft's railing and peered down at the nave, which was filled with empty pews on either side of a wide center aisle.

What time is it? This is Tuesday, so daily Mass should start soon, unless I slept through it. No, I would have heard it. By now, maybe someone unlocked the inner doors.

Lou stuffed his robe back into the Wal-Mart bag and descended the stairs to the vestibule. He jiggled the doors opening to the nave and found them unlocked.

That means someone else is here, maybe the sexton or priest. This would be a good time to sneak out, but Mass will probably begin any minute, and it would raise questions if people saw a stranger leaving now.

Just then, the outer door opened, and two women entered, engrossed in conversation, until they noticed the stranger. They nodded at Lou, and he opened the inner door for them. The outer door opened again, and an elderly man walked toward him, as if he would follow Lou into the nave. Lou had no choice but to join the parishioners and slipped into the end of an empty pew several feet behind the small group. He looked up and noticed a stained-glass window, which showed a man he assumed was St. Louis.

When he heard more people entering the nave, he buried his head deep into arms he'd quickly draped over the back of the seat before him. He held his breath, looking like a penitent deep in prayer and not to be disturbed. When he heard the opening words of the Mass, Lou let out a slow breath and looked at the altar.

Might as well pray for a good cover story. I'm going to need it soon.

Lou's relief when the others ignored him after Mass evaporated when the priest stepped down from the sanctuary. He held his breath as the man approached him, hand outstretched in welcome.

"Hello. I'm Father Don Tomzak, but everyone calls me 'Father Don' or 'FT.' Take your pick. Welcome to Saint Louis Parish. It's good to see a new face at Mass."

Lou stood, knocking the Wal-Mart bag onto the kneeler, and shook the priest's hand. It felt hard and calloused, like his own at one time. Father Don was an older man, with searching hazel eyes that locked onto him, making him squirm under the man's steady gaze.

"Hi, Father. I just arrived here yesterday. Name's Lou, Lou Sca-Scanlon. It's nice to meet you."

When the priest nodded and lifted the shopping bag from the kneeler, the brown monk's robe slid out and draped itself over his foot. He cocked his head and silently awaited an explanation.

"Yea, about that. I left the monastery and have all of five dollars and change to my name. I'm looking for work and a place to stay."

Can't get too fouled up with the truth. Less said, the better. Don't lie well, anyway.

"What monastery?"

"St. Dismas. It's fifty miles west of here."

"I think I heard something about it. Kind of low profile, right?"

Lou nodded. "Cloistered."

"Ah yes, that would explain it. What did you do at the monastery?"

"I mostly worked on its farm. I was in construction before I entered."

"And you say you're looking for a place to stay and need to find work?"

Lou nodded, hoping the priest might leave his questioning at that. Father Don frowned and looked Lou in the eyes, and after what seemed forever, smiled.

"Did some construction work in my day, too," the priest said. "Still do, on and off. One of our parishioners, Manny Vazquez, is putting together a homeless shelter for men downtown. He's bought the space, but it needs work, and I've been helping him when I can. I'll introduce him to you. You could be a big help to both of us."

Lou recalled his prayer for help when he had been wandering in the night hours ago. God had answered with more than he could have imagined. He smiled, and said, "Thank you, Father."

CHAPTER 39

CASE CLOSED

Father Tomzak parked his Toyota in front of the homeless shelter-to-be, which already bore the sign "The Good Samaritan." With the carved date "1943" barely legible on its cornerstone, Lou wondered what its original purpose had been. Store? Office? Bar? Since it took up a large corner lot, he estimated it should have enough square footage for its new life as a shelter.

The priest opened the door, stepped inside, and called, "Anyone here?"

"Yo," a voice echoed from the rear.

Lou followed Father Don into a room that could hold enough tables and chairs to serve at least 50 people. Smells of fresh paint mingled with sawdust took Lou back to his workdays, and he closed his eyes, inhaling deeply.

Could this be my future if I somehow get Rudy free? Will I ever return to my old life?

Footsteps brought Lou to the present. The man walking toward them was short and stocky, with a mass of black, curly hair surrounding a face etched with lines that hinted at hard times.

After introductions, Manny Vazquez led them to what he called his office, now a space surrounded by studs awaiting drywall. It held a desk and a few chairs, while building blueprints, numerous lists, and the remnants of a taco cluttered the desktop. Lou's stomach rumbled.

Once everyone settled in chairs, Manny leaned back and regarded Lou for several seconds. Lou returned his gaze until the man finally spoke.

"You sit here in the only clothes you own, carrying a Wal-Mart bag FT told me holds a monk's robe. You gotta know that raises questions. If you left the monastery properly, either your friends or family would have picked you up, or you would have planned for yourself ahead of time. I suspect you simply walked away, and that raises more questions. Are you running from something? Do you have any plans beyond today and tomorrow? Are you even who you say you are?

"I've worked with a lot of homeless people. It would surprise you how many of them once lived the typical American life — family, home, work. Then something happened, either addiction, layoff, losing the home or family, illness, you name it. Everyone has a story, so what's yours?"

Lou looked down at his sandals and told as much of the truth he could.

"You're right. I once had a home and family, but lost everything. And I walked away from St. Dismas because my best friend needs help desperately right now. I can't go into the details, and I haven't figured out what to do yet. Whatever I do, I can't do it from inside the monastery. I decided, because Rudy's situation is so desperate, it was better to ask forgiveness later than permission now." Lou shrugged and looked directly into Manny's eyes. "So I just walked away."

"Is your name really Lou Scanlon?"

Boy, you get right down to it, don't you.

Something in him respected that, so he answered truthfully, then held his breath.

"Lou, yes. Scanlon, no. Let's leave it at that."

"Are you running from the law?"

"No."

"What are you running from?"

"The monastery, for now."

"How long do you think it will take to save your friend once you decide whatever it is you must do?"

"Days. A few weeks at the most."

"Then what?"

"I honestly don't know."

The three sat silently for several seconds. Lou prayed. *Please God, let him trust me enough to give me the break I need.* Finally, Manny looked at FT, who gave an almost imperceptible nod.

"FT and I go back a long way, so I trust his judgement. God knows I need all the help I can get, and if you have the skills I need, I can offer you a place to sleep and food, and that's it. All we have to work with is donations, so we need to do as much as we can."

Lou nodded and coughed, his whispered "thank you" barely audible.

"Okay then," Manny said as he stood. "Let me show you what will pass as your sleeping quarters."

Abbot Anselm rolled his eyes, pressed the speaker icon, and slid his cell phone to the center of his desk. Brother Malachi leaned forward, turning his ear toward the phone. The old monk need not have bothered, because Director Muller's voice was forceful.

"To recap your report, Abbot, in the last four days, a reporter gained entrance to the monastery, where he remains as we speak. A resident, now deceased, set fire to your barn, and another resident, the reporter's friend, simply walked away during the confusion from the fire. Is there anything else?"

Anselm ignored the man's tone. "Yes. The arson squad investigated the fire yesterday, and a detective will arrive this afternoon, supposedly to tie up loose ends."

He locked eyes with Malachi and waited for an explosion of words from the director. Instead, Muller responded, "Of course. That's to be expected. I'm on the way now with the paperwork to support our protocol, which I assume you followed."

"Yes. I identified him as Curtiss N-e-e-b-o-l-d-t," Abbot said, giving Kurt Niebold's name the alternate spelling.

"Excellent. I'm bringing the paperwork to verify that identity. Hopefully, the alternate spelling, plus the paperwork, will block a computer match to Niebold's trial and execution. Pray that will be enough verification to satisfy them, and they'll have no reason to test the remains' DNA. That would bring us down, so I hope our relationship with certain county officials will prevent that. Meanwhile, keep the residents, and that reporter, away from the authorities, even if you have to lock them in the monastery's underground storerooms."

Four hours later, Director Muller and the Abbot met with Detective Roberts in Anselm's office. After Abbot Anselm requested a monk bring them coffee, Muller immediately addressed the investigator, making it clear to Anselm that his role in this meeting would be minor. That was fine with Anselm.

"As the President of the Board of Directors for the St. Dismas Monastery System, I appreciate your swift investigation, so we can heal from this unfortunate disaster. I'm here to work with Abbot Anselm to answer any questions you may have. We hope to lay Brother Curtiss to rest soon."

Roberts gave a perfunctory smile. "Our investigation so far confirms Abbot Anselm's description of events. Obviously, your monk died because of the fire, but the question remains why he used gasoline as an accelerant and lit the fire while he was still in the barn. Why did he commit suicide? Did he leave a note? Did you notice any change in his behavior recently?"

All eyes turned to Anselm, who took a moment to answer. "There was no note, and Curtiss has always been a loner. While cordial, he rarely smiled and spent most of his free time by himself. Recent change in behavior? He may have been more quiet than usual, but none of the monks mentioned any conversations with him that would raise a red flag."

"How long has he been a monk here?"

Muller opened a manila folder and scanned the first page before answering Detective Roberts.

"Curtiss arrived almost five years ago. According to the information he provided, his parents were deceased, and he had no siblings, family, or friends to notify in case of illness or death. He noted he was an independent accountant in Ohio until his business closed. Curtiss joined us a year later."

Muller handed Roberts the folder that held only a few pages. Roberts leafed through them and looked up.

"Did you verify any of this information?"

"It's our policy to accept a novice's CV at face value. By the time they arrive here, they're what we call seekers, and are ready to embrace a contemplative life. Other than Abbot Anselm's and Brother Malachi's cell phones, there's no contact with the outside world, and we have no television or internet. We limit access to music and reading to the hymns sung at prayer services and to the library, which holds only faith-based non-fiction. There's nothing of worldly value here, so we assume our candidates are sincere in their wish to deepen their relationship with God."

Roberts nodded and handed the folder to Muller. "We'll need a copy of this for our records."

"Of course," Muller said and asked how soon they could inter Curtiss.

"You should receive his remains no later than next week, if not sooner."

"It seems straightforward," Anselm interjected, hoping the inspector would agree. *Would this satisfy the authorities so they would not pursue the evidence any further?* Hope flickered when Roberts nodded, imitated a smile, and left.

Brother Malachi arrived with coffee. The old monk raised an eyebrow. "Gone already?"

Anselm smiled. "Let's hope that's a good omen. Coffee, gentlemen?"

Muller filled his cup. "Now to our next problems — the reporter and your escapee."

CHAPTER 40

THE BISHOP AND THE ABBOT

The next morning, Lou was alone in The Good Samaritan. Manny had left to snag a restaurant's used gas range and refrigerator at a bankruptcy sale. Working alone in what was to be Manny's office, Lou wielded the hammer with accuracy and power; just right, just so, and the nail sank into the stud. His muscles settled into a familiar groove, as if he had never left a work site, and he greeted each task like a familiar friend.

Doing work he had done for years took him back to those days when he would drive home as the sun faded, the soft glow from house lights promising warmth and comfort. Sally would have dinner simmering on the stove, while Becky's music floated from her room. He ached for that life as never before.

Lou regretted the years he had not shown Sally the love she deserved, and worse, withdrew when she needed him most. He had been such an idiot. What he would give to hold her in his arms and kiss her. He wondered if it would be possible to start again with new identities in another state.

Sally believes I'm dead. But what if…?

Misericordia may be hunting for him, but the state of Texas believed he was dead. With a low profile and a new identity in, say, Alabama, could the new Mr. and Mrs. Scanlon live happily ever after? Would Misericordia give up after a while and let him live in peace? Maybe, if he kept its deadly secret.

But where would that leave Rudy? How could he engineer his best friend's release without blowing the whistle on the entire organization?

Lou imagined Brother Jerome shoved into a holding cell to await processing for kidnapping. What would happen to the monk, his spiritual mentor, Abbot Anselm, Brother Aaron, and Malachi? Malachi had treated him like a son more than his own father had. And what about Predmore and the other prisoners? Would the state release them, re-incarcerate them, or worse, execute them for real this time?

Rudy would be free, but can I do that to them?

He slid to the floor and released his hammer. A wave of nausea swept over him, and he struggled to swallow. He closed his eyes and prayed.

Dear God, I need to know what to do. To speak and free Rudy, but put my friends in jail? Lord, they have been good to me even though I first saw them as jailers. How can I help Rudy without hurting them? Would it be possible to make a life with Sally after everything that's happened? Should I try? Please show me what to do. Jerome would tell me to trust you and not rely on myself. He would tell me to pray and wait for your guidance. There is no one to help me but you.

After a few minutes, Lou glanced toward Manny's desk, covered with a jumble of papers, one pile held down by the office phone doing paperweight duty.

No time like the present to get at least one answer.

"Operator," Lou said, relieved there were still human telephone operators. "Do you have a listing for a S-k-a-l-n-e-y in the Dallas directory? The person may use the initial S with the name."

He prayed Manny would not come back just then. He prayed the operator would find Sally's number. Then he prayed she wouldn't. Lou drummed his fingers on Manny's desk while jiggling his legs. *Come on, come on.* He jumped when the operator returned to the line with a number for "Skalney, S."

"Do you want me to place the call for you?"

"Um, not right now, but if you would give me the number. Thank you."

After several minutes of trying to think of what to say to Sally, he gave up.

Just do it. I must know, so I can get on with my life.

He dialed and counted the rings. *Maybe she was not home. Maybe it was not even her number, but a Sam's or a Stan's.*

"Hello."

Lou caught his breath. It was his Sally. He opened his mouth, but not one sentence came to mind. Suddenly, it was not about him. What would Sally feel hearing him speak when she believed he was dead? Would it terrify her, or would she feel overjoyed? Suspicious that someone was imitating him for some ulterior motive? Did he have any right to intrude into her life now?

"Hello?" Sally said again, sounding a bit irritated.

Then he heard the voice. It was male and soft spoken. "Just click off, darling. It's probably one of those robo calls."

Darling.

Lou hung up.

Kathy leaned into her uncle's embrace and fought threatening tears. She hated the fear that had turned her stomach into a war zone and colored her every thought.

"You look exhausted and upset, Kathy. What's going on?"

"I'm sorry to barge in like this, but I don't know what to do." Kathy fished a wadded tissue from her pocket and blew her nose.

Bishop Keenan guided her into his office. He grabbed a box of tissues from his desk and placed it on the coffee table, sitting in front of a leather sofa.

Once settled, Kathy grabbed another tissue. She explained Rudy had once again gone undercover, and told her, as usual, not to worry. She updated her uncle on Rudy's conviction that Lou Skalney could still be alive and there could be a connection between Lou and St. Dismas Monastery.

The Bishop nodded. "I remember Rudy asking me about it. As I told him, it most likely is not a Catholic monastery. I later checked with Bishop Haggerty, and he said he believed it was nondenominational. Did Lou find the connection he was looking for?"

"I have no idea, but the monks hired a local cattle rancher for stud service at the monastery. The rancher called Rudy and asked him if he wanted to ride along as a farm hand, so Rudy was going to use that to get into the monastery undercover."

"He's done this before for his work. From the stories he's told me, he knows how to handle himself. What troubles you about it this time, Kathy?"

"It's been a week, and even though he told me not to worry, I have a horrible feeling something's wrong. If he just asked questions and checked out the place, he would be home by now. He hasn't contacted me on his cell in days and I can't even reach his cell phone anymore. I called the rancher, Hank Campbell. He said when the monks invited Rudy to stay at the monastery, they left and drove back to the ranch. Campbell hasn't heard from him but said he didn't expect to."

Bishop Keenan frowned. "Did you go to the police?"

Kathy shook her head. "No. They'd say I was worrying about nothing and to just wait. I've never been this scared for him before, Uncle, even when he was investigating criminals. I want to go to the monastery and find out for myself."

"And why would they talk to you or even let you on the grounds?"

"I'm his wife. I deserve to know what happened to my husband."

"Do you really believe he's in danger in the monastery among those monks?"

"Who's saying they're really monks? They don't allow visitors on their property, and for all I know, they could be running a drug ring or manufacturing meth. I just want Rudy home and safe."

He took her hand. "How can I help?"

"Come with me to the monastery. Maybe the Abbot will talk to you and let you in as a kind of professional courtesy." She shrugged. "I don't know. Could that work, or is it a dumb idea?"

"Not at all, my dear. It's a start." He leaned back in his chair. "Hmm."

Kathy wiped her eyes and observed her uncle. She could almost see the cogs working in his brain while he stared at the wall and his fingers played an imaginary piano on his thigh. She remembered family stories about how he had turned down a full scholarship to Julliard to enter the seminary. Family lore held his father was furious his son would walk away from years of music study and intense training to become a priest. Kathy smiled. If he could face down his father, the stern grandfather she vaguely remembered, the Abbot will be a piece of cake — she hoped. After several minutes, the Bishop nodded and turned to her.

"Let me change into my formal cassock."

Kathy's eyes widened. She grinned. "Now?"

"Absolutely."

Kathy watched her uncle walk toward the monastery gate. He wore the black robe, short black shoulder cape edged in red, with the wide red sash of his clerical office circling his waist. He gave the bell's pull rope a hearty yank, and the gate swung open. She saw the black-robed gatekeeper do a quick double take at the sight of his visitor. Before the monk could gather his wits, Bishop Keenan, Kathy's Knight in Shining Armor Uncle, stepped inside. She would have given anything to hear what he was saying, but it must have worked because the heavy door closed. He was in.

They agreed she would wait in the car while he went inside to speak with the Abbot. Out of nervous habit, Kathy checked her phone once again. Nothing. She tried to pray, but her mind flitted from one scenario to another, none of them good. They all featured her husband in danger, tied up, hurt, lying in a ditch, or locked up somewhere. She shuddered, closed her eyes, and tried to empty her mind. Breathe in. Breathe out.

When the Bishop opened the car door, Kathy jumped, and her eyes flew open. She did not wait for him to get settled.

"Did you talk to the Abbot? What did he say?"

"He said Rudy had entered the monastery under false pretenses, pretending to be a ranch hand. He later identified himself as a reporter and asked about a friend of his, whom he had reason to believe was living at the monastery. The Abbot said Rudy would not accept that his friend was not living there. He even took Rudy through the monastery and invited him to join the monks for dinner. Since it was late, they put him up for the night, and the Abbot said he left the next day."

"What do you think, Uncle?"

"I believe they are monks and the Abbot's version of events seems plausible. The police would most likely believe him. Still, I wonder if he's telling the truth."

CHAPTER 41

HORNS OF A DILEMMA

Lou gritted his teeth, clutched the hammer in a death grip, and attacked a nail with such force he bent its head. Muttering, he slammed two more nails into the stud before he stopped. No amount of physical work would numb the pain from that one word, "darling."

Of course, Sally has every right to a new life. She believes she's a widow and has a lot of love to give. Whoever that man is, he'd better cherish her. She deserves more than what I gave her.

At the same time, Rudy's situation played at the edges of his mind.

Even though I let Sally down, I'll be darned if I let Rudy down too.

He recalled a message Abbot Anselm delivered one morning after Lauds about making decisions in difficult situations. He said knowing God's character would help a person decide what to do, because knowing who God is, leads to knowing his will. Put the "who is God" before "what should I do," Abbot advised.

Well, let's put it to the test and see.

After Manny returned at four, flushed with kitchen appliance success, they shared submarine sandwiches and French fries. Then Lou asked to borrow Manny's Bible.

"Sure. In fact, the case of Bibles I ordered arrived yesterday. Now we can get them out of the boxes and onto the shelves you built. I'll give you your own after we're done."

Two hours later, Lou settled on his cot, new Bible in hand, and read late into the night. He read about a just God who tolerated no sin, yet was a loving, merciful Father who sacrificed everything to make it possible for people to come to him. This God laid it all on the line for his creatures who could not save themselves. That is his character.

Although the words he read were familiar from the Bible studies he had done in the monastery, they went straight to his heart tonight. Not choosing to love and serve Jesus was the same as rejecting him. He was all in or all out, there being no middle ground. This was his moment of decision. If he were to be a follower of Christ, the way was clear. Or was he going to continue to run his life his own way? How had that worked so far?

Lou had been unaware of how tense he had been until he felt his arms and legs relax. The answer seemed so obvious now. This decision would cost him everything, yet an unexpected peace filled him and dissolved his fears.

Father God, I am sorry more than I can say for killing Beauregard Abbington. Even if he was guilty of murdering my Becky, I should have left justice to you. I regret not loving Sally as she deserved, and pray she finds happiness. I ask that the plan I have is from you and results in Rudy's freedom. Dear Lord, take my life for what it's worth. It's all I have to give.

"I need three favors, Manny. Could you hand deliver a letter I wrote to the St. Dismas monastery this morning? I hope it will solve my friend's problem and I can get out of your hair. If the letter works, I'll need to use this place for a meeting. I wish I could tell you more, but trust me, I spent the night praying over this. Also, can you ask FT to be the contact for arranging the meeting here? I don't want them to know where I am right now. At least, not until the meeting."

Manny extended his palm for the letter. "Sure, if it's that important to you. But don't think you're in the way because you've been a Godsend and this place will be ready for ministry in a week because of all your work. You're always welcome here, and I hope this solves your friend's dilemma."

"I should know soon."

CHAPTER 42

WHAT PRICE FREEDOM?

Abbot Anselm paced in his office. Pressure was building. Now a Bishop, Rudy's in-law uncle, was nosing about and who knew how far his connections led, even here in the Bible Belt.

A shaft of guilt pierced him because he had lied to the man. He had taken vows to obey God as best he could, and now he was a liar.

Whatever we decide, we'd better move fast. Dear God, I know it's wrong to keep Rudy from his family, and now I've sinned even more. What am I becoming? What sins am I leading my monks into?

Fists clenched, he was staring out the window when a knock on his door broke his reverie. Anselm turned to see Brother Aaron proffering a thick envelope.

"Someone delivered this and said to be sure you received it immediately. Before I could ask questions, he drove off."

"Thank you, Aaron. Wait a moment, if you will."

Anselm took the letter and settled behind his desk before opening the flap. After scanning the three pages, he let out a long breath. "Please ask Mr. Muller and Brother Malachi to join me here."

After Muller and Malachi read Lou Skalney's letter, Muller turned to the old monk. "Brother Malachi, you know Lou best. Do you believe we can we trust him to keep his end of the bargain?"

"Absolutely. He offered the one requirement he knew we would demand of him."

Anselm cleared his throat and looked from Malachi to Muller. "Do you think Rudy will go for the deal?"

"If he wants to return home soon, he will. Besides, everyone has their price," Muller said. "Lou and Rudy have been friends since childhood, and I doubt Lou would present a deal Rudy would refuse. Things are about to fall apart, and I couldn't have come up with a better solution. Or any other solution, for that matter."

"You know it will change everything," Anselm said.

"Yes, but the monastery system, and its people, will survive, and that's all we can hope for at this point." Muller frowned and crossed his arms. "We must tread carefully now. Before we present this to Rudy, I'll take it to the Board of Directors for their approval. If we get the green light, we'll go forward. It shouldn't take more than a week."

A week later, Rudy and Malachi joined Anselm and Director Muller in the Abbot's office.

"Rudy, this is Director Muller, who heads up the Executive Board of Misericordia," Anselm said.

"So my fate rests in your hands. Is that it?" Rudy asked. He grabbed a chair, leaned back, thrust out his legs, and folded his arms against his chest. He glared at Muller.

Before Muller could reply, Anselm rested clasped hands on his desk and leaned toward the reporter.

"Rudy, please believe it has not been our desire to keep you from your family, but the situation up to now has been impossible. Unless you agreed to kill your story, we could not allow you to leave. The ramifications of publicity would go far beyond what you already know, and we cannot allow that to happen. Until now, you have refused to agree to silence."

"I'll find a way out of here, whether you approve or not." Rudy glared at Anselm. "My wife will find me, and you will pay."

"Kathy is a determined woman," Anselm said.

Rudy startled at the mention of her name since he had not told the monks the names of his family members. Anselm pushed his advantage.

"Her Uncle, Bishop Keenan, came calling the other day. We told him you had left after spending the night with us."

Rudy sagged, and his arms and legs felt like lead. He had been so sure Kathy would find him. He gave her credit for calling on her uncle for help, but apparently, they were both misled by Abbot's lies.

If they put even Bishop Keenan off the scent, I could spend years here.

Rudy stared at Anselm as the Abbot lifted a paper from his desk.

"Your friend Lou sent us a list of demands that we believe will accommodate your, shall we say, journalistic scruples and allow you to return to your life. Now that he is free of the monastery, he promises to keep silent about our system, but only if we release you. Otherwise, he will go to the authorities. Frankly, we believe him."

Rudy recalled the conversation he and Lou had in the chapel when Rudy realized Lou had acclimated himself to life in the monastery and regarded the monks as spiritual guides. It had shocked Rudy then, but now he believed Lou would keep silent about the monastery system because his friend had never made a threat he wasn't ready to carry out. He knew Lou would turn them in if Rudy did not agree to kill his story, but it would break Lou's heart.

Could I live with that on my conscience? Or the executions that might follow?

Director Muller added, "We promise you exclusive access to write about the monastery's new prison ministry of rehabilitation. We'll no longer interfere with executions. We believe the government will use us simply because we're successful and cost less. Not to mention prison overcrowding."

Rudy snorted and challenged Muller. "Forgive me for being skeptical, but that would require transparency on your part, which would be new to Misericordia."

"We are more than capable of submitting to oversight. Do not underestimate us or what we can do."

The director's sudden smile banished his threat like the flick of a light switch. "Not only will we give you a retainer to write exclusive copy for us as we may require, but as recompense for holding you against your will, Misericordia will pay the undergraduate college tuitions for both your children. Of course, you may continue your other freelance work as you wish."

A hint of a smile played at Rudy's lips. He had believed keeping silent would make him an accomplice in repeated kidnappings, but now, his silence could put an end to them. Rather than the scoop of a lifetime, if he accepted their offer, he would have exclusivity on a terrific series, even if it was not what he had planned. And no article could bring in as much money as tuition for Lisa and Gabe's college educations.

Lou, you dog, you thought of everything.

He realized this was the only card Lou had to play, and he was playing it for all he and Rudy were worth.

Besides, if Muller is telling the truth, and I have no reason to doubt him, more good may come from this than if I blew the thing wide open.

As if he knew what Rudy was thinking, Anselm leaned in and stressed, "Rudy, nothing you write will change what has happened. But because of who you are, and the stand you have taken, the monastery system will now operate within the law. We can't offer anything beyond that."

Rudy closed his eyes and saw Kathy, Lisa, and Gabe standing before him. He swallowed threatening tears.

"When could I leave?"

Anselm looked around the room. "If everyone agrees, we are to contact a Father Tomzak at St. Louis Church in Arkdale, and he will arrange the meeting."

Every head nodded.

The wall clock in the main room showed twelve minutes after ten. Having downed his fourth cup of coffee, Lou was about to set a record for pacing.

"Take it easy, buddy," Manny advised. "Traffic, construction, anything could hold your friends up. Didn't you say you prayed about this all night?"

Lou jammed his hands into his jeans' pockets. "Yeah, but I'd feel better if God sent an angel with three forms of ID to tell me it was the right decision."

Manny chuckled. "Wouldn't we all. Sit, will you? You're driving me nuts."

Just then, a black sedan pulled up in front. Lou recognized Anselm behind the wheel, and he turned to Manny. "Will you let them in? I'll be right back."

Without waiting for a reply, Lou headed toward his sleeping quarters, leaving a puzzled Manny to greet the visitors. After assuring them Lou would be out in a moment and showing them to the meeting table he had arranged, he offered coffee. The older monk and the man in a black suit declined, but the man in jeans and striped shirt asked for tea.

Manny smiled. "I think I can scare up a tea bag." He was about to add that he must be Lou's friend, but before he could say anything, Lou walked in.

All eyes turned to the brown clad monk who stood holding a Bible in his right hand. Manny's lips formed a silent "oh" before he excused himself to make the tea, curiosity slowing his pace.

Lou regretted he could not explain everything to Manny, who had helped him in every way possible without knowing the facts. He wished there was a way he could thank him again, but right now, he needed to focus. He sat across from the trio and smiled at Rudy.

Anselm introduced Director Muller, who pulled Lou's letter from his pocket, reviewed it point by point, then fixed his gaze on Lou.

"Rudy has accepted this agreement. Knowing him as you do, can you vouch for his word?"

"Absolutely. I put it together, knowing what would and would not be acceptable to him."

Muller looked at Anselm, who gave a nod. He continued. "I see you are wearing the robe. Are you prepared to return to St. Dismas for the rest of your life?"

The rest of his life. The words echoed in his mind. Months ago, it was a prison sentence, and he would have preferred death. He recalled his aborted attempt to scale the monastery walls, Sargan and Caesar snarling at his feet; his fellow prisoners hooting at his newbie escape attempt. He thought of Predmore and realized, with surprise, that he looked forward to seeing him again. Lou thought of each day sliding into the next, overflowing with work, prayer, and friendship. He missed the library and, yes, even the monastery's endless vegetables, not to mention the blasted oatmeal.

"I am." *Dear God, what work have you done in me?*

Anselm smiled. "Welcome back, Lou."

He turned to Rudy. "And you ..." He pulled his cell phone from his robe's pocket and handed it to him. "Your cell phone had to take one for the team. Use mine and call your wife."

Hearing his wife's voice, Rudy smiled. Every man in the room listened to Rudy's one-sided conversation.

"Kathy, stop crying. I'm fine. I'll be home by this evening at the latest."

They heard snatches of Kathy's words. Rudy nodded his head, listening to his wife giving him a version of "I love you, thank God you're all right" followed by "I'll kill you for what you just put me through."

"Honey, I'll tell you everything when I get home."

Rudy gave the Abbot and Director Muller a warning look, as if to say, "Don't even think of asking me to keep something from my wife." They both nodded.

After Rudy ended the conversation with Kathy, he and Lou stood and gave each other a bear hug.

"Thank you," Rudy whispered. A frown creased his forehead. "You really want this?"

"Yes, I do."

"Well then …" Rudy's words trailed off.

CHAPTER 43

HOMECOMING

It amazed Lou how much his return to the monastery felt like a homecoming. As he stood between Brothers Aaron and Malachi at the edge of the wheat field, a glance to his left caught Frank Predmore smiling at him. This time he felt gratitude for a friend who was glad to see him.

I don't deserve his friendship, but I am so grateful for him, and the others as well. I wouldn't be standing here with men who have become like brothers to me If it hadn't been for the fire and Rudy.

Still, a man died, and now monks and residents gathered for Kurt's memorial service. Abbot Anselm held the box containing what remained of Kurt Niebold.

Lou struggled to erase the hellish memory of the man engulfed in flames. He recalled their many conversations over coffee. Niebold had so much insight into others, but so little into himself. He knew when Lou was planning to escape, and he also knew that Lou's screams one night had been theater in search of facts.

Anselm's words returned Lou to the present. Surrounded by his people, the Abbot offered praise to a loving God who knew Kurt's heart more intimately than anyone could, who knew the pain he had suffered from his mental illness; to a God who judges his creatures with more wisdom, justice, and mercy than man can comprehend. After singing Amazing Grace, the men watched Anselm open the box and disperse its contents into the late morning breeze.

"May God release you from the sins and shackles that bound you in life, Kurt Niebold."

They uttered a collective "Amen."

Brothers Jerome and Aaron sat across from Frank and Lou during lunch after Kurt Niebold's memorial service. Talk circled around practical subjects, ignoring the elephant in the room.

"With your construction background, I'm pretty sure Brother Malachi will use your expertise to build a new barn," Aaron ventured.

Lou grinned. "I'd like that. I did some work for a homeless shelter during the few days I was out, and it felt good to use a hammer again."

"Speaking of which," Jerome said, leaning forward, "were you planning to escape from here when the fire broke out? Did you grab your opportunity?"

"I wasn't planning to escape. But when I had the opportunity, I took the chance without thinking. It amazed me it worked, so I kept going. Looking back, I see how God supplied the ride to Arkdale with a trucker who handed me fifty dollars because he felt sorry for me. I didn't know where I would sleep that night, but came across a church with an unlocked door."

Lou told his friends about Father Tomzak, Manny, and how studying the Bible led him to find a way to free Rudy. When he finished, he looked up to see tears brimming in Jerome's eyes. Lou looked down at his empty coffee cup and thought, *God meddled in my life and his timing was perfect, although it didn't seem that way when I was going through everything.*

"Good to have you back, Lou," Aaron said and chuckled, bringing Lou back to their conversation. "Now maybe it won't take three monks shadowing you to keep you here."

And the elephant lumbered away.

Lou sat alone in Anselm's office after the Abbot left him to think and pray.

Stunned, Lou frowned. Was he the man Abbot Anselm said he was? That person did not square with someone who could ignore his wife's pain, kill another human being, or treat a fellow prisoner with the disdain he had treated Predmore. He cringed just thinking about the old Lou Skalney.

Have I changed that much? Can I trust myself to be the man Abbot Anselm thinks I am for the rest of my life?

After a half-hour of prayer, Lou surrendered once again. "Thy will be done," he said to the Unseen Presence in the room.

Brother Jerome shook him. "Wake up, Lou. It's time to get up."

He sat upright on his cot. "I wasn't asleep, Brother. Is it three a.m. already?"

Jerome smiled. "Indeed."

They walked to the chapel, where black-clad monks already filled the pews, and Lou was the only resident present. Abbot Anselm stood at the foot of the altar, a privacy screen to his right. As Lou followed Jerome down the center aisle, the monks chanted a psalm of praise. When they reached the end of the aisle, Jerome slid into the pew to his left and Lou knelt before the Abbot.

Anselm directed the formal question to the figure kneeling at his feet. "What is it you wish?"

"I wish to become a monk and dedicate my life to serve God."

"Are you making this request freely?"

"I am."

"Do you vow to obey the God-appointed authority set over you, to remain poor in spirit and goods, and to respect the dignity of all who cross your path, especially those in need of your care?"

"I do so vow, with the help of God."

"As Abbot, I believe you are worthy of the trust we place in you. As you step with faith into your new life, by what name do you wish to be called?"

Lou Skalney did not hesitate. "I choose the name Jonah, because I have lived in the belly of this whale far too long."

A hint of a smile crossed Anselm's face as he extended his hand to his newest monk. Lou took his Abbot's hand, rose, and walked behind the screen. Within minutes, a black-clad monk, with the red cross emblazoned on his chest, joined his fellow monks in a closing prayer.

Then Abbot Anselm took Brother Jonah by the arm and said, "Let me introduce you to your fellow monks."

Lou, now Jonah, cast Anselm a quizzical look, which Anselm ignored. The Abbot brought Brother Jonah to Malachi. Malachi shook Jonah's hand, congratulated him, and said, "I also was executed for murder. I grew up in a Mennonite community, but married someone from outside. We left the community to run our own farm, just the two of us. When Margaret died of cancer, I tried to manage without her, but couldn't. Bills piled up, and I knew I would have to give up the farm, but couldn't bring myself to leave. When the federal Marshall came to evict me, I pointed a gun at him, desperate to hold my ground. I didn't mean to kill him, but before I knew it, the gun went off."

Speechless, Jonah stared at Malachi. Rather than judge him, Jonah's heart ached for his old boss. He understood how the pain of the loss of his wife, his farm, the only life he knew, could have driven Malachi to that terrible moment. He thanked God for this man in his life.

Next, Brother Luke, the physician, spoke.

"When I was on staff at the hospital, I judged who would be better off dead than alive. I targeted the severely handicapped and used medication to relieve them of what I thought was their misery. By the time they caught me, I had killed fourteen people."

One after the other, Brother Jonah "met" his fellow Brothers. They were all like him — redeemed killers. At last, he stood before

Brother Jerome, his gentle, wise mentor. Jonah closed his eyes and wished he could close his ears as well. Jerome spoke.

"My wife and I were going through a tough time in our marriage. There were arguments, noisy arguments the neighbors could hear. The day she was murdered, we had another blowout, and in a rage, I slammed out of the house. I spent the rest of the day and that night holed up in my bookstore. When I returned home, I found police cars surrounding the house. Someone had stabbed Daisy in our kitchen, but I was arrested, tried, convicted, and executed. I was guilty of many things, but not her death. Without an alibi, I was just another guilty black man."

Brother Jonah squeezed Jerome's arm and smiled.

Abbot Anselm spoke to his newest monk.

"When I was younger, I led a street gang. We owned the streets on the south side of town, extorting business owners, drug dealing, running gambling rings, and taking down anyone who got in our way. I was guilty of many crimes, but they got me on racketeering, and I did 20 years in the state pen. When I got out, I didn't know how to live on the outside. I couldn't return to my past life because I had found salvation in Christ while serving my time. My family would have nothing to do with me. In desperation, I joined a Benedictine monastery and lived as a monk for five years. But I was restless and felt called to help prisoners. In time, I left the monastery and became a prison chaplain. I loved the work but hated the executions. Somehow, Misericordia heard about me, and because of my history, thought I could serve them as an Abbot.

"As I told you in my office, we cannot allow residents to know the monks were once prisoners like themselves. It is not a position for the ambitious, or something to work toward. That's why you cannot continue to live here as Brother Jonah, so tonight you will move to another monastery.

"A monk must be a man of integrity, a man of strength, tempered with gentleness. Because they are dead to the world, our residents are vulnerable to any cruelty we could inflict. This must never happen. Instead, our monks are guides leading our residents to the foot of the Cross, where each makes his eternal choice."

"That's why people disappeared in the middle of the night," Jonah said. He sniffed. "And we thought…"

"I know what you thought; that we were murdering people. Better you believed that than a resident becomes a monk for the wrong reasons and harms someone. We transfer prisoners in the night as well. Colin Mackey needed a monastery with tighter security, and so we transported him while everyone slept."

Jonah remembered Niebold's assertions that the monks were murderers. *Well, he was half-right.*

Abbot Anselm continued. "Brother Jonah, stand before the altar and I will give you your final blessing. Following that, I wish to speak with you and Brother Malachi in my office before you leave."

Raising his hand above Jonah, Anselm made the Sign of the Cross as he spoke the ancient words Moses had spoken to Aaron.

"The Lord bless you and keep you;

the Lord make his face shine on you;

the Lord turn his face toward you and give you peace."

Abbot Anselm's desk lamp bathed his office in a warm glow. He waved his visitors to a trio of chairs across from his desk. Jonah cast Malachi a quizzical glance as they took their seats. Anselm handed each a glass of wine from a decanter parked on a side table.

"A celebration, Brother Jonah." Anselm lifted his glass in a salute. Malachi frowned. "I don't…"

"I know, my friend, but you soon may change your mind."

Anselm settled into the third chair and took a sip from his glass. After a long pause, he said, "As you know, you will leave us this night, Brother Jonah. Director Muller informed me Misericordia has designated you to direct the first rehabilitation unit in our monastery at Granada. The current residents will transfer to existing monasteries, including here in Trinity County, so their way of life will continue unchanged."

On hearing that, Jonah's heart raced, and his hand shook as he brought the wine glass to his lips. His eyes widened in astonishment. After swallowing a generous mouthful, he spoke in intense, low tones. "I know how to build a rehabilitation facility out of stone, mortar, and wood. But I have no clue how to run one. If they want the new mission to succeed, they should select someone who has some experience. I-do-not."

He aimed a fierce look at the Abbot, as if to say that was the end of it.

In the ensuing silence, Jonah recalled how his life had gone off the rails every time he had been in Anselm's office. The first day when he awoke in the monastery, Anselm informed him he would never leave the place alive. The second time, Anselm told him Rudy would not be leaving the monastery because he knew its deadly secret — unless he swore to remain silent. And at his last visit, Anselm offered Lou Skalney a new life as a monk.

How much more will my life be twisted beyond recognition?

Jonah turned to Malachi. "Bear me out, why don't you. Tell him I'd be no good at running things. You were an Abbot once. Why don't they ask you instead of me?"

But his friend and mentor remained silent.

Anselm said, "Brother Malachi will accompany you, and be your mentor in everything from Krav Maga to your new administrative role." He smiled at his second in charge. "I'll miss you, my friend, but I know you will help Brother Jonah as you did me. By the way, I'm told they have a kitchen garden they're looking to expand into a farm."

Malachi heard Anselm out and said nothing for a long while. Jonah thought, I can't imagine this monastery without the two of them. They're like old lions, sometimes growling at each other but keeping the pride in check. How can Anselm kick him to the curb with just an "I'll miss you?"

Jonah's eyes widened when he saw Malachi take a sip from his untouched glass of wine. The old monk gave Anselm a small smile and said, "I remember your first days as Abbot. You had much to learn."

Anselm sighed. "Without you, I would have been insufferable as an Abbot."

Malachi's eyes sparkled. "Would have been?"

"Without you here, I may revert."

They smiled at each other in a private code. Suddenly, Malachi put down his glass and said, "According to God's will."

Newly minted Brother Jonah exclaimed, "Wait! What? You accept that? This is crazy, you know that, don't you?" His eyes flicked between them. "The both of you know better. Just tell Misericordia they're wrong. This is nuts!"

Anselm covered his mouth with his hand while Malachi spoke.

"Brother Jonah, you just vowed to obey commands from those in authority over you. Did you think it would be easy?"

"No. But I thought the commands would make sense."

"So you will obey only if you agree with them?"

"Well, no, but…"

"Brother Jonah, the second you repented of your sin, came before Jesus and surrendered your life, your very eternity, to him, you became a new person. Don't think for a moment your life in Christ will be comfortable or easy."

Malachi leaned toward Jonah, his eyes boring into his. "Know this, and you will ride on eagles' wings. Ignore this, and you will crumble. In the book of Romans, Paul writes, 'And we know that all things work together for good to those who love God, to those who are called according to his purpose.' In other words, Jonah, trust him and hang on for all you're worth—for you are worth everything to him."

· Jonah ignored his tears as he left Anselm's office and stepped into his future.

ABOUT THE AUTHOR

Photo by Alex Boutakov

Fueled by coffee and an overactive imagination, Sue LeDoux creates fiction that draws from her years as a nurse and wife of a CSI chemist. She blends her fascination about church history with life's raw experiences. Her flawed characters navigate messy lives. She does not write for the spiritually comfortable.

Visit Sue at www.sueledoux.us.
Or
write her at 3177 Latta Road,
PO Box 157, Rochester NY 14612

TOPICS FOR DISCUSSION

When Lou Skalney believed Beauregard Abbington's acquittal was a travesty of justice, he rationalized killing him. People have shot, hung, or stabbed criminals since Cain killed Able. What are your feelings about justice outside of the judicial system?

How do you feel about the death penalty?

If you were running things, how would you deal with serial killers, murderers, people who commit treason, etc.? Be as creative as you want.

Americans mostly believe we need prison reform. If you agree, what do you believe is the most important thing that should be addressed?

Following that, in what other ways would you reform the penal system?

In 2019, 36% of people in Texas owned guns, not counting guns purchased on the black market or at gun shows. Texas is the gun toting capital of the United States. In *The Divine Meddler,* some in the monastery killed someone with a gun. What are your views about gun control?

Lou Skalney was raised in the Catholic tradition. In *The Divine Meddler*, a priest and Bishop help Lou, as do non-denominational monks, including one who had been a Mennonite. What is your view of Christianity and its many denominations?

Have you found your spiritual home? Are you looking for one? If so, How would you know you found it?

Is there anything that could make you leave your current denomination?

What do you think of ecumenicism?

Made in the USA
Columbia, SC
22 December 2022

73681345R00186